Within the Frame

Book 1: Captured

By Victor Alexander

A D.o.J.O. Tale

Table of Contents

Chapter 1: Lorenzo

Have you ever created something you hated?

If you're a creative person, or consider yourself one, think about it deeply. Have you ever written, sketched, drawn, sculpted, or painted something and then... been disgusted by it? Have you ever put something out into the world, given an idea physical shape and form in some way, and then looked at it... and then despised it?

That's how Lorenzo Wallace felt. He felt it every time he caught himself looking at the most famous portrait he ever made – *Mermaid under Glass*. The painting itself, as one might expect, was a mermaid – one based on a woman of African descent from the waist up, with natural thick black hair pulled up in an afro puff that swayed with the current and dark eyes – topless and swimming before a window. The effect was made to show that in her face was a confusion and growing fear as she'd apparently thought she was free in the ocean until she'd swam upon the unnatural clear wall and realized she was in captivity the whole time. In her shock, she held out her hand towards the glass as if she wanted to believe it was fake, but was terrified it wasn't.

It was a great concept, it really was. The problem was that the execution wasn't perfect, and the imperfections ate at Lorenzo. They ate at him because he knew they were there, he knew they were his fault, and he knew that if he'd had a bit more time they wouldn't be there at all.

He'd rushed this. He'd rushed it for a deadline, and what started off as a passion project for him, something he'd been proud of and worked hard on… but it had turned into something he'd just done to meet a deadline. In his haste he'd missed things, things he'd consider easy mistakes he should have caught… and the gallery owner, much to his horror, had either not seen the errors or didn't care, because next thing he knew it was up on the walls and displayed to the world.

Worse, people liked it. People loved it! Every time he came to see the piece, there were people from all over the city and of course some visitors from out of town, all gawking at something he wasn't proud of with muttered words of awe and joy.

It sickened him inside. Seeing people loving this piece, a work that in his mind was a failure, and loving it, sometimes made the young black man so mad he couldn't see straight. He'd made so many paintings he'd worked harder on, for longer, putting more painstaking effort and care into getting them just so. But despite all his work on the other portraits, what did the people fawn over? The one he'd hurried through.

"What a beautiful piece!" said a voice from behind him, the words making his skin crawl. Oh, if it wasn't in public he'd have ripped it off the wall and smashed it! He'd have splintered the frame over his knee, then stomped it again and again! Just knowing people were staring at it thinking it was good when he knew he could do better made his entire body feel hot and uncomfortable, like he wanted to rip his way out of the building. He didn't even recognize the voice at first, until the person behind him continued talking.

"You can see the level of detail was most focused on the eyes," the voice said. Now that he paid attention, it was obviously female, though a bit lower than your average woman's. "The artist made her expressive and so beautiful in her obvious fear and pain. I'll bet the artist is a sadist; only they see that much beauty in suffering."

Lorenzo turned slowly, putting a face to the voice at last. He recognized this woman, in her blue and lime-green jogging outfit, with her braids pulled back into a pony-tail. She had the jacket open, showing off a sports-bra and the type of toned physique some would kill for and others would kill to be near. Despite the definition of her muscles that could be seen under the jacket and sweats, she also had a softer, rounded face with big cheeks and expressive bright-brown eyes that gave her whole countenance a rather deceptively youthful experience that, when combined with her smooth rich brown skin gave the general impression she was anywhere between the ages of a freshman in college and a graduate student. Only a few key glances and tonal hints, or her taste in music, would give away her real age.

As she looked at Lorenzo, she smiled a big and wide smile. It was one of those smiles with imperfections that just made it nicer somehow, a warm and infectious grin that started as a thin line and slowly spread ear-to-ear in a way that was infectious, making Lorenzo smile right back despite himself.

"It's good to see you smiling again, Z-No," she said, placing a hand on his shoulder gently. "I'm glad you still know how; I was beginning to think you'd forgotten."

"Tati…" he said, rubbing his right eye slowly, "that is, by far, the sappiest thing I've ever heard you say. Like, that's Barney the Dinosaur doing a crossover with the Care Bears levels of cheese."

The woman, Tati, outright laughed, covering her mouth a bit as she did so.

"I see your sense of humor is still alive and well, too!" she said between chuckles as her laughter finally subsided. "I take that to mean you're still keeping that wit of yours sharp?"

"Mostly by accident," he admitted, still smiling despite his earlier melancholy. "Most of who I spend time with these days are assholes from work. They don't provide much challenge."

"You should start keeping better company again, then," Tati said, stepping closer to the painting as she spoke. "Everyone back at the Dojo misses having you around, you know. Sola and Luna both ask about you all the time, along with Dante and Vergil. Hell, you know Gomez and I miss you, of course…"

Lorenzo sighed, staring back up at the painting. He did miss the Dojo, and all the guys and girls therein… silly code names aside, he'd never had more fun than when he was part of the community with them. He missed the games, the bonding, the snacks, the training… but then, there was the whole thing of having a job that not only took most of his time but was filled with nosy-ass prudes…

"Yeah, I know…" he muttered, rubbing the back of his head. "I don't get around as much as I used to. Hell, I don't do half as much of anything as I used to, these days… Is 26 too soon to be over the hill?"

"You're talking to a 42 year old woman who jogs 3 miles a day," Tati said, crossing her arms. "You do the math, big guy."

"Fair enough."

"So, when you're done staring at your old work and gloating about it-"

"Wasn't gloating, Tati."

"I'll believe that never…" she said, smirking slightly. "I've known you too long to buy that humble act, 'Z-No'." She patted the younger man on the back, smiling that warm smile of hers once more. "You're one of the best painters I've ever met, clearly… and one of the best photographers. Speaking of which…"

Lorenzo looked back at her, folding his own arms and grinning. As much as he hated to admit it, he missed being called by that name. It felt good to be Z-No again, even if only briefly. It brought back the warmer memories. And even though he hated the piece on the wall, despised it even… it felt good that someone he respected enjoyed it. The artist in him was happy to have the validation.

The cynic in him was the one who assumed she needed something from him, and asked Tati what she wanted. She looked a bit saddened but eventually, she did explain it;

"We're having a big event weekend for the Dojo's 5th Anniversary," she said at last, hands now locked behind her back. "We'll be welcoming some new members, we'll be hosting some special teaching events, and of course, we'll be having a special munch to bring in new people. And since you were with us from Day 1, it wouldn't be the same without you. Also… we need a camera man."

"And you want someone who knows the score and won't ask too many stupid questions," Lorenzo finished for her. "Well, that makes sense; I'd imagine it's hard to find reliable, discrete, trustworthy camera folk for a night in the Dojo."

"Yeah, Gomez and Dante especially don't want to trust outsiders," Tati replied after a while, resting one hand on the young man's shoulders. "So we decided to reach out to family. And, even though you haven't been seen around for a while… you're always family, Z-No."

The words felt unfamiliar to him, strangely warm and kind. He dealt, once again, mostly with people at his job these days – stiff, superficial, and fake were always the orders of the day. There were no meaningful connections in

12

the halls of Merriks and Hines Advertising Company; everyone was surface-level only in all their interactions, just plodding along and keeping things light and fake and friendly. Lorenzo had even noticed that, as long as he kept his tone positive, he could say almost anything – he responded 'terrible' when coworkers asked how he was doing, he joked about his own death, he casually slipped in to his boss how the job was killing him inside... and no one batted an eye. Actually having someone care about and listen to what he was saying, after all this time... well, it felt nice. And feeling nice was unusual.

"Well, nice to know I'll be welcomed home," he said, smiling again despite himself. "I probably won't be up to mixing it up too much, but as far as the meet-and-greet stuff and the photos? Color me there. Just let me know the time and place."

Tati lit up brightly and hugged him, then began explaining some of the particulars as she walked him out of the gallery. Casting a last look back at the painting, Lorenzo couldn't help but realize from this distance, he couldn't see his failures… and he wondered if that's how everyone else saw it.

It was nice… which is how Lorenzo knew it wouldn't last.

Afterwards, back home a few hours later, Lorenzo thought it all over as much as he could while looking over some of his old photos from the glory days. Back before the job began to bleed him dry, he had dreadlocks down to his shoulders. He wore a lot of black leather in those days… a lot of spikes and acid-washed denim. He owned like 3 shirts in those days that weren't black and full of holes.

He was happier. There were bad days then – days where he wasn't sure when and how he was going to eat next, or if the rent would get paid – but comparatively, even the struggles from back then were better than the days now where he had plenty. At least in those days he still had his friends, his secondary family. He almost forgot why he left all that behind.

Then he swiped through the photos and discovered a picture that hadn't been deleted yet, one of him barely conscious with a stupid grin next to a beautiful bronze-skinned woman with shoulder length curly hair and thin eyes throwing a peace sign at the camera with a devious smirk across her face.

Memories flashed back to him, hitting the young man in the chest like a sledgehammer. He suddenly couldn't breathe, his vision began to blur, and as his breath seemed to catch in his throat without ever going down to fully inflate his lungs, he heard a distinctivel ringing in his ears.

Not again. Not right now. Hold it together, hold it together!

He staggered to his feet, through his apartment, bumping up against the walls as he made it into his bathroom and snatched open the medicine cabinet, grasping at bottles and rattling them before his hazy eyes before he found the one he needed, wrestling the top off his Xanax and shakily breaking a single bar in half, throwing it back with a few gulps of tap water.

It may have been psychosomatic, a case of mind over matter, but he began to get his grip moments after swallowing the pill and his steady breathing began to restore some order to his world. He closed the cabinet and stared at himself in the mirror, seeing the sweat that was already beading up on his raw umber skin as he slow-breathed his way back into reality. It was his first panic attack in a while… damn. His therapist would most likely have a lot to say about this one, given the cause and all. He gripped the sink for a moment, then threw some water on his face and let it bead up on the miniature afro where his dreads had once been.

The ringing faded last, as it always did. There were a few seconds where he felt he could still hear it, drowning out all other noise at first, then an undercurrent to the residual noise of the apartment as if reminding him it would never truly go away. His therapist told him he personified his panic attacks like that – giving them motivations and thoughts of their own – because he needed something to hate. And he did hate them; he hated the loss of control, he hated the pounding of his pulse, he hated the dizziness and disorientation.

Most of all he hated how, after they were gone, he was just a bundle of nerves and pain that had to self-soothe into calmness.

"It's over now…" he reminded himself out loud, splashing more cold water on himself before speaking again. "It's over, she's gone, and she's never coming back. You're okay, Z-No. You're okay."

It felt pathetic to have to say it out loud, but it did help. He walked back to the computer, deleted the picture as quickly as possible, then leaned back in his chair as the chemical calm continued to wash over him. He wasn't going to let her continue to govern his life; like he had to keep reminding himself, she was gone now… and letting her govern his life this long afterwards was pointless. It was time, long past time, he get back to living his life. And with that in mind, he pulled up the Dojo's website to check the current goings on status.

"Welcome to the Dungeon of Joyful Obedience!" read the website banner, in appropriately gothic cursive font. He'd have to applaud Vergil later about the website's overall design; the layout was much better than it had been in previous years and looked far more professional. There was a section with their mission statement – "Discipline brings Joy, but Obedience is Earned" – featured prominently, as it should be. The two phrases were separated slightly, just below the name, giving everything that came after a sort of coherent feel with each portion of the mantra. All things related to the Bondage and Discipline, as well as Sadism and Masochism, were under the "Discipline brings Joy" side, while things related to Domination and Submission fell under the "Obedience is Earned" portion to put emphasis on the importance of Dominant partners having obligations to their submissive partners. Other links explained more about the Dojo, Membership, the members-only image and video gallery… and, highlighted as being recently updated, were the events.

The most recent event, the updated one, was of course the Anniversary event. It featured in large bold letters that there would be a special return for the special occasion; the return of Dojo's own prominent photographer and one of its founding members, Z-No.

He was booked for the event now, officially. A bit of anxiety crept back up, but it met the cold wall of 'nope' that the Xanax had build up in his mind and went back down. What would be would be, at this point… nothing left to do now but start formatting his camera and the memory cards properly… make sure he didn't have any work-related stuff tied to this camera, for one thing, so there was never a reason to connect the two even accidentally.

Also, he had to decide if he wanted to dust off his toys and join in the fun during the Anniversary Party. It had been a long time since he dusted off his toys…

Chapter 2: Kristina

Days off are for junk food, anime, and long naps to get away from the existential dread. Or at least, that's what Kristina Shank believed – after all, what else was there to do? She could take and send in more pictures to modeling agencies, only to have them say bullshit about how they were looking for someone 'less urban' at the time; she could dwell on her day jobs as a dog walker and hotel staffer, which were rewarding and fun but not what she saw herself doing for the rest of her life; or, she could play some video games, eat some candy, and take a wine nap. She opted for the third, and was fast asleep on the couch after a couple of glasses of wine and an hour or so of Fallout when her phone began to buzz and rattle around on the coffee table. She reached over and picked it up, not bothering to sit up from her face-down position as she groaned in the direction of the receiver;

"Lisa, this better be important."

Her friend on the other end of the line, Lisa, squealed the moment she answered the phone. Kristina moved the speaker of the phone away until the sound stopped, then put it back up to her ear with another loud groan.

"You done?" she asked, grumbling a bit more. She was starting to sit up a bit, tugging at her oversized black Batman T-shirt to make it easier to dust some crumbs off it. It was her day off, so she was sporting this shirt and no pants because that's what freedom looks like, and her natural hair was securely tied up in a satin scarf.

If you looked up "Don't Fuck with Me" on Google Images, one of the results would probably resemble her to an almost comical degree.

"Kris! Get up, right now, and go to your computer!" Lisa said. She sounded out of breath, like she'd been hyperventilating or something. Usually Kris would care more about that, but at this point… she couldn't muster up the energy needed.

"Give me one good reason," she growled back. "And it better be a *damn* good reason."

"*Z-No is back!!*" Lisa screeched into the phone.

Kris bolted upright as if she'd just heard a gunshot, rubbing her face in an attempt to wake herself up as she got to her feet and began jogging towards her laptop. She set the phone on speaker and laid it down next to her laptop, clicking away to input her password before opening up her browser.

"Bitch, I swear if you're lying to me-!" she said, already booting up the device and going to the bookmarked home page of the Dojo

"Not lying!" Lisa said, still obviously over excited. "It's real, it's really real! Look for yourself on the events page!"

And sure enough, there it was in plain text: the announced return of the Dojo's best photographer, Z-No, confirmed for the Dojo Anniversary!

Now it was Kristina's turn to squeal, which she did quite loudly.

"I know, right?!" Lisa replied. "This is huge!"

Lisa had introduced Kristina to the Dojo's website a few years ago when it first went online, inspired by the fact they both had more than a passing interest in BDSM and the fact that Kris, like most of the patrons of the Dojo, was black. Though there had been many other draws to the Dojo in particular – the layout, the proximity to their home town, the mission statement and the fact that the majority of the members looked like Kris but were very all-inclusive

– what kept Kristina involved was the presence (and the abrupt absence) of the mysterious Z-No.

She'd followed the site and its members quite closely since being introduced to it, and ever since had become fixated on him in particular. He was never the signature focus of any picture he took, nor was he ever that exposed – the few pictures in which he was prominently featured had him wearing a full-face mask like all the other Dojo patrons. But his artistry when it came to photography… the way he drew in the eye while taking pictures, the way he could focus every picture just so to express what he saw and wanted others to see… that was unique. And before she was a model, Kristina was a photographer… and the style of this mystery man Z-No drew her further into the Dojo and its dealings. She memorized several of their mantras, joined as a private donor, and checked their site faithfully for 2 whole years now… all because of Z-No and his photography. When he stopped being the main photographer about 8 months ago, she'd stopped bothering with the site as much – she still checked in and donated to them, but her interest waned without the mystery man of her fascination behind the camera. But this meant he was back. And she felt warmth, a specific joy flowing through her veins as she gazed at that announcement.

You've come back to me…

"Kris? Kris?! Bitch, are you listening?!" Lisa chimed in, disrupting the daydream Kristina had been having.

"I-i-i… I'm here!" Kris managed to get out, putting the phone up to her head. "What's up?"

"Now that I have your attention," Lisa said in an overly snarky tone "Look! Look at the next event!"

Kristina rolled her eyes, reminding herself that the tone Lisa was using would have to be addressed with her white female counterpart later… but it was mostly forgotten when she pulled the full calendar into focus. 'Munch Brunch meet-and-greet Breakfast Buffet', the event title read in red text. 'The following founding members of the Dojo will be in attendance:'

She scanned through, and suddenly her heart slapped her ribcage. There it was, plain as day – Z-No. He would be at the meet-and-greet Munch, he would be where she could meet him and shake his hand and-!

"Oh my god…" she hissed softly into the receiver, picking up the phone without even looking down as she found herself staring at his name on-screen like an answered prayer. "He's gonna be there. The man himself… I can't even process that…"

"Don't bother trying to process it," Lisa said with a smile evident through the phone. "We're already signed up. I'm your plus one, so you can bail if he turns out to suck or be a creep or something."

Kristina felt like her eyes were going to pop out of her head. Meeting her hero, the icon? Oh no, she wasn't NEAR ready. She had to do so much research, she had to impress him, she had to get clothes and make up, she had to brush up on his works to see what he liked and how he liked it…!

"Munch is at 1:20 P.M, this Saturday," Lisa said while Kris was still tripping over her words. "I'll be at your house at 12 to get ya, so… be ready! Bye~"

And with that, she hung up the phone and Kris was alone. Alone with her thoughts, alone with the site, alone with her ideal of a man whose works she'd been infatuated with for too long. Lisa was forcing her to meet him, which should have made her happy but... but..!

What if he sucked? What if he was just a bland, boring, shit person who took great photos? What if he was a jerk? Or worse yet what if he was great?! What if she met Z-No, this being she'd likened to a god, and he was exactly as magical and wonderful as she'd always hoped... but he found *her* pedestrian or boring? What if she came off like a basic bitch to him, or a groupie?! What if she creped him out?! What if he didn't like black girls?! Yeah, she was fairly sure he was black too but that meant little to nothing these days!

In the midst of her panic, she clicked a few pictures on the Dojo's gallery page and instinctively opened the gallery of photos prominently featuring the man himself; all 45 pictures of Z-No. In a large number of them, he was wearing a distinctive mask, a white dress shirt with the sleeves rolled up, and a black silk vest to match his pants and belt. Her heartbeat calmed somewhat as she found the gallery, and clicked onto one picture of him walking towards the camera. He was in the process of rolling up the left sleeve with his right hand as the picture was taken, a brutal-looking flogger in his left hand. She could only see his eyes, but she swore that he looked both in control and bored of it; as if he were staring right at her with this otherworldly calm and centered nature. It was a look you saw in the movies, when a gladiator was storming towards a downed enemy intent of finishing them off. He had the energy, in that picture, of a man who'd broken women better and stronger than she. Those cold, calculating, dark brown eyes that were almost black... staring out from behind that mask with a mixture of disdain and absolute confidence in himself.

That same picture always made her melt a bit inside. More than any of the more explicit pictures or videos in the premium gallery, this one captured her imagination and let it run wild.

"You'd probably think I'm pathetic..." she hissed at the image, full-screening it at making sure the most prominent feature was that face. "I guess I kinda am, fawning over you like this..." She bit her bottom lip, staring at him and trying to picture the face under that mask the hands under his gloves. "You're probably used to it by now though, aren't you? Mmm, I'll bet you're a smug prick who gets off on how much control you have over women without effort. Then again, you have every right to be cocky..." She paused, panning down. The pants he was wearing left little to the imagination and she could clearly see the outline of his dick. Fuck... Was it bad tailoring or was it just that big? I mean, judging by those hands... those big, powerful-looking hands, with strong vascular definition that captured her mind's fantasy of how powerful his grip must be...

She was imagining it, without realizing it; in her mind's eye she was still in her chair as that *being* the captions called Z-No stepped out of her computer and loomed over her, ready to punish her for being a weak, soft, spoiled little brat and break her into a proper fuck-toy.

She bounced in her seat a bit, letting her mind carry her away.

"I bet you enjoy knowing how flawed I am, you god-like fucker..." she hissed through her teeth, eyes slipping closed as one of her hands began to caress her chest. "I bet it makes you hard knowing you could do whatever you want with me and you haven't even spoken to me yet..." She paused a bit, clutching at her left breast as her thighs instinctively squeezed together. "Mmm, I bet you're getting off on the idea that you don't even need words to control me... that you could have me at any time... Nnngh... That you don't have to be gentle... and that I'll love every second of it." She gripped her own neck as she whispered out the words breathily, free hand panning the screen back up to his masked face. Those eyes, those fucking *eyes*, yes-!

In her dream she was helpless, defenseless as he pressed her against the wall. She felt that hand (her own hand) grip her throat even tighter as she lost herself to the fantasy and knew she should be scared... but all she could think about was how much stood between them at this moment. He had a mask between his lips and hers; a shirt between his chest and hers (for in her fantasy, she was already naked); he had jeans and boxers between his hot, throbbing dick and her eager, wet little mouth and pussy...

Too many layers. Please, take some of them off? She begged mentally, seeing herself struggling futilely to get closer to him, just a bit closer... to smell his cologne, to rub her head against his neck, to feel her own sex grind on instinct against that print pressed through his pants, to show him how earnestly she wanted him, needed him.

In the fantasy she moved up towards him as much as he let her, focused on those eyes, as she panted and let herself get lost in him. Part of the fantasy for her wasn't getting what she wanted, but getting as much of what she wanted as he allowed her to have. He controlled when and if she got anything from him more than the time of day, and she was to be grateful for even that.

"Mmmph, Fuck…" she whispered to the empty room, her hips gyrating back and forth of their own accord as she felt that pressure and need for pleasure building between her thighs but ignored it just as she imagined he would. "You know how bad I want you, don't you? You know I need you, don't you? But you're still gonna make me beg, aren't you, you cruel motherfucker… Huh?"

A smirk crept up her lips and she envisioned his voice in her ears telling her what to say. He was cruel in her fantasy, but his voice was sweet… that paradoxical element was always important to her. In her fantasy, she slid up and forward, licking his mask as she groaned out softly;

"You're gonna make me say it, aren't you? Fine… *Please*, use me *Sir*… *Please,* taste me *Sir*… *Please*, touch me *Sir* and see how fucking wet your worthless doll has become for you..?"

Her hands were between her thighs, busy because she couldn't stop them from pretending they were his larger, stronger hands tormenting her pretty little pussy through her silken black panties. She could almost taste her own desperation in the air, and then… the chair flew backwards, leaving her suspended in the air for all of 1 second as reality crashed in. She rolled out of the chair and towards her couch, hitting it with a quiet *thud* that startled her dog and made her glad her roommate wasn't home. Groaning and disoriented, the 22-year-old woman opened one eye slowly and checked herself for damages. She was embarrassed, despite no one but her Great Dane mix Rex being there… but aside from wounded pride, she was indeed alive and mostly in one piece.

"Well, that wasn't my most spectacular moment…" she mused up to the ceiling as Rex bounded over to check on her. She gave his massive forehead a gentle shove with her clean hand. "Thank you, baby, but Momma's just fine…" she assured him. "Biggest bruises are to my ego…"

She got to her feet, sighing and rubbing the back of her head gingerly. Nothing like a ruined orgasm to put things back into perspective, she thought. Also, it didn't really bode well for meeting her hero in real life if meeting him in her fantasy ended with her absolutely embarrassing herself. She made her way back to her computer with no slight amount of disgust in herself, staring at the computer screen again.

She did want to meet him. Attraction and fantasies aside, she wanted to meet the guy who took all these lovely pictures of bondage and sadomasochism she so thoroughly and routinely enjoyed in her alone time – not just because of her own perverse enjoyment but because of his purely artistic way of framing it. He saw the world as she saw it, she thought – the beauty in acts most people were all huffy and judgmental about.

Besides, it's not like she'd *literally* start masturbating as soon as she saw him. She had a bit more self control than that… right?

Maybe if he asked me to… in like a deep, rumbly voice… she admitted in her own head, giggling slightly at the thought as she bent over the desk to begin finishing things up.

Sighing and steeling her resolve, she went through to her calendar to find the day of the Dojo munch, finding she had little to move around to make it happen and the few things she did need to move were all personal – meaning she wouldn't have to worry too much about negative fallout if she did go. She was just about to text Lisa and let her know she was free on the day of when an email alert buzzed on her phone. She checked it out on her laptop, seeing that she had a callback audition for a small modeling agency she'd applied to work with a few months ago. Better yet, it was the day before the Munch!

If that's not a sign, I dunno what is…

With that, she programmed both events into her calendar, then set her chair back up before texting Lisa the words "I'm in." She then turned her phone off, locked the rolling wheels of the computer chair, and pulled the picture from before back up before taking a second to bite her index finger – the same finger still a bit moist from being between her thighs earlier. She smirked playfully at the image of Z-No, then slid her panties to the side as if she were displaying her still moist little slit to him personally, feeling the chill of the air against her sex.

"Now… where were we, *Sir*?" she asked, ring finger lightly brushing her clit as she whispered the words to him. "Would you like me to continue? I think we were just about at the point where I was continuing to debase myself for your attention… You were enjoying that, right *Sir*? You smug fucker…" She bit down on her bottom lip, head rolling back slowly and her eyes slipping closed. "Come on then… enjoy it more, you sick bastard… drink me in with those piercing black eyes of yours, looking at me like some piece of meat…"

She lost herself to the fantasy again, biting her bottom lip to stifle moans as she pictured him standing over her as she whispered filthy words of lust. He took photos of her as she begged and pouted and whined for his approval, for him to continue watching her, and inevitably for him to let her cum as she stroked a single finger against her g-spot and another furiously flickered at her clit.

She was almost fully lost in the fantasy when she heard the door downstairs open. Her roommate was home, and would probably need help with the groceries. Kristina groaned audibly into the air, closing out the tab on her computer and resigning herself to have to wait for later to full enjoy herself.

Honestly, though… in her head, Z-No would probably make her wait anyway so no harm done, right?

"Kris!" came the voice of Jason, her roommate, as if on cue. "Mind helping me with the-?"

"Does it require me getting of my glorious ass and/or putting on pants!?" she yelled back, interrupting him before he could finish. Tit-for-tat, since he'd unknowingly just done the same.

"Yes to the first question," Jason said, chuckling. "The answer to your second question depends on how comfortable you are with the neighbors seeing said ass."

Kris rolled her eyes and marched off to her bathroom, washing her hands clean and staring into the mirror to practice not looking like she just had her orgasm ruined for the second time today. Then, she headed back into her room, mumbling and grumbling as she did so.

*Days off are **not** meant to be spent wearing **<u>pants</u>**!*

Chapter 3 – First Meeting

The biggest downside to being back in the fold with the Dojo was it gave Lorenzo something to look forward to outside of work. Normally, that would be a good, thing, but when one already despises their job before it becomes something that keeps one away from what one would much rather be doing, every minute spent at work seems to drag on at the pace of a slug on morphine. He found himself listlessly staring at the clock on his computer screen again and again, marveling at just how long it took for the numbers to change.

It also didn't help things that Z-No had over-shot his goal a bit. To make sure there was no reason for the job to interfere with his trips to the Dojo, he'd gotten a jump on all his additional work – taking and editing all his photos just the way the boss would like them, the way that killed them inside, staying late at the office to get it all wrapped up in advance of the big anniversary event (now just 2 days away) and the Munch (now just 3 days away). In his Zeal, he'd wrapped up all his remaining workload for the week, which not only made it clear to anyone paying attention he could work faster, but it meant that his already miserable and boring job was even more dull – he had literally *nothing* to do but pretend he was busy.

I could be at home getting stuff set up right now… he thought to himself, growling slightly under his breath as he did literally nothing to the same picture for the 12th time. His mind wandered to all the stuff he could be taking care of had he not been stuck behind a desk. He could be making sure all his personal camera stuff was in order to take perfect shots, he could be going over the Dojo's space to plot out his gear layout, he could be practicing his knot-tying skills in case he was asked to do a suspension demonstration…

God, how long *had* it been since he tied someone up? It had to be nearly a year now, if not more. In that much time, his skills had to have atrophied a little bit at least… A shame, too. He used to weave intricate designs and patterns with rope like a spider would with silk…

"Hey, Lorenz? Lorenzo?! You there, bud?"

The sound jolted Z-No from his faux busy work, blinking rapidly like a child awoken from a dream and unable to reconcile it with reality. He glanced around and finally his eyes came into focus on… *him.*

"Oh, Hey Zach," he said, faking a smile. "Sorry, I was over here working so hard I didn't hear you!"

"I can tell!" Zach replied, placing one hand on Lorenzo's shoulder. "It looks great bud, I can really tell you've been working hard."

Inwardly, Z-No gritted his teeth. On a list of 20 reasons to hate working for Samuels' Photography and Advertising Company, numbers 3 through 15 all related back to the owner's son Zachary Samuels. Zach was everything Z-No – the younger, more passionate and less compromising Z-No – hated about some people in the field of photography. Zach was a trust fund baby with greased-back hair, cliché tattoos that he didn't even bother hiding under his shirts (in fact if anything, he moved the shirts around to display them), and he had never had to work a solid day in his life. He got his dad to take some of their seemingly bottomless supply of wealth and buy him all the camera equipment under the sun, and thought that made him a photographer. Zach knew nothing about great photographers like Gary Winogrand or Gordon Parks... he was just an obscenely wealthy brat who used his expensive gear as an excuse to get close to beautiful women so he could have an excuse to see them undressed, throw out the only real photography lingo he knew, and then try to fuck them.

Z-No felt his skin crawling from being touched by this creepy bastard, even on the shoulder through his clothes.

"So, it looks like you're about done…" Zach said, smiling that creepy long smile of his. "And I could really use your help my man. We got some new talent coming in to get some photos done, and Papa Zach needs a wing-man. Besides, you're way better at picking real talent than me, eh? I mainly look for 'other' talents on 'em…"

The bastard even had the nerve to chuckle and nudge Lorenzo as he said it.

Z-No – the original Z-No, the teenage to 20-year-old Z-No – would've decked this guy. 16 year-old Z-No would have slammed an elbow into Zach's throat, and 21-year-old Z-No would've done the same and followed that with a head-butt to the nose while he was winded before he kneed the rich bastard in the gut a few times while telling the prissy fucker he was a disgrace to the field.

But Z-No back then wasn't Lorenzo now. Z-No didn't have as many bills to pay. Z-No could live life just fine couch surfing and eating cheap fast food. Z-No could drop a job and just assume he'd survive 'till another popped up. Lorenzo, on the other hand, had a nice comfortable apartment he'd grown rather attached to, and in order to keep things that comfortable and nice he couldn't break the jaw of his boss' son. Even though said boss' son so richly deserved it.

Not during work hours, especially…

"Sure, buddy…" Lorenzo said, surprised his pants didn't literally catch fire from that statement. "I can help out a bit, whatever you need."

At the very least, it's something to do… he thought. *Besides, someone should probably be around to keep him from scaring off the new talent.*

Speaking of the new talent themselves, the girls were, as one might expect, all various degrees of beautiful. Some had a bit of experience modeling for this and that, some had never done it before but had always wanted to, and in some way or another each young woman here was expecting something big out of this meeting.

Of course looks weren't everything, as they always had to explain – there was also being able to pose properly and convey emotions.

"Uhm, I've seen like, every episode of project runway, Papi~" said a bleach-blond overly tan girl near the middle of the group, "I know how it works, don't you worry~". She was, as one of Lorenzo's best friends would put it, alarmingly Caucasian – making the use of 'Papi' and a forced Latinx-American accent that much more insulting to the culture she was attempting to rip off.

I don't know if there's enough caffeine in the world to get me through a day like this, Lorenzo thought as he popped a Red Bull can open and took two big swigs.

"Alright people!" Zach said, clapping his hands together. "We're gonna line you guys up alphabetically, and then we're gonna ask you to give us a few looks. We need energy from the word go, so this line doesn't move slower than molasses. We got a lot of you girls to go through today… ooh, bad choice of words! Or was it?"

Some of the girls forced giggles, figuring it would be best to play along with the guy who'd introduced himself as having the same last name as the company itself. Others looked around nervously, clearly uncomfortable, then went back into stage presence mode. Two of the girls rolled their eyes, having heard such stupidity before.

49

Lorenzo decided that unless those two absolutely tanked, they were in.

The rest was basic work as usual, with the models posing in front of a green screen and taking direction. Lorenzo didn't say much at first, just adjusting equipment and snapping photos when appropriate while trying to not to let the disgust he felt for Zach and the job in general show in his face. All these girls were, in one way or another, beautiful... and Zach being Zach, he was flirting with the most stereotypically beautiful. It made Lorenzo sick to the stomach to know he shared a gender with this bastard, let alone having to take orders from him. Somehow he managed to keep up a professional presence, and was able to politely remind Zach to remain on subject.

Part of him always felt better behind the camera – even when he wasn't given the freedom to do as he pleased, at least he was doing one of the things that made him feel completely at ease and complete. So long as he was behind that lens and snapping photos, capturing the beauty of women, he knew who and what he was – an eye beholding beauty. The outside world faded away, and he could capture those rare moments and angles from which the world seemed absolutely perfect. Each click of his finger on the shutter caught the world and the women as he saw them through his view finder (which he preferred using as opposed to the LCD display); those few moments where everything was perfect.

He was adjusting things a bit more when he heard Zach talking to one of the girls who'd rolled her eyes before. The snake bastard had taken a moment while Z-No was away from the forefront to start snapping pictures and pretending he knew what he was doing.

The day I no longer need this job, Zachary… you'd better run.

The young lady was obviously uncomfortable, and Zach was of course making it no better by continuing to talk to her like an invalid. She was gorgeous – one of the prettiest women they'd shot all day – with the same type of smooth brown skin, soft brown eyes, and plush full lips that could drive a man insane. Plus the way she was built… slim-thick, as a lot of folks would call it. She was petite in most places, with curves that were just gradual enough to be natural but still added such a surprisingly shapely figure to her… it was hard to ever put words to how women like her looked. People paid millions to have girls like her in music videos next to money and guns and CGI explosions.

And Zach couldn't get her to look good to save his life.

Idiot.

"What seems to be the problem here, bud?" Z-No asked, trying to pretend he wasn't daydreaming about strangling Zach the whole time he walked over.

"Well, you see it," Zach said with a sigh, gesturing to the young lady. "I can't get a decent shot out of this one. Good grief, she's giving me *nothin'*!"

Smart girl, Z-No thought.

"Lemme try, Zach…" he said, still forcing that smile. "After all, you did bring me down here for a reason…"

"You're the wizard, it is true," Zach said, backing away from the camera. "I humbly acquiesce to the master."

That word choice, though… Z-No thought, suppressing a laugh.

Once Zach was out of the way and headed to the crafts services table, he walked up to the young lady and introduced himself, calmly.

"What's your name, miss?" he asked, holding out his right hand to her.

"Kristina," she said, obviously still frustrated. "Kristina Shank." She took the offered hand, then paused and looked at his for a moment. She almost seemed to be studying it

Well, that's odd...

"Well, Kristina... I'm Lorenzo Wallace," he said, managing a smile. It was a bit more clinical than the smile he gave Tati at the gallery, but it wasn't his fake business smile either. It was that smile someone gives another person when they empathize with them for having to put up with bullshit. "Now... you've done some modeling before, I take it?"

"Some, yes." The responses she gave were still very curt, but that didn't bother him.

"I figured. Do you usually smile or just pose in your photos?"

"Pose."

"Perfect." He took the camera off the tripod, moving around a bit with it. "Now, we're gonna try a couple looks. Give me…" he paused, then smirked and let her see him glance at Zach – who was currently flirting with one of the models from earlier – and then back to her with the word, "*disdain.*"

She followed his eyes, and reflexively her eyes showed exactly the expression he was talking about. With a click, he captured it.

"Perfect!"

She blinked, not expecting him to take the picture until she looked back in his direction.

"Don't lose momentum," he encouraged. "Keep that focus, whatever it is. Give me that face one more time."

She paused, then seemed to get the message. The look she had returned, and he snapped a few more candids while moving around her.

"There it is, that's what we need to see!" he said proudly. "*Now* follow the camera with your eyes… there we go. Keep those looks going – you're above it, you're beyond it, you're a princess!"

She smirked a bit at the word 'princess' and he made sure to catch that from a few angles.

"That's it! That's the look a queen has, baby! Glamorous, absolutely!"

In moments he'd lost himself in the shoot. He was taking photos of her the way Z-No took pictures... the way he wanted, highlighting all the angles of her he knew would draw just the right amount of both critical eye and lewd imagination. He'd briefly imagined her in sheer satin fabric, cuffs on her ankles and wrists as she posed before him – no longer in the office studio but in the Dojo after a long scene together. She drew that mindset out of him – her skin, her figure, the unique scent of her –

"Lorenzo?"

The sound of Zach' voice yanked him back into the here and now, and he realized he was sweating. He'd gotten carried away – he wasn't even sure how many pictures of her he'd taken.

"I'm fine," he said after a short pause, stepping away and rubbing his forehead. " Just... got a bit caught up, is all." He looked over at Kristina, and smiled. "It was a fun shoot… thanks for being patient with me."

"Not at all!" she said, her face flushed. "Thank *you* for taking your time with *me!*"

Zach whispered something to him about preferential treatment, but Lorenzo shrugged it off. She was the last model of the day, and besides… he'd found something when he took the photos of her. As he explained this and showed Zach the pictures, the boss' son whistled.

"That's what I get for questioning the master…" he shot back, smiling that obnoxious smile. "Disregard what I said – you keep taking pictures like that, take all the time you want."

You damn right I will, Lorenzo thought. There was a tension in his muscles that eased away once Zach's grip on his shoulder left, Lorenzo grabbing the rest of his Red Bull and swallowing down his revulsion at having such a bastard touch him *again*. He didn't think anyone noticed, but… a glance at Kristina saw she noticed. She offered a coy smirk, and suddenly he felt that same strange tug he'd felt before. Whatever had drawn him to take pictures of her that way, or fantasize about her that way… it was there every time she smirked or smiled.

It's just wishful thinking, he told himself. *Get a grip and stop projecting, Z-No.*

Back in his professional form, he showed her the pictures and she picked out which ones she was most satisfied with. Lorenzo made sure she had her paperwork and dismissed her, trying and failing not to watch her leave.

"You're a damn idiot if you don't hit that," he heard Zach mutter from behind him.

Part of Lorenzo was revolted by the very implication of him doing something so grossly unprofessional. Another part, almost as large a part, was indeed imagining not just hitting that but claiming that.

He sighed, as they were done for the day, and headed outside for a breath of fresh air. All day cooped up inside... it was no way to live. At least he got outside in time to watch the sun set today... and as he leaned against the wall cracking open bottled water, he couldn't help but marvel at the sight of the city's skyline framed against the bright oranges and muted purples of the sunset.

In a practiced motion from his childhood, Lorenzo held up an imaginary camera and made a shutter-clicking noise with his mouth.

"Let me know how the prints turn out!" called a voice from behind him.

He spun around, surprised to find the young woman from earlier standing there, hands behind her back and a slightly nervous smile on her face – the kind one gets when telling a joke they weren't sure was funny. Lorenzo chuckled a bit, if only to alleviate the tension and his own embarrassment at getting caught taking imaginary photos.

"I sure will... you're Ms. Shank, right?"

"Only when I'm getting paid or getting in trouble," she said, the smile on her face a bit more easy now. He could tell she'd used that joke enough times before to be comfortable with it. "Please, just... call me Kris."

"Kris it is, then," Lorenzo responded, smiling. "The company pays the models, not me... and I don't think you're in any trouble just yet."

"That's surprising, considering how Mr. Samuels was talking," Kris replied, shaking her head slowly and letting the long black hair bounce a bit around her head. "Way he looked all displeased I thought I'd blown it."

"Zach doesn't call the shots around here," he told her with a roll of his eyes. "His dad part-owns the place, but he has less control over what models we pick than the catering staff."

The two of them shared a short laugh about that, then went silent and stared up at the sunset together.

"I'll definitely put in a good word," Lorenzo said at last, giving the same sort of slight smile she gave when she walked out. "Anyone who doesn't take shit from Baby Samuels is alright with me."

"Really?!" Kris asked. Her eyes lit up, and she actually bounced in place just a bit. "Wow, that's... wow! Thank you, thank you so much Mr. Wallace!"

"Hey, nobody calls me Mr. Wallace but the government..." Lorenzo responded with a smirk. "You call me Lorenzo, okay?"

"Got it," she said, smiling back at him. There was another long silence, during which she mimicked his hand motions and took an imaginary picture of her own before saying, quite breathily, "It really is a beautiful sunset."

Not as beautiful as you, the cliché part of Lorenzo wanted to say. But he caught himself and went with a reserved silence instead, leaning back against the wall.

"Say, Mr. Wal- I mean, Lorenzo..." Kris asked slowly, looking over at him with a puzzled stare. "Can I ask you something?"

"Sure," he replied. "Anything."

"What made you take pictures of me like that?" She titled her head, looking at him. "I mean... that other guy, Zach, he didn't take pictures of me like that at all."

"That's because Zach doesn't know the front end of a camera from the tip of his dick," he said, practically spitting the words. "He shoots at women like a horny teenager: no idea what makes them appealing besides T & A. Heavy emphasis on the T, like the momma's boy, nipple-deprived, orally fixated child that he is." The words were just pouring now, but he couldn't stop them. He had no desire to stop them; it felt too good getting it off his chest. "Any real camera man could have seen what angles to take pictures of a woman like you from." He stared off into the setting sun, then back over at her. "You should let me do some reshoots sometime too. Better lighting, natural lighting like this… really makes your eyes pop."

"I'd like that," she said, pulling some of her hair back from covering her ear. Lorenzo could see the outline of her neck so clearly… and suddenly he wondered what it would feel like to bite into it… how she would taste… what sounds she would make.

"It should go without saying," he told her, "but if anyone heard what I just said about Baby Saumels, I'd lose my job so…"

"Oh, don't worry about that!" she said, giggling. "Your secret is safe with me, I swear. If anything, I respect the honesty… you being willing to admit your boss is a cunt means you haven't drank the Kool-aid… but still being able to keep your job means you're a consummate professional. I can dig that."

For a few moments, neither of them said anything. There was just the sunlight basking over them both, the ambient noises of the street, the lingering smell of the hot dog vendor on the corner and the gyro stand on the other corner… and for that moment, Z-No wondered what it would look like from outside. He held up his fingers again, this time in a portrait position rather than a landscape, and prepared to take another fake picture. Then he glanced over at the young woman.

"Wanna get in on this one with me?" he asked.

"A selfie?!" she said, scoffing incredulously. "Why, Mr. Wallace, I hardly figured you for the type…"

"I'm full of surprises," he replied, rolling his eyes. "You want in on this photo or nah?" Then, before she could respond, he smirked and added, "And what did I tell you about that 'Mr. Wallace' crap? Say that again and you're in trouble."

"Sorry, Lorenzo…" she said, mock pouting. "I'll be good."

If you knew what that phrase does to someone like me… he thought quietly.

Kris skipped over, pressing her chin slightly against his shoulder. He could smell her – the coconut oil smell from her skin complimenting the smell of strawberries coming from her hair. He felt the warmth of her arms as she wrapped both of them around one of his. And for a moment, he wished this was like a real picture, a moment he could freeze in time for an eternity. He also found himself wanting to kiss her... then his smart watch began buzzing and chirping off a merry tune.

"Shit... that's my time for the day," he said, slowly pulling his arm away. "We'll have to talk more another time."

"Oh... alright," she said, looking a bit disappointed. "You, uh... You guys have my contact info, right?"

He nodded.

"Alright. I should probably be heading out as well." She sighed, looking up at the sky again then over at him. "Thanks again, for working with me and being patient. I've never had a photographer who just got my angles right like you did."

"Well, we'll hopefully be working together again!" Lorenzo said, smiling. He then shook her hand, headed inside, and jogged to the bathroom to down another Xanax – first one since breakfast. Nothing activated his anxiety quite like a pretty woman he didn't know showing interest in him.

She's up to something, the doubting voice in the back of his head told him. *She **has** to be up to something, why else would she talk to **us**? I mean, no woman talks to **us** unless she wants something... **She** proved that, didn't she?*

It was getting worse. It was getting louder. He couldn't hear the world around him as he power-walked into the bathroom and threw himself into a stall – just a nightmarish rush of his own blood in his ears punctuating the negative internal monologue that mocked and tormented him. He locked the stall door and let it hammer him like waves in the ocean: the sound of his heart pumping a mile a minute and his own voice reminding him of his failures, of his loneliness... of the woman known only as 'the cur' now, and her coy little smile in that picture of them together.

Then there was the familiar feeling of suffocation – the struggles to get air becoming harder, the exhaustion setting into the tense muscles, the blurring vision. It was like his own blood was drowning him from inside his body. He had to take the pills because his body and brain were constantly at war, he reminded himself. It was supposed to make him feel better as he frantically fumbled with the failsafe top... but really, it only gave the echoes that pulled him down more ammo.

Needing drugs to shut up your own head, he heard in his own voice. *Gosh, Z-No, how punk rock of you.*

He didn't even lie to himself and say he was only going to take a half. The whole pill went down his throat with a hasty chug of water that left him coughing and choking and sputtering... and afterwards, calm. The brain-blanching neutrality spread from his chest outward in a familiar wave, returning his heart rate and thought process to something like normal. He didn't usually have panic attacks at work... but then again he didn't have many nights as big as tonight ahead of him either. He blamed his nerves on that instead of Kris. After all, he photographed beautiful women all the time. That wasn't any different...

He went about getting cleaned up, and informed Zachary the work for the day was done so he would be headed out. He went to his desk to clock out and gather his things... then the rest of it became a blur. He vaguely remembered signaling for a ride using his smart phone... then he was outside of a storefront martial arts dojo called Black Tiger Mixed Martial Arts Dojo: the public, business face worn by the Dungeon of Joyous Obedience. He saw

Tati teaching a class, and signaled her over once she had a break from teaching some preteen kids how to properly use stances from Tae Kwon Do. She jogged over and hugged him.

"You're early!" she said, grinning.

"Have to set everything up," he reminded her. "Speaking of which..."

"It's the same path as always, Z," she said, giving him a shove. "You do ya thang; we'll see you down there."

And with that, Lorenzo went around to the back room behind the training area, past the mats and sparring gear, to a specific locked door. He produced the key for it from his pocket and was greeted by old, familiar concrete stairs he took down into the basement... the cool, empty darkness he illuminated with a flick of a switch. Here was the waiting room, laid out with soft and comfortable leather couches kept meticulously clean, upholstered in the Dojo's signature colors of black and bright green. Here was where people decompressed after and between scenes, and where they amped up before scenes.

Past the waiting room was the true Dungeon – a playground for adults with twisted fantasies. It was a spacious, well-lit area with a concrete floor like a modern gymnasium, with strategically placed mats on the floor that matched the furniture in the waiting room. The bondage furniture was already laid out, positioned atop the aforementioned mats and with enough space between the different pieces to allow for full range of motion – even if two Dominants needed to use one or more submissives at the same station at the same time. On the wall were the communal toys – floggers, paddles, ropes and restraints in that same Black and Green color scheme that characterized all other customizable aspects of the Dojo, organized with care in accordance to type and purpose. Lorenzo took a moment to observe each of them, silently greeting them like they were his old friends instead of the people upstairs. He'd help build some of this furniture, after all… and he'd personally helped with the acquisition of some of the communal implements. He touched them all in passing, then sighed before setting up his personal photography equipment. He needed to make sure every station had perfect lighting… and once that was set up, he went about white-balancing and setting up his camera, along with taking a few practice snapshots of the empty room just to make sure he had the proper illumination on the proper places. Once all that was done, he took in a deep, cleansing breath and smiled a warm smile before reaching into his bag for the last thing he'd need tonight: his mask.

He wanted to put it on already. He wanted so desperately to be behind that mask again, to be the *true* Z-No again. To wear a mask like his was to be removed from the all-seeing eyes of polite society and conventional reality; the obscuring of his face meant his freedom. People might be free to judge Lorenzo behind the mask, but Z-No was annulled from the anguish of authority by his anonymity. He stared at the mask, about to put it on, when the others arrived. And then Tati – no, Morticia: in this place she was Morticia, just as everyone else went by their dungeon names – came downstairs, leading the rest of the pack. Gomez, Dante, Virgil, and Titania were all there. He remembered them all, like there'd been no time since the last time they met… and the hugs and calls of joy were so many it was drowning out his anxiety and fear from before. This was where he felt the most at home and at peace; here with his family of fellow freaks. There was no judgment, no condemnation, no evil; just love.

Finally, as everyone settled down, Gomez placed one of his massive hands on Z-No's shoulder and smiled.

"Welcome home…" he said, smiling.

"Good to be home," he replied. "So… masks on, folks! We need a picture of the founding roster."

Chapter 4: The Munch

"Why aren't you in bed yet?" Lisa asked Kris via their Skype connection. "We have to be up early as balls tomorrow, remember?"

"I don't sleep before stuff like this anyway," Kris replied with an exasperated sigh. "Too excited, too anxious... too many decisions on what to fucking *wear*!"

She was on outfit number 12 thus far, the others all collected in a heap on the left side of her bed as a jumble of dresses, stockings, and small accessories. Beside the bed on the floor, a matching heap of heels lay in a discard pile as well. On her night stand, there were different lipstick colors and nail polish types, all in an array. Her options, stretched out before her, were almost endless... which gave a restrictive level of freedom. The choices weighed on her with the oppressive inevitability of making a decision and the possibility of that decision being the wrong decision.

And as she held up outfit 12… it was clear it was weighing on Lisa too.

"God, woman, you're *killing* me!" she groaned out before thudding her head down on her desk. She looked it, too; her hair was pulled back in a messy ponytail, her makeup long gone, her reading glasses on a bit crooked once she sat back up and stared into the camera… but she made no indication or mention she was going to sign off and leave Kris hanging.

"I know I know… but I can't go meet *him* looking any ol' way!" Kris said with a stamp of her foot. "I'm not going to bed until I have an outfit that will **slay** at the Munch. And I'm talking make 'em stare so hard, when I walk by and they snap their necks – *that* level. I want to cause tears of thirst and bitter jealousy, bitch! Now *help me!*"

"God, FINE!" Lisa snapped, adjusting her glasses and looking her over. "You should go with… the dress from outfit 3, the stocking from 5, the makeup from 6, the heels from 10, and the belt from 4. Oh, and the lacey underwear from outfit 7 too, plus purse from 9.

Kris, like most people would in such a situation, stared at her friend with a flabbergasted and confused stare.

"Just trust me," she said. "Grab them in this order: 3, 5, 6, 10, 4, 7, and finally – 9, the purse. Then tell me what you think."

Kris hesitantly picked out the items requested: a red sundress with white diamond designs, a black belt, some stark white heels, and contrasting black lipstick. She tried them on and stared herself down in the mirror, surprised by how it all came together.

"Lisa, babe," Kristina said, staring at herself in the mirror and toying with a few different poses, "Have I told you recently how much I love you?"

"Like 10 times a day," Lisa responded with a wry smile. "Which still isn't enough but hey, I'm forgiving."

"Well, again… thanks," she said, pausing for a moment to get out of the selected outfit and back into her sleeping clothes – this evening an oversized "Bad Religion" t-shirt and some black satin panties. "I just needed to be sure of stuff again… especially after yesterday."

"That reminds me," Lisa said. "You said you had a photo shoot, right? How'd that go, hun?"

"Well, it could've been better... lots better," Kris admitted. "The first part was embarrassing as fuck… the guy whose dad owns the whole place took pics of me at first, and… let's just say it didn't go well."

"Was he a jerk?" Lisa asked. "Or was he just a creeper?"

"Worse, he was both."

Lisa sucked in air between her teeth, then offered up a soft "yikes".

"Well, it wasn't all bad," Kris said shortly after. "This other guy took over... real professional type, super nice. He took some *amazing* pictures, too. Seemed a bit stiff at first, but..." she paused, drifting off a bit.

"What?"

"Say Lisa, you ever..." she paused, placing one hand on her chin. "You ever like... I dunno. You ever listen to someone talk and just know they're..."

"'Bout that life, as the kids say?" Lisa finished for her.

"First, never talk like that again…" Kris said with an eye roll and a slight laugh. "But yes, that's what I mean. Like that new photographer, the one who took over after the Daddy's Boy… he just had this air about him, y'know? Something about the way he talked, and how he held himself…"

"Was he hot?" Lisa asked, cutting her off.

"Well, I mean…" Kris paused, biting her bottom lip.

"That's a yes!" cried Lisa, clapping her hands.

"Shut up!" she snapped back.

"So, you think he's competition for Mr. Z-No?" Lisa asked, leaning forward.

"I work with him, Lisa," Kristina reminded her with a roll of her eyes. "Sleeping with someone at a new job seems like a bad move, wouldn't you say?'"

"Valid point," her friend admitted. "Counter-point; it's only a bad move if you get caught."

Kris couldn't suppress a laugh at that one... but as she continued to talk to her best friend she couldn't help but wonder if there was a point to that little line. She'd read plenty of romance novels and short literotica stories about having sex at work, and they always made it sound *hot*. Sure it was wrong, but that was half of what made it so amazing; the risk of getting caught made the sex that much more compelling and difficult to resist, with the added risk of job loss moving the thermostat up higher. It was something to consider...

After a while, Lisa signed off and left Kristina alone with her thoughts. Lorenzo was nice... attractive as well. She'd noticed his brilliantly white and straight teeth, his smooth mocha skin, and when she'd held his arm for the fake selfie there'd been enough time for her to detect a satisfyingly solid amount of musculature and tone. Maybe it would be fun. He seemed like a consummate professional... maybe he was too professional to bend a pretty young thing like her over his work desk and make her beg for mercy – or beg for more. But maybe she could convince him to break the rules, just once. She loved the idea of that stiff and rigid persona cracking because she made him unable to resist...

It's still a bad idea, she reminded herself. *It's stupid, it's stupid, it's* **stupid.**

Of course, her libido didn't really seem to care how bad an idea it was... and she needed to get some sleep anyway. She resolved to check her email one more time before resigning to a quick masturbation session before bed, and was met with a pleasant surprise; an update from the Dojo.

Of course she clicked it.

"THE FAMILY IS BACK TOGETHER!" the header text announced proudly in all caps. "We had a blast tonight at the anniversary expo, and boy… you missed out if you couldn't make it."

Rub it in, why doncha… Kristina said to herself with a huff before scrolling down to read more.

"We took PLENTY of pictures, but our beloved Z-No is a perfectionist and isn't letting us release them until he's had time to make them look even better than they already do. ☹ He's such a spoil sport sometimes… but we love him anyway! For now, this is the only picture he's allowed us to release early. Enjoy it now!"

The picture in question was a portrait of the founding Dojo family. She recognized the fit woman near the front sporting a black faux-leather dress as Madame Morticia, and the burly, hairy-chested giant holding her on his shoulders as her husband and submissive, Papa Gomez.

On either side of them, posing like characters from some Renaissance painting, were the adorable couple known as Dante and Virgil. Standing in front of the ox of a man Gomez was Titania, the ruthless Domme know affectionately as the Fairy Queen, posing with a bull whip in her hands and her tongue sticking out. And in front of her, doing one of those 90s hip-hop album cover squats, was him… Z-No, the man himself.

I'll be meeting him tomorrow.

The thought alone set her heart to fluttering. She found her fingers dipping between her thighs and pressing into the satin fabric as her fantasies began to blend. One moment she was in Lorenzo's office, being placed gently onto his desk… and the next she was bent over a piece of dungeon equipment and at the mercy of Z-No.

"Mmmph… fuck…" she whispered to herself, fingers kneading more insistently at her labia and clit as she lost herself in the dueling fantasies. "Don't just tease me…"

The worlds couldn't be more different in her fantasies. On the one hand she imagined Lorenzo to be sweet but strong – what she called 'vanilla with an edge'. He wasn't kinky, in her eyes, but he had enough of an authoritative manner and cold glance to at least rev her engine. She wouldn't put a bit of spanking or neck biting past him… but otherwise he'd be sweet and loving, like something out of a novella. He wasn't in a hurry, and he knew what he was doing… the type of guy who'd make eye contact when he pressed his fingers against your g-spot just so you knew he did it on purpose. The idea of it, the stare he gave, made her slide her panties slowly to the side and delve two of her own fingers into the wet mess her pussy was becoming. Just a little press in and a slight hooking of the fingers… and there it was. Her palm was able to brush her clit as her middle and ring fingers caressed the inner tenderness, the ridges against her nimble

digits sending a white-hot flash of pleasure directly into her

brain that switched the fantasy channel back to Z-No.

Z-No was a whole different beast. She'd seen the

pictures… he liked to tease the lucky woman he'd tied up

by making them kiss the toys he was going to use on them

before each session. He would alternate between gentle

caresses and harsh strikes, seemingly without a warning or

discernible pattern. His bio on the website stated his biggest

kinks were orgasm control, begging, and… something else,

she couldn't remember, it was a long word and didn't

matter. All that mattered was in her head his big strong

hands were slapping her tits as he coldly and quietly

observed her, the free hand moving in and out of her pussy

slowly, methodically, drawing the orgasm he'd never let

her have closer… and closer…

Soon the images blurred in her mind, locations and

persons all swirling. One moment she was on the floor of

the set from earlier with Z-No on top of her instead of Lorenzo, choking her while he fucked her against a green screen… and the next she was against the walls of the Dojo's Dungeon, Lorenzo kissing her slowly as he called her beautiful. Then things began to mix further, with Lorenzo treating her to the business end of a flogger while Z-No lifted his mask enough to swirl his tongue over her throbbing little clit…

The mash-up overwhelmed her. She clutched her left breast hard, staccato fucked her pussy with the other hand, and imagined him – no them, *both of them* – ordering her to cum.

The tight warm walls around her fingers squeezed, her body went white-hot with energy, and she felt like an explosive charge detonated – one second a bundle of potential and the next a supernova of wondrous chaos. She shook in her chair as she came but couldn't stop her own hand, too lost to the blended fantasy. Her head pressed against the cool fake wood of her desk as she bucked her hips and whimpered out soft curse words and plaintive noises as the pleasure and pain collided. Then the exhaustion sank in as her muscles confirmed she was spent, and she stayed against her desk panting a bit longer before deigning to look up.

That was twice. Twice in a single week, she'd caught herself pawing away at herself looking specifically at Z-No or his work. And tomorrow she was going to be meeting him.

This is going to go absolutely wonderfully, she thought to herself sarcastically, leaning her head back to stare at the ceiling. Everyone always talked about what a mistake it tended to be to meet those one looked up to, and most of those stories didn't even have the added complication of wanting to get your brains fucked out by said hero. It was going to be a disaster... but she'd already signed up for it, whatever happened. Too late to pull back now. She stared a bit more at the ceiling, then finally gazed back at the screen... at him.

Then she clicked off and distracted herself with Netflix and red wine until bed.

The next morning came sooner than she'd expected, and she found herself lunging out of bed and frantically moving from place to place in the house trying to get ready. She was in such a hurry she did her makeup before getting in the shower... which resulted in about 2 straight minutes of swearing before hopping out the shower to redo the ruined makeup. Then there was the moment she spilled nail polish whilst doing her toes, stubbed her foot in an attempt to keep it off the rug, and ended up falling into her closet face-first. This resulted in a bit of poignant grumbling and defiantly kicking her feet, before getting up to clean the mess and make a third pass at her makeup. By the time she got dressed up, she felt like she'd run two marathons and done the 100 meter dash… but it was worth it when she caught herself in the mirror with her hair perfectly laid and her outfit coordinated fawlessly, showing off just enough skin and shape to tantalize the eyes. All that was left to do was grab a light breakfast – granola bar and soy milk – and wait for Lisa to pick her up while avoiding Rex's enthusiastic attempts to nuzzle up to her and lick her face.

"Sorry, sweetie!" she told the overgrown pup, smiling. "Momma's gotta look her best so no kisses, okay?" She patted him on his head, set out his food and water, and made it outside just as Lisa was pulling up.

"There's my girl!" her best friend called out the window. "God, you *always* make the shit look effortless… c'mon, hop in!"

"Oh, you know…" Kristina replied, dusting a bit of Rex's hair off her skirt, "… the hardest part is waking up."

The whole way there was filled with music and idle chit-chat, a welcome distraction for Kris… but eventually it ended and they pulled up to the legendary Top Hat bar and grill – a place known for miles for their whiskey cocktails and Texas style barbecue menu.

"A-1 cooking but messy as all hell," Lisa teased as she pulled into the parking space. "If there's anything more fitting for this, I dunno what it is."

Kristina, meanwhile, was psyching herself up to not bolt out the car and run away screaming. For a moment, all she could really think was 'don't freak out' over and over… and by the time she was sufficiently calmed, Lisa had somehow gotten her inside the restaurant.

FREAKING OUT. I AM FREAKING OUT!

As tense as she had been, however, everything that followed was very laid back. The first person she met other than the hostess was Morticia... who was dressed in a track suit, insisted she be called Tati, and complimented Kristina's dress by clapping and saying, "YAS, bitch!"

Nothing eases tension in a room like track suits and colloquialisms.

Tati led the two younger women over to the table, where she introduced them to the rest of the family – her husband Gomez, real name Daruis; Titania, real name Tasha; and last but not least Dante and Virgil, real names Terrence and Ulysses respectively. They were all super friendly, and so were the other, younger members the pair were introduced to. After a moment, Kris was making fast friends with another pair of outsiders, and was wondering why she'd ever been nervous in the first place. But then she heard Tati behind her;

"There he is! Hey, Z-No!"

For a split second Kristina felt like a few thousand ice cubes running up and down her spine, her whole body a mess of nerves and chills and tension. This was it, this was the moment – she was going to come face to face with *the* Z-No. She thought for a moment this was what rabbits must feel like when they hear a wolf behind them in the snow – like prey, like vulnerable raw meat, just begging the fates and gods for mercy since it was too late to run. She took in a deep breath and turned slowly towards the sound as her curiosity trumped her fear... and that's when she looked back and looked over at none other than Lorenzo Wallace.

So... remember the prior freak out? Her brain reminded her. *That was about 4 out of 10. PREPARE FOR A LEVEL 11 FREAK OUT!!!*

There was a moment where she was swearing to herself it wasn't him: that it couldn't be him, that there was no way. He actually fed this delusion at first, by acting like they'd never met. But as the Founders and other members of the Dojo starts talking, and she heard his mid-tenor voice with that dry witty tone… it couldn't be anyone else. He was dressed differently – in a Black Flag t-shirt and jeans as opposed to his usual dress shirt and slacks from the pictures, but that body type was definitely Z-No… and that voice was definitely Lorenzo. They were one and the same, she knew, and she knew he knew she knew… which, aside from being a confusing mixture of thoughts was actually pretty terrifying. Would he tell the group and have her removed, or tell the people at work and have her fired? Both options were anxiety fuel of the highest grade… and for Kris, the best option was to get out in front of it. The moment that the introductions were over and everyone was allowed to mix and mingle, she saw him starting to slip off. Following the cue of many action movies before, she gave Lorenzo a 10-second head start then followed, trying to be inconspicuous while also keeping him in her line of sight. He went out the back and she waited, then followed… and the next thing she knew she was watching him, by the dumpsters, pulling out a flask with a built-in cigarette case full of already-rolled joints.

God he's so cool… she thought for a moment longer, fading out to daydream. Then, as he was putting one of the joints in his mouth, she decided to step forward.

"Hey," she called out. His reaction was a startled noise and then him almost dropping his joint before turning to face her.

"Jeez!" he snapped, exasperated. "I thought you were the fuckin' cops for a second there…" He then paused, then put the joint behind his back before looking her over. "Don't tell the guys inside, okay? I didn't bring enough to share."

"That's not why I'm out here!" she said in a hoarse whisper. "But, I mean... if you're offering..."

"Only because you caught me," he reminded her. "And if you say a word to anyone..."

"Who am I gonna tell?" she said, rolling her eyes. "I'm gonna walk into work on Monday, stand around the water cooler and say 'Hey guys, I was at a bondage club brunch and smoked a joint with one of the photographers'?"

"You have Monday off," Lorenzo stated in a bland, matter-of-fact tone.

"That's so not the point!"

Lorenzo grabbed her wrists and shushed her, the way a parent might a child. She was about to protest the indignity of this before she found the joint in her mouth, put there by him. He then produced a Zippo lighter from his pocket and lit it in a single, smooth motion before holding the flame up to her.

For a moment she watched the fire dance between them, swirling around in front of her and reflected in his eyes. The warmth from it was palpable, removing some of the chill and tension of the morning and the moment. She leaned forward and let the tip of the J dangle in its tiny roaring embrace, then took a deep puff inward as she noticed how well the rich bright fire reflected in those dark brown, almost black eyes of his.

Then he snapped the casing shut and put the lighter away, breaking the spell. It didn't help either that the joint appeared to have something potent and stout in it, making her start to choke a bit after just one hit.

Lorenzo, the man she'd stormed outside to confront, had to give her a sip of his water and pat her back to get her breathing right. *If one could die of embarrassment*, she thought, *this is when and where I'd do it.*

For what felt like a long time they sat in silence – just passing the tightly packed paper full of ganja back and forth between one another. As it was starting to kick in for her, she finally felt the irrevocable urge to speak.

"So... am I in trouble?" she asked. "I mean, for this... coming to this. Am I like, busted?"

Lorenzo made a face, then shook his head and passed the joint back to her.

"You said it yourself..." he told her, bit of smoke still curing out of his nostrils, "... how would I go about telling anyone where I met you today and why? Besides... I've been a member of the Dojo longer than I've had the job. What would I gain by outing you?"

"Valid points," she replied as she took a slow puff. Then, inevitably, she followed with "Damn... this is some good shit."

"Medicinal," he told her. "It's specifically grown for stress... and I'm trying out something new. What brought you out here anyway, Ms. Shank?"

"I thought I told you to call me Kris," she hissed, glaring at him before taking another small puff. "You don't get to call me Ms. Shank in a situation like this. That's way too formal."

"Kris it is, then..." he said, sighing and taking the joint back when she offered. "Still doesn't answer my question."

"I just wanted to see if it was you," Kristina said with a shrug. "No offense, but... you're one of the last people I'd have expected to be here."

"None taken," Lorenzo told her. "That's by design; I go outta my way to look too square to be here."

"Mission accomplished, then," she said with a smile. "I'd never have guessed you had a kinky bone in your body... let alone that you were Z-No."

He gave her a glace when she said that name, but then otherwise said nothing and just passed her the joint back.

"Can I call you that?" she asked, suddenly realizing she might have crossed a line. "Z-No, I mean. Can I call you Z-No or is that awkward?"

"I'm smoking a joint at a munch with someone just met I met at work," he began, pulling out the flask once more, "and I'm not the one who invited her. It doesn't get much more awkward than this."

"So... is that a yes on the Z-No thing?"

"Yes, it's a yes."

Kris caught herself clapping, then caught Z-No snickering at her clapping. She then stared down at her hands before placing them squarely in her lap.

"Sorry," she said, still looking down. "I'm just a bit excited. The whole reason I came here today was because of you... the Z-No you. Like... I'm a big fan of your photos. Like, before I found sites like the Dojo I thought black people being into BDSM was weird and unhealthy. I kept trying to bury or repress it. Then... I saw your photos and... I dunno. You made it beautiful. You made it art."

"It was always art," Lorenzo said, pulling a long gulp from his flask. "I just captured it as art instead of as an oddity." There was a hit, an exhale, and a pause before he spoke again. "The idea of black love shouldn't be some oddity or myth... and it shouldn't only be for those who have missionary vanilla sex twice a week. If anyone tells you that you're not normal for being black and liking

BDSM, tell them to fuck off." He stared off, and for a

moment she saw the flames dancing in his eyes again. He

had a sort of passion about him, when he talked about this

especially, that made him seem to almost glow. He was

alive with this slow-burning energy, just waiting for a

moment to release it…

There was a moment where she realized just how

badly she wanted to sit on his face. Then there was a

moment of panic where she wondered if she'd said that part

out loud. Then there was a second moment of panic as she

wondered how long she'd been blankly staring at him while

stoned, eyes fixated on his lips as he spoke so softly yet

powerfully. Then there was a moment of flinging her

fingers around and cursing when the neglected joint burned

her middle and index fingers.

"Calm down, calm down…" he said, taking hold of

her hand calmly. "Let me see…" He led her hand for a

moment, examining it… and if there were ever a moment Kristina felt more like a groupie she couldn't think of it. Here he was, examining her fingers… one of those fingers being among the same ones she used to masturbate to his pictures and likeness... and she was torn between too high to make a move and so high if she didn't make a move her pussy would make one for her. She had that weird, weed-induced, cotton mouth horniness – the kind of arousal where it felt like all moisture in her mouth had left to make sure her pussy was extra wet.

Damn you, Libido, why do you betray me!? She thought, staring angrily down at the throbbing, needy bundle of nerves between her thighs. This state (which her roommate affectionately dubbed the 'stoner boner') wasn't unfamiliar… hell, she used to smoke all the time. But it had been a while since she last hit a joint and never before in her smoking history was someone she had a crush on babying her and taking care of her fingers like this.

"So, listen…" he said, standing up slowly and stretching as he stomped the last embers of the joint out. "I think it goes without saying that you and I never saw each other here today, as far as the office is concerned."

Kristina nodded, not willing to do much else.

"Good." Lorenzo sighed, rubbing the back of his head, before looking down at her for a moment. "If you want to keep coming to munches or attend classes, or even become a full member of the Dojo, feel free. It'll be nice having someone around I can talk to about this stuff anyway."

"What if I want more than that?" Kristina asked before she could stop herself. She kept her voice a bit low, or tried to… but he turned to her like he heard her and she felt her whole body glow hot with embarrassment.

"And what else might you want?" he asked after a bit of a pause.

"Well… remember when I said I was a big fan of yours?"

He nodded.

"Well… I've always wanted you to take pictures of me," Kris said, not looking up. "And not like… not like the ones you took for the company the other day, either. I mean like… like the ones you take for the Dojo."

"You mean, for a portfolio?" asked Z-No.

"No…" she said timidly, hands folded in her lap. "I want something more… private. Like, just between the two of us. You understand, right?" She stared down at her hands again, fingers knitted together and gripping each other. She felt the steady thumping of her heart now, her pulse still relatively slow even as she felt nervous.

Shit.

What she'd just confessed to him was something that she'd never confessed to another soul other than Lisa… and it didn't feel like the typical way of doing things. In the books and movies, the scene was always so different; usually it took place in some high-rise apartment that cost thousands of dollars, with an epic view, with a well-dressed man in a suit saying something romantic. Here instead they were puffing medicinal pot outside behind a barbeque joint, both dressed in casual clothing, and she'd made the first move. How many rules had she just broken? How badly had she just screwed this up? God, she could only imagine how absurd she must seem to him at this point, how out of place… how desperate.

"Hand me your phone," he said after a long pause.

Kristina blinked for a moment, confused… and then she reached into her purse and pulled out her phone, handing it over nervously. He took it, then looked down at it before shaking his head and handing it back with a smile.

"Helps if you unlock it first."

"Oh!" she said, frantically fumbling with the touch screen buttons for a moment or two before managing to put in her pass code properly and open the home screen. She handed the device over to him, and he began typing away on it.

"I saved my name and number," he said, "and sent myself a text so I know yours. If you wanna discuss this later, when we're both more clear-headed, feel free." He handed the phone back to her, then took his own out of his pocket as it chimed to alert him of her message.

Kris felt like her heart was doing backflips. "Was that a yes?" she asked immediately, short of breath a bit.

"It wasn't a 'yes' or a 'no' yet," Lorenzo replied. "It was a 'we'll see how it goes'. I mean… best we get to really know each other first, before we move into the fun stuff."

Kris wanted to scream that she *did* know him. She wanted to point out all the nights she'd studied his photo composition, how she'd devoted hours to analyzing his unique shooting style, how she'd almost memorized his bio on the Dojo page. But before she could do any of this, she attempted to stand up… and failed.

That changed her perspective right quick.

"You've got a point…" she said. "To reiterate… that was some good shit."

"I'm well aware," he told her, shaking his head and smiling again as he helped her up.

"So… should we head back in?"

"We can if you want," he replied.

"If I did what I wanted, I'd probably get in more trouble than I've made already," she said with a nervous giggle.

"Well, you're not in any trouble yet," Lorenzo assured her. "So... what was it you wanted to do that might get you into trouble?"

Kris took a deep breath in. She was starting to feel the effects of the weed more now, but instead of relaxing her it was making her second guess herself at this point. She knew she was stoned, and thus knew what she was proposing was a bad idea. But she was also just stoned enough to ask.

"I... I want..." she started, hands once again clasped in front of her. She stared down at her dainty little feet in those size 7 heels, then over at his large black boots. Her eyes nervously drifted up his jeans, stopping at his groin by instinct just long enough to see a slight bulge in the denim that made her wish he'd been in gray sweatpants... then she forced the perverted side down and quickly made her way up to his eyes.

"I want… to ask you… to kiss me," she said. "I know you said it's better if we talk later and all, but…"

"I said," he interrupted, "it would be better if we talked about the other things later. A kiss, on the other hand… I see no harm in going for now. All you have to do is ask."

And then she felt his warm, large hand on her cheek. She brought her head up to meet his gaze slowly, still taken away by those dark eyes of his. He had other handsome qualities; the well-manicured beard that showed off his chin and jawline, a very becoming nose, full and soft-looking lips… (god, those lips…) but the eyes were still what drew her in. When he was in his Z-No persona, how they'd first 'met', those intense dark orbs were all she could see… and now again they were all she could focus on. They were like black holes: their gravity was infinite, drawing in all things surrounding them, including her. She felt like she would fall into them and never cease falling, adrift in the sea of those pool-like pupils until she was so far gone the light from the surface was a distant memory.

She relaxed her body against his, letting herself sink and not bothering to fight the gravity that pulled her down towards and into him. The only effort she could manage was to place one of her own soft hands against his face and feel the leftover scruff of his beard tickling her palms as she dangled limply across his form. She felt the strange contrast of his heartbeat against her chest, out of sync with her own circulatory rhythm enough to be distinct but close enough that they formed their own thudding rhythm… like a double pedal beating slowly on a bass drum.

"I already said I wanted-," she began, only to stop as his other hand gripped her right hip and gave it a light squeeze.

"Exactly," he replied, smirking slightly. "You said you *wanted*. And I want to give you what you want. But you have to *ask*."

He was arguing semantics. Part of her wanted to rebel and not say a word just for that. But here he was, so close… smelled richly of coffee and cologne, of cocoa butter and hair oil… feeling warm against her fingertips, looking like a rich dark-brown statue of her own desires made flesh.

It didn't exactly help the cause that being forced to beg was one of her kinks anyway.

"Fuck… I…" she started, wanting desperately to get the words right. She held on for a bit, fingers slightly twitching against his cheek, and then – "Please. Please, will you kiss me?"

"That'll do for now," he said. Then his lips were against hers and his arms were around her and she felt the air inside her rush out in a huff. Her lips parted to move with his, to make room for his, just as she exhaled to make room for him. Her flesh prickled with small sparks of electricity as her brain shot fireworks of alertness and awareness through her nerve endings of pleasure heightened as much by the THC in her system as they were by the fulfillment of her fantasy.

I'm kissing Z-No, she told herself in disbelief. *God, yes, I'm kissing Z-No!*

Her hapless libido, earlier kept in check, would allow no further restraint or hesitation. She kissed back greedily, ravenously, her hands both around his neck as her hips pushed forward against his to line up with that outline she saw earlier and feel it against her and *oh,* **yes** she could feel it… So close and yet so achingly far from pressing against her and then into her and..!

Wet wasn't the word; she was soaking.

The kiss ended, all too soon for her tastes, and she felt the lightheaded daze take over her brain as she tried to remember where they even were and what else was in the world.

"We should get back inside," he told her.

"Mhm. We should."

"You don't want to, though, do you?"

"Nuh-uh."

"One more kiss?"

"Please?"

And so they did. She lost track of time, of space, of self… but then this kiss was also broken and he slowly pulled his hands off her skin

"That's enough for now," Lorenzo told her. "There will be others."

"Promise?" Kris asked, still stroking his face.

"Guaranteed," he assured her.

And with that, she managed to pry her hands off him and they went on back inside – her first, then him so as not to raise suspicion. On the way back in, she stopped by the restroom to fix her makeup and recollect herself mentally at the same time, reorganizing her thoughts as she touched up her lipstick. She let the restaurant's AC cool her down a bit, then sighed at herself in the mirror. She'd never felt so depraved and desperately needy and horny as she did after that kiss.

Good thing it worked out. God only knows how she'd have been able to handle it if he'd said no.

She opened her phone to see 2 missed texts from Lisa, both wondering where she went, and responded with a heart-eyes emoji and the words "BITCH DO I HAVE A STORY TO TELL YOU" in all caps.

Chapter 5 – Z-No

What the hell did you just do?!

Lorenzo gripped his head with both hands, sitting on his couch at home contemplating that very question. He'd always had a strict rule to not mess with women he worked with in any capacity. His entire working life he'd always avoided 'dipping the pen in company ink', as his father had so colorfully put it – even back when he was working menial part-time jobs he didn't care about losing. Now that he had a career... now that he was making good money and paying his own bills, he picked *now* to break that cardinal rule?!

Still it had happened. It happened and he had to tell someone. First instinct was to call Tati, but he thought better of it; with all she had on her plate when it came to keeping the Dojo organized and running smoothly the last thing he wanted was to stress her out.

What he needed was someone who would have the time to listen to his plight and understand it. And that meant he needed Tasha. Tasha, aka Titania the Fairy Queen, was one of the few members of the founding Dojo team Z-No never really lost contact with – in part because she wouldn't allow him to do so. She was always keeping in touch, either calling or texting him at least once a day to check back in. She had her own mental health issues, and had also been friends with Cozbi… so she more than anyone else knew what he'd been going through. He sent her a text first, just to make sure she wasn't busy… and after she confirmed she wasn't doing anything of import, he called her.

"Wuddup, Z?" she asked, her voice a mellow baritone. "You alright?"

"Kinda," Z-No replied, sighing. "Not gonna lie, part of me is really freaking out right about now."

"What's wrong?!" Tasha asked. Her voice immediately shot up a few octaves, and Z-No could practically hear her clenching her fists through the phone. "What happened? Who is it? When do I kill them?!"

"I love the enthusiasm," he replied, "but it's nothing like that. It's on me: I made a mistake and need to talk to someone about it, that's all."

"Oh…" Tasha sighed, and the tension went out of her voice slowly. "So, we talkin' messed up, screwed up, or fucked up?"

"What's the difference?" Z-No asked. "I mean, aside from social acceptability?"

"Simple," said Tasha. "Messing up is like, I dunno… forgetting your sister's anniversary – it's not really a big deal, but it's kinda a bummer. Screwing up would be like getting them a present, but misspelling her husband's name. And fucking up would be accidentally sending him a picture of you naked and causing an argument that almost ruins their whole marriage."

"… Dude."

"It was a for instance! If I sent my sister's husband a naked picture, it would be on purpose and you know that."

Z-No snickered. It was good to hear that typical side and cynical sense of humor typical of Tasha. It always relaxed him a bit.

"In that case," he told her, "I definitely messed up. It's not big… not yet… but it's bugging me right now."

"Wanna talk about it?" she asked.

"Sure… in person," he replied.

"I dunno about that…" Tasha said. "That's a bit out of the way, and I have work to do, and-!"

"I got weed."

"Be there in 20 minutes."

Next time, Z-No thought to himself, tossing his phone aside, *I should probably lead with the 'I have a weed card' card.*

About 25 minutes later, Tasha and Z-No were leaning back on his couch, smoking a joint and listening to Ska like they were back in undergrad. Tasha was blowing smoke rings, her boots kicked up on the table. She was a bit like the opposite of Tati in some ways; where Tati was always dressed to work out or jog, Tasha dressed like the punk rock princess she was; black boots that went up to her shins, studs and piercings in her ears, nose, and lip (a Labret, a Monroe, a nose ring, and .05 gauges), eye line sharp enough to slit a man's throat, and matching nails.

"You haven't changed a bit," he noted with a smile, recounting how he used to look equally punk rock back in the old days.

"Sure I have," Tasha replied as she passed back the joint. "I eat healthier. Plus, I do Yoga now."

"Tati?" Z-No asked.

"Who else could get my ass into yoga pants at 6 in the damn morning?"

"Shit… I guess we all grew up."

"Speaking of changing," Tasha said, staring at the joint in her hands, "Since when are you smoking again?"

"Since I got a prescription," Z-No told her. "I was using Xanax for my anxiety, but then… I was using them too much and too often. So, I decided to try something new."

"Makes sense," she replied. "Weed's more natural, and way easier on your kidneys."

There was a long pause as Z-No hit the joint… then as he exhaled his first puff, he explained everything. He explained meeting Kristina, from the beginning – including the part where they met at work – and all the way up to earlier when he'd kissed her. He took a second, smaller puff, then blew the smoke out through his nose like a dragon.

"I'm supposed to be messaging her back on Monday," he said with a sigh before passing the weed back over to Tasha. "Thing is I dunno if it's a bad idea or what, if anything, I'd even say to her."

"Well, there's 3 things to consider," Tasha said. "Thing one; she's a model, meaning she doesn't exactly work with or for your same company. Technically, she's a freelancer and not a coworker so your 'company ink' policy remains intact."

She paused, taking her boots off the table and sitting forward, not looking at Z-No at first as she spoke.

"Second thing; she has as much to lose if you two get exposed as you do. If there's anything you can count on in this world besides Taxes, Death, and Trouble, it's the fact people will usually act in their own best interest. Mutually ensured destruction is the main reason we don't have nuclear war. And third…"

At that moment, Tasha paused and put out the L. She rubbed the buzzed sides of her head, then tussled some of the longer locks up front out of her way. She toyed with her chemically relaxed hair a bit longer, then finally looked over at Z-No again.

"I still have your back, Z-No. We made a promise and I will keep it. So… if you're worried about her pulling something like the Nameless Cur did to you… know that if I catch even a hint of that particular brand of fuckery… and trust me, I know it by smell at this point… I'll drown her in her own blood."

Her hands were clenched tightly as she said this, as if she were imagining strangling an invisible neck. She kept her eyes locked onto Z-No, and he could see the sincerity in them. He knew she meant every word of it, of course… after all, he'd seen what she could do when someone hurt someone she cared about first hand.

"Hopefully, it won't come to that," he said, placing one hand on hers. "Besides, I already promised Tati the next time someone destroys me, she gets to take their head off. You're gonna have to take that one up with her…"

"I suppose we could share the rights to beat the bitch to death," Tasha said, snickering. "Although… a tag-team tandem ass beating from me *and* Tati is probably some class of war crime at this point."

"Yeah, we'll only go with that if she really screws up," Z-No confirmed with a snicker. Then he paused and gazed up at the ceiling. "Of course, the plan is to never let her get that far…"

"You have a lot more control this time," she said in an assuring tone, placing a hand on his shoulder. "She came to you directly, and already seems quite smitten with ya. Just press the advantage, Z… and maintain control."

Z-No didn't respond at first – he couldn't. For a few moments, he let the guitars and trumpets of Streetlight Manifesto play as he kept his mind traveling. As Toh Kay sang out the lyrics to *A Better Place, a Better Time* – one of his favorite songs by that band – he drifted off with the idea one day he would wake up and the world would be fine. Even if it was a myth, it was a myth he wanted desperately to believe in.

"Maintain control…" he parroted, his words slow and deliberately chosen. "It honestly feels odd to be in control again, after the Cur and all. Feels like it's been ages."

"You think you're up for it?" asked Tasha, taking her hand off his shoulder. "I mean, if you're not, that's perfectly alright…"

Z-No felt his body tense up instinctively as she said that. Tasha meant well, and he knew that… but also hated being pitied. Nothing took more of the wind out of his sails than people treating him like he was something fragile, like he might shatter into pieces at any moment… it was revolting to be seen as weak like that. Yes, he had been in a

sorry state when Cozbi H. Bingham moved through his life,

leaving nothing but debris and wreckage in her wake as all

powerful storms do… but that had been a long time ago. He

was better now, he was stronger now… and it was time to

prove that.

"I'll be fine," he told her with a sigh. "Worst comes

to worse, it's like you said; I'm in control this time.

Besides, after all this time… not living my life just means

she wins."

Tasha sighed and grumbled, taking her feet off the

table as she contemplated his words. Then she placed her

hand on his shoulder again.

"Just remember, Z… whatever happens, we still got

your back," she said. "Me, Tati, everyone at the Dojo… we

all got your back, bud. We're still your family."

"I know," he told her.

"So next time someone fucks you over and hurts you like the Cur did…" she said, patting his arm, "Don't shut us out and avoid talking to us like last time. We worry."

"I won't," he assured her, patting her arm back and smiling. They sat in silence for a bit long time, passing the rest of that joint back and forth, before Z-No looked over at Tasha and asked the obvious question:

"Why do you call her Cur?"

"Well," Tasha replied as she put out the joint, "most people would call her a bitch. But bitches are just female dogs. I like dogs. And a dog, male or female, has the redeeming quality of being loyal, and lovable, and teachable.

"And she's none of those things."

"Exactly," Tasha said, tapping her head. "I run with plenty of bitches; hell, some of my best friends are bitches. But you'll never find a Cur in my circle."

Zeno laughed a bit at that, then sighed a bit.

"I miss nights like this," he said.

"Me too," she replied. "It's nice. And, if you're starting to feel like your old self again, there's a *Koffin Rat* show downtown tonight…"

"Thought you had shit to do today," said Z-No.

"I did," she replied. "But hey, I can cancel for a good friend. In fact…" she pulled out her phone, and sent one text. "Fuck 'em, it's my night off.

"Fine…" Z-No muttered, getting to his feet. The songs on the radio switched gears, shifting over from Ska to hip-hop with the sudden bumping of *Hands on the Wheel* by Schoolboy Q and A.$.A.P. Rocky. "But you got the first round of drinks."

"Moi, pay for drinks?!" cried Tasha with a false insulted tone to her voice and a posh accent to match. "Why, Mr. Lawrence, I thought you were a gentleman!"

"This gentleman just let you smoke up half his weed," Z-No replied with a snicker. "And I believe in reciprocity. So you're payin' for my drinks."

Tasha laughed a bit, then hopped off the couch after Z-No.

"Yep, he's back…" she said, throwing her arms around her old pal. "Welcome home!"

And with that, a few moments later, they were out the door and catching an Uber to one of the sleazier bars downtown – the wonderful dive bar known as Debris. The music was loud, the drinks were cheap. Koffin Rat was one of those bands that brought big-time metal to little stages…

and in the middle of the crowd, causing as much havoc and

chaos as possible, were Tasha and Z-No. Elbows and

bodies were being flung as far as the eyes could see, and at

one point Z literally lifted up Tasha to let her kick as many

people as possible – a move they'd been using at shows

like this since they needed fake I.D.'s to get into places like

this.

The next thing Z-No effectively remembered, it was

morning and he was asleep on his couch. His whole body

felt like one giant throbbing bruise from all the impacts,

and the residual liquor in his blood made standing seem

like an impossibility.

All signs of a good evening out.

He staggered to his feet and made his way from the

living room to the bathroom down the hallway, washing his

face and taking a quick look at himself in the mirror. His

hair was a mess… which pointed out again that his hair was growing long enough to get noticeably messy to begin with. He kinda liked it, despite the mess of naps around his head. It looked more like his old self… and he missed that. He missed having nights like that, too… and after brushing his teeth to get the taste of leftover whiskey out of his mouth, he went into check on Tasha.

The Fairy Queen in question was sprawled out on his bed, atop the covers as was usual of a long night drinking. During the night she'd somehow stripped down to her panties… and thrown on one of his shirts, a black t-shirt with **MAYHEM** scrawled across it in blood-red letters. Z-No rolled his eyes and ever-so-gently kicked of the legs on his 4-Poster until she started to stir.

"Mornin'…" she muttered with a yawn, stretching slightly as she rolled over onto her back. "Sleep okay?"

"Like a drunken angel…" he replied with a shake of his head. "Then I woke to the hell of you stealing my shirts again."

"Someone spilled cheap beer on mine last night," she explained, sitting up slowly. "I wasn't gonna get on your bed in a wet t-shirt that smelled like bad booze… nor was I gonna sleep wearing a bra, fuck that."

"So you stole my shirt?"

"You're just mad you don't get to see my tits," she sneered.

"I've seen your tits more times than I can count, Tasha…" he said with a grumble. "Or should I call you TIT-Tania?"

"Har-har…" she mumbled, flipping him off. "So original, Z…"

"Seriously, how many times have I seen you topless or naked, or both?" he asked.

"Fair enough…" she replied, sighing. "But what if one of your side-chicks comes over and I'm passed out on your bed naked? They might get mad at you… or worse, leave you for me and get their hearts broken."

"Since when do I have women lined up like that?" Z-No asked.

"I'd estimate you've had what I call 'pussy on retainer' since…" she paused, making motions in the air like she was doing math in her head before continuing, "since high school. Or at the very least, since freshman year of undergrad."

"You give me too much credit," he replied. "Never forget I was an awkward nerd for years."

"Awkward nerds still get laid," she said mater-of-factly. "I should know – I've fucked plenty of 'em."

"Because you're a huntress of the wild, seeking whom you might devour."

"… fair point. Plus nerdy dudes try harder. They eat pussy like they got something to prove, lemme tell ya…"

"I'll take your word for it…" he interrupted, covering his eyes with his left hand. "You want breakfast?"

"I *want* my pussy eaten and another joint…" she said, flopping back down o the bed. "Got me thinkin' about getting head first thing on a Sunday… you a heathen, Z."

"You think about getting head 20 times a day," Z-No countered. "Besides, I wasn't gonna let you fuck some rando from the club on my bed, fuck I look like?"

"I wasn't gonna fuck him on your bed!" Tasha assured him. "I was just gonna ride his face on the couch, then kick him out. Nothing major…"

"So my couch can smell like pussy I'm not even getting until I get the upholstery cleaned?" he asked with a cynical tone and a raised eyebrow. "Again, fuck I look like?"

Tasha kicked her feet back and forth like she was having a temper tantrum, whining the whole time to go along with it.

"You keep acting up, I'm calling Tati," Z-No warned her.

Tasha gave him a dirty look, then went silent. She was stubborn, sure… but even at her worst, she was not up to tango with her big sister Tati.

"Fuck you, Z."

"Not right now, Tash…" he said sarcastically. "Now, come on. I'm gonna need a hand with breakfast… since someone talked me into 3 extra tequila shots…"

So between the two hung-over black 20-somethings, they managed to form enough of a coherent human being to make scrambled eggs, toast, and two bowls of cereal. As they began to feel better, chomping down on the food, Tasha took the opportunity to ask a pressing question:

"So… you think getting back in the game is the right thing to do?"

Z-No sighed, then looked down at the table for a moment. He wasn't sure it was the right thing to do. He wasn't sure he was ready… or that he could handle it. He only knew one thing with any certainty, so that was the only thing he said to his old friend:

"It's this or lay down and wait for death," he said flatly. "And I've tried that already. At this point... might as well live."

He let those words hang in the air for a bit, and the pair ate in silence.

Finally, Tasha broke the silence.

"Well," she said, spinning her spoon in the air. "If you start to backslide, just remember one thing."

"What?"

"I can and will kick your ass till you're back to your old self." She finished this statement with a laugh, then sighed. "seriously, Z... don't let something like this be what changes you... for the better or the worse. Whatever happens... stay you, okay?"

Lorenzo nodded. But he was already unsure if that was a promise he could keep.

Chapter 6: Kris

Kristina had gotten used to not having real days off. When you work two jobs, you seldom have the day off from both – best case scenario, she had the day off from one and could either sleep in later or go to bed earlier. And now that she technically had three jobs – Z-No had been a man of his word and gotten her on retainer, the modeling equivalent of being a freelancer on call – she had even fewer days off. If she wasn't walking dogs, she was behind the desk at the hotel slaving away. In the unlikely even she was doing neither of those it was either because she'd just gotten done doing either or both of those, or she'd been stuck on location for a shoot all day.

"It's starting to get a little absurd," she admitted to Lisa as the two sat together in the latter's flat, cotton balls between toes as they propped daintily painted up toes on the coffee table to watch some Netflix together.

"Yeah, having more jobs than you need will do that…" Lisa commented dryly as she selected 'keep watching' on the list of Netflix options.

"More than I need?" Kris countered incredulously. "The hell do you mean?"

"I mean, you're a model now…" said Lisa, staring at her toes for a bit and wiggling them. "It's your dream, isn't it?"

"I'm a *part-time* model on retainer," Kris said. "You don't quit a full time gig for a part time gig, Momma taught me that."

"Even when the part time gig pays full time money?" asked Lisa.

"It doesn't pay *that* much…" Kris assured her with a dismissive eye roll. "Besides, I'm not sure how long I'll have it. Don't get me wrong, I love being able to put 'professional model' on my resume now… but the place has more Nepotism than the Roman Empire."

"That's still a thing, huh?" mused Lisa, staring fondly at her toes. "Well, if you ever wanna smash some patriarchy, you know I got your back." She looked over at her best friend, smiling warmly. "Let me use my powers for good this once, ah?"

The 'powers' of which Lisa spoke were mostly tied to her unique ability to network and connect in a way that was nothing short of extraordinary… with an emphasis on the 'extra'. In a seemingly effortless way, Lisa could make her way into the most surreptitious of social circles and somehow come out unphased by any filth she might encounter therein. Part of why she was able to work only one job and live remarkably comfortably was that strange network of hers: she knew coke dealers who sold to state senators and circuit court judges; she knew tech nerds hired out by bankers to scrub their computer history clean; and her brother was a white-collar pimp (proper term 'Escort Security Provider') whose 'girls' serviced some of the most powerful people in the tri-state area.

Anyone who ever needed humbling, Lisa could break them down like a birdhouse made of toothpicks.

"As tempting as that sounds…" Kris said, stretching slightly as she spoke, "I'd like to keep my nuclear option until I really need it."

"Aw, I'm your nuclear option? That may be the sweetest thing anyone's ever said to me…"

"I know, I know… I'm wonderful," Kris said. "Now, let's get some snacks before we work on the fingers, ah?"

The reason the girls were getting so gussied up was because Kristina had put in enough work to make the stars align and give herself the day off from all 3 jobs at once.

And the reason she'd done such a monumental and difficult thing to herself was simple:

She had Dojo classes to attend.

Attending one munch was not enough to open the doors to the Dungeon of Joyous Obedience. At best, it could be considered to be on par with putting in a job application, and the first interview equivalent was being invited to attend an open Dojo class. The open classes were held in a separate location from the actual dungeon, and were, according to the emails Kristina and Lisa received, 'tame enough to be done in daylight… and with your clothes on!'

"In other words," said Lisa when they first looked over the emails, "we don't get to do any *real* fun stuff till they know for sure we're not fakers, creepers, or both."

This made sense to Kristina. As the email put it, the point of these was to assess where someone's skills were at that moment as they sought entry into the Dojo. 'There's no shame in not knowing', it said. 'We simply want to make sure we know where you are so we can provide the safest, most fun, and most informative experience possible.'

This put Kristina's mind at ease quite a bit; she was no spring flower virgin waiting to be plucked, nor was she some completely naïve damsel who thought kinky was having sex with the lights on... but she wasn't all that experienced in BDSM, at least when it came to real world one-on-one sessions. She'd had one prior play partner, who'd since moved away... and other than that she was loathe to admit most of what she knew came from books, films, and her own vivid and illicit fantasies put together from pieces of those books and films she'd read and watched.

Lisa, on the other hand, was threatening not to go at all. She was more experienced than Kristina in many aspects – she'd been a rigger, she'd been part of another dungeon, she'd had a prior dominant – and made it no secret she thought her 'resume' alone should let her jump ahead in line so she could skip straight to the fun stuff.

It took Kristina reminding her about *why* the Dojo was such a big deal to make Lisa calm down and go with the program, though that raised another set of questions… namely, why they were bothering with low-level initiate shit if Kris had a main-line on a founding member.

The Dojo, like many other dungeons, had a sort of unwritten policy that basically said 'if you're in a relationship with an existing member, we waive the paperwork and let you waltz on in based on their word alone'. One had to assume this went double for founding members, too: the website for the Dojo quite literally had shrines to each of them. And one of those founders was in Kristina's phone, saved under the nickname 'Sir' with little heart emojis around the word.

Kris rebuffed this idea for three reasons: one, because she wanted to take the classes anyway and see what new fun stuff she could learn; two, because she wasn't officially *with* Z-No (though she hoped to change that soon); and three, because she wanted to earn her spot in their ranks based on her own merits.

Lisa rolled her eyes at Reason 3, calling it "overly dramatic, semi-cliché bullshit', but agreed nonetheless to give it a shot. So, with that part taken care of the two were off to their first ever semi-open Dojo Class.

The Dojo had rented out a literal classroom in a local Civic Center for this particular class, complete with old-school desks and the familiar sights and smells of 'K thru 12' all about. It had desks large enough for adults and older teenagers, but the walls and singular window still had childish drawings and art projects hung up that indicated much younger students also graced these hallowed halls at different times. What put Kristina into full-on nostalgia mode, though, was the smell of arts and crafts. The room had the overly familiar aromas of water-soluble paint and clay, and of crayon and permanent marker; that wonderful, cheery scent of playtime and mirth which never truly went away no matter how often the room was scrubbed. It all reminded her of the classes she'd most enjoyed in school, the ones that gave her the freedom to be creative.

For a moment, Kristina thought about going to look for some construction paper and scissors before the instructor came in… but she decided it would look far too unprofessional. She did, however, make a mental note to purchase some of that wonderful stuff the next chance she got.

She and Lisa picked seats in the middle of the room, made themselves comfortable, and watched the other prospective members milling in as they waited for the Dojo rep that would be teaching them to file in and chatted idly to themselves about who it might be.

Lisa lit up like a Christmas tree when she saw their instructor, and Kristina couldn't help but marvel herself. The website covered faces in masks or blurred them out, but body types of the founders were very unique to them – no two were exactly alike. As such, when they saw the buff, thick black woman at the front of the class, sitting on the teacher's desk with one leg over the other as she idly chewed on gum... they knew it was no one else but Titania, the Fairy Queen.

Titania was one of the founders Kris had met during the munch, but was also the only person Kristina had studied almost as frequently as she had studied Z-No. Being bisexual, Kris felt a certain and undeniable attraction to beautiful women who looked like she some sort of goddesses and made mere mortals worship them as such... and that's who Titania always was. As she stood at the front of the class with a duffle bag beside her, sporting form-fitting jeans and a white t-shirt, Kris was reminded of the cliché term her Father once used to describe some women: she was, in fact, 'thicka den a snicka'. She was a marvelously proportioned woman, far from slender, with plushness of hips and thighs that she wore with pride.

At one time, yes, Kristina had fantasized about being with a woman like Titania. At the same time, a bit of 'exploration' (in other words long nights of study and a bit of masturbation) had led Kristina to conclude she didn't want Titania but instead wanted to *be* her. She wanted, more than she wanted to be under the sway of the Fairy Queen, to be like her. She wanted to walk into a room and command adoration without a word. She wanted to break hearts with her hips and snap necks when she crooked her finger.

She stumbled, once, upon a paid subscribers only picture of Titania laying in repose as shirtless men massaged her feet and fed her grapes. That was what tipped the scales for Kristina. Though she had to admit, if the other opportunity ever came up…

"Alright class!" came the low female baritone from the front. "Sit down and hush those pretty mouths cuz Teacher got a hangover."

A bit of mild chuckling followed, during which Kris couldn't help but glance about. She noticed there seemed to be so many people here: probably candidates from other munches. The Dojo, she knew, accepted in only 5 full participating members per cycle of inductees… and there were 20 in this class with her.

Oh no…

As Titania (who introduced herself using her real name, Tasha) began to explain that she was exactly who they thought she was, Kris kept running those two numbers through her head.

I have a one in 20 chance to make it in! she thought. *Might even be less than that, because there may be one other person who is already accepted... I really, **really** don't like those odds.*

"Alright, first things first," said Tasha after a long gulp of coffee. "Who in here was ever in the Scouts?"

A surprising number of hands shot up, at least half the participants. Kris was starting to put two and two together... and again, she felt she was at a marked disadvantage. This reduced her odds that much more, she thought. They were one in 30, if not lower.

"So, those with their hands up probably have some decent knot-tying skills," Tasha responded. "That much is good to know. The rest of you, don't sweat it; we're all here to learn, and even those of us who've been at this for years can still learn something new about ways to utilize rope. Thus, today's class... knot-tying made simple."

This title sent a slight murmur through those there assembled, and Kristina didn't need much thought to figure out why. The group was relatively diverse in terms of gender and the choices in clothing alone – ranging from suit and ties and cocktail dresses to sweatpants and tank tops, and everything between – meant their personalities had to be different as well. This meant some of them had to consider themselves submissive types, just like Kristina did. And most submissives, in her limited experience, weren't all that adept at being the rigger rather than the rigged.

And that increases the odds a bit...

Tasha raised a hand, quieting the chatter.

"Now, I know some of you may be wondering why I chose this topic," she said. "Some of you may even see it as unfair to have a class on rope tying when your strong point is being the one getting tied up." She smiled as she

155

mentioned that, drumming her fingers a bit on the desk as if experiencing a flashback. "Trust me; I know how hard it can be to do things that seem like they're outside your skill set. But, there are plenty of reasons for a submissive to know their way around both sides of the rope."

"First…" she continued, stepping away from her desk and sauntering slowly towards the students, "erase the idea that only Dominant types can be interested in being riggers, or that only submissives enjoy getting tied up. Being the one who does the ropes for others can be a form of service, both meditative and rewarding. As for being the one bound up… take me for example." She came to a stop at Kristina's desk, resting a hand on it as she addressed the crowd. "I'm sure everyone here has been to our website… and if you've seen my pictures on there, you know the 'submissive' role isn't one I'm noted to take often."

A mild chuckle broke out among the crowd, Kristina joining the nervous laughter while trying not to make direct eye contact with the buxom goddess towering above her. The tone with which she spoke was that authoritative, powerful, "Head Bitch in Charge" timbre that sent electric chills down Kris' spine. It was the kind of thing she hoped Titania wouldn't notice, but had a distinct suspicion she somehow picked up on it.

"I've always been of a mindset..." said Tasha as she stepped backward towards the front of the class again, "that a Dominant leads by example. And besides that, I didn't start off my journey as the queen you see before you. As such, I've no problem being bound up... even if only to prove a point."

She paused for a moment, then pulled up the bottom of her shirt just enough to expose a latticework of black cotton ropes tied around her body that Kristina recognized at once as part of a Karada, or 'rope dress'. She became flabbergasted by this while the rest of the class let out slight noises of disbelief.

"There's a lot more than knot tying skills you can learn from use of rope," Tasha said, lowering her shirt slowly. "Which is why it's often the first class we teach prospects: it shows us where your head is at. So, with all that out the way…" she paused, then opened up the duffle bag next to her, procuring a few large bundles of the same simple cotton rope. "Class is officially in session."

The class itself was a simple enough thing; people were to split up into pairs, then each pair was handed one bundle of rope and one piece of paper with some visual guides on commonly used ties. Once those were distributed, each person in each pairing was to take turns being the binder and then the bound. Pictures would be taken with smart phones to prove which knots were done, and have them critiqued by the instructor.

"If I had my druthers," Tasha said, interrupting the handing out of ropes just as she got to Lisa and Kris, "you'd all line up for inspection. But that takes longer, and the main door has windows. We don't wanna go scaring the vanilla folks walking by."

Another bout of chuckling emerged, during which Kristina reached out and accepted their paper and bundle. Rather than release it, Tasha held onto them a bit longer, long enough for Kris to make eye contact.

She had the most gorgeous hazel eyes…

"Good luck, kid," she said, before winking and walking off to the next grouping.

Kris and Lisa both stared after her for a moment, star-struck. After that moment, Lisa dropped her voice to a hushed whisper and asked what was going on.

"You know Titania now too?!" she asked her friend, almost accusingly.

"Of course I don't!" said Kristina, equally cross.

"She seemed to know you!" Lisa hissed, hands over her mouth.

"Well she doesn't!" Kristina shot back. "I swear, I just emanate subby pheromones or something. Either way… let's get to work!"

As the pair did indeed get to work, however, Kris couldn't help but wonder if Lisa was right. She'd easily written it off the same way she wrote several encounters off: Dominants seemed to have this strange ability to sense submissives and vice-versa, like sharks tracing the scent of blood in water; she used as much to explain how she'd been drawn to Lorenzo before she even had the slightest inkling he and Z-No were Bruce Wayne and Batman. But was there more to it? Did Titania know her somehow? And if she did, what did that mean? Was it good, was it bad? Should she be overjoyed or start running?

While she fretted over all this, Lisa finished up putting her hands in the first bound position, tightening it before reaching to grab her cell.

"Christ, that was fast…" she said aloud to no one in particular.

"If I had a nickel for every time I had to say that," replied Lisa with a chuckle. "Really, though… it's just muscle memory. I can tie a knot like this one in my sleep."

"Knowing you?" said Kris. "I'd be surprised if you hadn't done that at least once already."

The first part of the exercise went off without a hitch. Lisa excelled at tying and untying knots, and within 20 minutes she'd done all the required rope work on

Kristina – including the section marked 'bonus' – and taken the prerequisite photos to show their instructor.

Then it was Kristina's turn, and things became a bit… difficult.

Kris was barely used to being on the bound side of bondage, and had no practical experience with the opposing side of things whatsoever… so much so it felt like part of her was rebelling at the thought of doing the inverse. Every step she saw on the print-out, her hands seemed to veto it by committee decision without her brain even attending the meeting, and she kept ending up with vast tangles of rope that weren't even remotely appealing or aesthetically appeasing.

"You're making a mess…" said Lisa with a slight smile.

"I know!" Kris replied, untangling her bundle of bullshit for the 5th time.

"Not the sexy kind of mess, either..." continued Lisa.

"Shut *up*!"

"Look, you're going too fast..." Lisa informed her, taking on a more motherly tone. "Try slowing it down and going one step at a time."

"That doesn't help if I can't get past step one," Kris shot back, finally done undoing the jangled mess she'd made.

"Well, it might help if you stop fighting the rope," Lisa suggested. "You're treating it like you're mad at it... try treating it like a friend! Here, let me show you..."

And with that, Lisa began walking Kristina through the first few exercises again, this time going slower. With this lesser speed, Kris was better able to see how her best friend actually treated the rope; she was delicate with it, almost lovingly moving each piece into place. She really was treating the rope like she cared about it as much as she cared about Kris… and it was almost as insulting as it was impressive. Impressive and, Kris was loathe to admit, very sexy… she felt that familiar tingling feeling building that made holding still to be bound mildly torturous.

With this second walkthrough, and a bit of verbal encouragement, Kris was able to get through the majority of the print-out ties. Some came out a little wonky, but Lisa ensured her they were close enough.

She'd just finished the third-to-last tie – an extended double-column elbow tie – when Tasha's phone went off, signaling time was up.

No, no, no! Not yet, please!!

But it was over. After unbinding Lisa, there were a few moments where Kris just sat still, staring despondently at the ropes in her hands.

"C'mon, Krissy…" said Lisa, tapping her gently on the shoulder. "Think you're the only one who didn't finish?"

Kris mumbled indistinctly in response.

"You did great," Lisa assured her. "Better than I did the first time I tried tying someone up, that's for sure. Now, let's go get graded: worse comes to worse, I'll buy you ice cream!"

Kris looked up at the mention of this, and managed a smile.

"You're the best, Li-Li."

"I know!"

Because of the need for a pep talk, the pair soon found that they stood at the very end of the line to have their pictures reviewed. Most people had gone on ahead, and were already out in the halls. Tasha, as she had when the class started, sat on the desk as she carefully looked over and analyzed each set of pictures before sending the prospects on their way. Her face gave away very little, but occasionally she'd half-smile at something... though whether the smile marked derision or genuine pleasure was anyone's guess.

Lisa, being actually proud of her work, showed hers to their instructor first. Tasha looked over the gallery in her phone... and whistled.

"Someone's had practice..." she said. "Well done."

"Thank you!" she replied. She started to head off, but stopped near the door when Kris shot her a pleading 'don't leave me!' stare.

"Your turn, Miss Shank..." said Tasha, holding out her hand expectantly.

She knows my name?! thought Kris. *Holy shit!!*

She handed over the device as ordered, already unlocked, and began showing Tasha how to get through the camera feed. The analytical hazel eyes of the Dojo's great Titania seemed to be staring holes through her phone... and as Kris expected, she did not whistle at the end of this.

"You could have gotten your friend to do your knots for you..." said Tasha. "Why didn't you?"

"That... seemed like cheating..." Kristina replied, blinking profusely and feeling dumb even as she said it. "I mean, the point was to see what I could do, right?"

The half-smile returned to Tasha's face, and she pushed up from the desk to stand at her full height.

Kristina felt tiny by comparison.

"You're exactly right..." said Tasha, handing the smaller woman's phone back to her. "And despite this... a lot of people cheated anyway. Most thought I wouldn't notice... but I did."

"How do you know which one cheated?" Kris asked, struggling to make eye contact. Tasha was not only stockier, but taller, with each of her hefty breasts almost the size of the more submissive lady's head. And with the more endowed lady's breasts practically at eye level it was not the easiest thing to ignore them.

Kris pretended to look down at the phone, actually glancing at her own C-cup breasts for a moment as a comparison.

"They both did, as far as I'm concerned," Tasha said with a dismissive eye roll, shocking Kristina so much she looked up and sapped out of her self-comparative meditation. "You help a cheater cheat, you're just as bad. And either way... they both missed the point of the exercise. You, on the other hand? Well, you got a lot of work to do… but at least I know you're not afraid to do that work."

"Th-thank you!" Kris managed, putting the phone back into her purse. "I'll try to practice in my spare time, too! Once I stopped over-thinking, it was a lot of fun!"

"Glad to hear it…" said Tasha, extending her hand for a handshake. "I can't wait to see how you improve."

There was a moment during that handshake, feeling the latent power in that grip, that Kristina wondered if Tasha might pull her in and kiss her. How could she react to that? Would she be able to react at all? Would she blurt out something about being in a relationship as Titania bit her neck and pushed her onto the desk? Would she be able to resist this glorious woman if she so much as asked her to come with her for 'further study' after class?

Fantasies ran wild through her brain, most of them involving a bound Kris and a naked Titania towering over her in some fashion… but also, just for the briefest moment… the idea of Tasha herself offering to let *Kris* do the tying and the topping this time…

She was jerked forcefully back to reality by a cough from Lisa, which made her wonder how long she'd been limply holding their instructor's hand with helpless 'fuck me' eyes. So, rather than asking, she thanked her again and dismissed herself.

"Be seeing you, Miss Shank…" said Tasha as Lisa and Kris hurried away.

"That was hot!" Lisa said the moment they were out in the parking lot.

"That was a *mess*," groaned Kris in response.

"I could've cut the sexual tension with a butter knife!" said Lisa, grinning. "It was *that* thick, oh my *god*!"

"Just get me home so I don't die of embarrassment in public…" Kristina pleaded.

"More importantly, though…" said Kris. "She said 'be seeing you' and 'can't wait'. You know what that means, right Krissy?"

It dawned on her, that moment, that Instructor Titania, a founding Dojo member, did indeed just say all of that. And that meant…

"Holy fuck, I'm in…" she said, staring off into the distance as the clarity hit.

"We're in!" chimed in Lisa.

"We're in!!" shouted Kris, grabbing her friend and bouncing up and down.

After some slight squealing and hopping in celebration, they both got into the car to head back home. Lisa suggested they stay at her place a while, since it was closer and the class was draining… to which Kristina agreed before leaning over in her seat. She was fatigued… that strange workers' tiredness that only comes over you once you're finished with the task or tasks at hand, and makes you realize you must have been tired for a long time and just ignored it.

So, as Lisa drove with some mellow reggae music by Linton Kwesi Johnson playing, Kris began to drift off to sleep, visions of the smug smirk of Titania dancing in her head before she nodded off completely.

In two more days, she would have another class with the Dojo to get that much closer to joining an organization she so admired. And in one more day, she would have a date with Lorenzo Wallace.

Sometimes, just sometimes… life was pretty fucking wonderful.

Chapter 7: First Date

It had been a while since Z-No had been on anything he'd even consider a date. Other than when Tasha or Tati dragged him out somewhere, he'd become mostly a hermit at the tender age of 26. Between the job, meaning he had less free time and the world-altering event now known as 'the cur'... he'd had no real desire to go out and meet new people. But this one person, Kristina Shaw, had met him and drawn him out of his comfort zone. Now here he was, first time in what felt like ages, waiting at a restaurant for his date to show up. He hadn't been this nervous about meeting with someone since he was a teenager... right down to the sweaty palms. He ordered water while he waited and let it cool his hands, and idly wondered if he was overdressed for it – here most people were dressed casually, and here he was all dressed up in a black dress shirt, purple tie, slacks, and his best (and therefore least comfortable) shoes.

Maybe I'm over-thinking this shit… he thought, sighing. *I do tend to do that…*

His right hand was idly twitching on the table for a bit, and he wondered if he was okay enough to hold on without any Xanax or weed in his system… and then she walked in the door and he caught himself no longer wondering about it at all.

Kristina Shank was gorgeous. He always knew that, since the second he saw her… but damn if she didn't show out today. She was sporting a unique pin-up look; something like a black Marilyn Monroe in a slick black dress that hugged every single supple curve on her gorgeous form, and heels so sharp they could cut someone's throat. She had the perfect hairstyle for it, makeup laid so perfectly it should've been some sort of crime, and blood-red lipstick that made her already plush lips look so ripe and delicious it almost hurt him to gaze at her.

He hopped to his feet and greeted her with a smile, pulling out the chair for her and doing the whole 'southern gentleman' thing he'd been taught as a kid.

"You're too kind, Mister Wallace…" she said smirking slightly as she adjusted her dress and took her seat.

"Please…" he remarked, chuckling slightly. "I think we're beyond the last names, aren't we?"

"True…" she replied, tilting her head slightly. "I just wasn't sure how formal you wanted to play things, since you're dressed like a government official or something."

"Says the woman who would look perfectly at home in a black-and-white mystery movie…" he shot back, one eyebrow raised. "I'd say we're pretty well matched in that regard."

"Touché," she said, giggling slightly. "I'll take that as a compliment, by the way…"

"You should," he told her. "You remind me of a young Esther Jones… you even have a good voice for blues." He smiled, taking a sip of his water. "I'll bet you'd look fantastic in a fancy old-school car… top down, valet opening your doors, thirsty-ass fan boys sprinting behind you for a chance to light your obscenely long cigarette…"

She laughed outright at that one, and Lorenzo smirked a bit more and felt much more at ease. If nothing else, he knew he was funny at times… and laughter was one of the best ways to diffuse a situation. Besides, if you can make a woman laugh, as the saying goes…

"I've thought about that before, actually…" she admitted. "The whole aesthetic is really pretty, and I love Jazz music."

"What about the idea of being worshiped?" he teased.

"Oh, I can get that any time," she said with a click of her tongue. "I already have more than a few… let's call them admirers. Mostly white guys who use words like 'exotic' or 'chocolate' or 'mocha'… who want me to step on them. You'd be surprised how much white boys seem to love me."

"Look at where I work," Lorenzo countered. "Both places I work, I mean. Nothing surprises me."

"Fair," she admitted. "Still, the 20s would've been a great era to live in… minus all the racism, of course."

"That's every era, though, isn't it?" he asked. "Minus the racism, almost every era in America would be awesome... except maybe the times before cars."

"I guess," she replied. "Part of me wants to go back to when there were castles and kings and shit... again, without racism. I think every woman wants to be a princess or a queen at one point or another, y'know?"

"Makes sense..." he admitted. "Kinda like how every guy wants to be a hero once or twice, but... with more long-term stability." He chuckled a bit. "Think about it – most heroes don't get paid and have to work full time as a hero *and* get nine-to-five jobs. Kings and Queens, though? They have job stability for themselves *and* their kids... until and unless someone overthrows them, they're set for generations."

"What about Black Panther?" she asked. "King of Wakanda, and a superhero... best of both worlds."

"Valid point, also super hot you know comics…" he said, "but… then you gotta deal with running a country and saving the planet. Talk about pressure… and on top of that, you have shitty writers who can ruin your marriage on a whim? Fuck that."

"Now you're getting meta," she pointed out. "If you didn't know you were the one being written about, though, wouldn't that be a pretty sweet gig?"

"I guess…" he admitted. "But that's the case with most fiction. Hell, up until you know how the story's gonna end, life's pretty sweet for Hamlet, too."

That sparked a whole new avenue of conversation, as they got onto plays, and how she'd taken theater in high school and how he'd written a few plays in undergrad. They went on to literature they both loved, bouncing back and forth from the classics like Byron and the adored ones like Poe to comic books and manga, and how the two were 'not' the same thing (even as he pointed out the word manga just meant comic in Japanese).

"So, why are we meeting here and talking about books?" she asked him. "I have to admit… this wasn't quite what I was expecting when you invited me to lunch…"

"I try not to do what's expected of me," Z-No replied with a smile. "That's why I got in so much trouble in high school, and why I ended up focusing more on art than most subjects like math."

"I admire that…" Kris began, one hand idling on the table and cupping a glass of lemonade she'd ordered, "but that doesn't really answer the question."

"I wanted to get to know you," he said simply. "The first two times we've met, it was in places with expectations. First was at work, then the Dojo munch – places where you're kinda expected to put on a certain face mask and walk in with a certain persona. I wanted to see what you were like outside of those places – that's why I chose the most relaxed pub in town."

"And yet you came dressed to the nines," she pointed out. "So if we're letting our mutual hair down… does that mean you always walk around sporting a suit and tie?"

"I guess it's my turn to say touché," he admitted with a chuckle. "It wasn't the plan, trust me… I didn't really have a plan. But after we talked last night, when you said you'd be wearing something classy… I thought I'd match the aesthetic." He paused, picking up his mug of tea and taking a slow sip. "Plus… I can still be me in a suit. I'm sure you can still be you dressed to kill."

"Darling," she said, in a mock-up of the way old movie stars would speak, "I didn't come dress to kill; I came to attend the funerals of the men and women who break their necks staring at us."

They shared a laugh at that, but it was true and Z-No knew it; there were people throughout the restaurant giving them all sorts of glances. Not only were they both the most well dressed people there, but... they were 2 of only 10 black people there, including the staff. Add in that Kristina cut a silhouette most would kill for – to touch or to have for themselves, take your pick – and Z-No (despite his hatred of the formal attire) looked rather dapper in a suit, and well... they drew in attention. He noticed every time a man in the building stared over at her, or caught a quick glimpse while their date was distracted... and he noticed some shaky stares at his direction, wondering how he got a woman like her.

"I won't be attending their funerals, my dear," he said in his own theatrical voice. "I'll just send flowers along with your amazing ass; I'm sure that will more than compensate for me not attending."

"Roguish~" she teased. "Are you that insensitive? Or perhaps you just don't want any of the women who keep checking you out falling into open graves?"

"Flattery will get you nowhere…" he taunted. "Except, of course, my bedroom."

"Then by all means, I should up my flattery!" she said, making a grandiose gesture. "If I go back to your bed, I won't have to go back to work!"

Another shared laugh, then a pause as he placed his hand on hers on the table.

"You should smile in more pictures," he said in his normal voice, a bit softer. "Not those practiced smiles, either… smiles like this one. That's such a warm, radiant expression… like, at this point, I'm having a hard time not smiling myself."

"You *are* smiling, silly…" she said, tucking a bit of hair out of the way and blushing.

"See?"

"It's nice to see you smile too…" she admitted. "I always saw you as someone who didn't smile much… or, alternatively, did the slight grin like a Bond villain."

"I'll take that as a compliment…" he started, before pausing a bit and raising an eyebrow. "Wait… which Bond we talking here?"

"Pierce Brosnan," she said. "Connery was the best bond… but Brosnan had the best villains."

"Acceptable answer…" he replied. "You were on the edge there with that 'Brosnan' comment… but you pulled it out."

"I'm so glad," she teased with a roll of her eyes. "You should be just marveling I still know Bond; most people forget about any of them before Daniel Craig."

"Don't remind me," he said with a sigh.

From there the conversation went on to other classic movies, theaters, and other stuff... and soon enough the date was over. It was a perfectly nice, wonderful vanilla date that gave him insight into the world of the lovely Ms. Shank... and he liked what he saw.

Eventually, Kris had to get back to work... and Z-No offered her a ride there. On the ride, occasionally, he would give her a sly smirk or a nod, but otherwise didn't say much... and then about halfway to her job he gave her a smile as they stopped at the red light.

"Well... I think we can call phase one a success..." he said.

"Phase… one?" she asked.

"Yes. Phase one was seeing if I liked being around you. Phase two… is seeing if you'll make a good submissive."

"Oooh…" she replied. "I didn't know it was a test."

"You weren't supposed to," he told her. "Wouldn't mean much if you passed that way."

"So what's phase 2?"

"I'll be sending you a list of kinks," he explained. "It's my personal list, ranked in order of like or dislike. You mark down which ones you like, dislike, or are curious about… and we'll see how compatible we are on that regard."

"Makes sense…" she said. "Seems a bit more formal than I would've expected, though."

"So you'd prefer something more spontaneous?" he asked.

"Maybe…"

"Alright." He parked the car outside her job, then looked over at her. "Be a good girl and slide your panties off, would you dear?"

Clearly confused, she went ahead and did as she was asked, slipping down her pantyhose first, then the panties themselves, before pressing her thighs together and holding her hands in her lap.

"Good girl," he replied, holding out his right hand. "Now hand them over…"

With a slight look of concern, she did as he was told, placing the soft satin cloth gently into his outstretched palm. He stuffed them into the pocket of his jacket, then placed his hand on her right thigh.

"Very obedient…" he said in an encouraging manor. "Now… is there somewhere in this parking lot where people won't interrupt us?"

"Uh huh…" she said, biting her bottom lip. "Over there, next to the dumpster… no one will be over there for a while."

"You have to be at work soon, right?" he asked, hand idly squeezing her thigh.

"Mmhmm."

"Should I stop then?" he offered, even as he moved the car closer to the quiet spot she pointed out.

She shook her head.

"Speak up, I can't hear you."

"Please, don't stop…" she said, one hand lightly gripping his arm. "I have plenty of time, I won't be late for work…"

"You realize... he said, as he pulled her skirt up just a bit, "that I'm going to be sending you in to work after I play with your pussy, don't you?"

"If that's what you want..." she whispered, "who am I to say no?"

"You're that desperate to be played with? Naughty girl..."

"You bring it out of me, Sir..."

He took his free hand and cupped her chin, drawing him in to look at her as he pressed his lips to hers, at the same time his ring and middle finger found her slit under the dress and began to caress it slightly, slowly making its way up to her clit.

"Already wet?" he asked, chuckling.

"Your fault…" she replied breathily, her lips against his as she pulled in greedily for another kiss, gripping his tie with one hand.

"How is it my fault…" he began, gently making his way up to her clit, "that you're a filthy, wanton little girl?"

"Because I want you to treat me like one…" she hissed through her teeth, eyes flying open for a moment as she sucked in air through her teeth. "Seeing how you can treat a girl like that? Sir… you make me wanna be bad… so very, *very* bad…"

"Good of you to be so honest…" he said with a smirk. "Now in the spirit of honesty… you tell me when you're close. And when you're about to cum…" he paused, gripping her neck before continuing; "make sure you ask permission."

She let out a noise between a groan and a whimper as she pressed herself further against his hand.

"Yes, Sir…"

"Good girl."

He continued rubbing her clit and kissing her, gripping her throat as he growled playfully into her ear. After a bit, he pressed his ring finger into her pretty little pussy, followed shortly by his middle finger… then both fingers found her g-spot while his thumb rubbed away at her clit.

"Hnnng… S-sir… Please…"

"Please what?" he asked. "Speak up… use your words."

"Mmm, Sir… Sir may I please cum?"

"Good little doll…" he growled against her lips. "Now, look at me… look me in the eyes while you cum. Give it to me… give Daddy that pretty O-face…"

She moaned out seconds later, as if on demand, her hips bucking weakly against his hand before she shuddered and he felt the warm walls of her pretty pussy tightening around his digits, squeezing hard as she obediently came. Her brown eyes went wide, then rolled back in her head... then closed as she panted against him.

"Shit... shit..." she huffed. "I don't... I can't... with just your... *fuck.*"

"The fucking will wait..." he encouraged, kissing her forehead. "Now, off to work you go." He pulled his fingers away slowly, letting her see him lick them clean. "Don't worry, sweetie... if you obey as good as you taste, you'll be getting plenty of what you ask for."

She nodded, then sighed, tugging on her dress and collecting herself.

"Behave yourself…" he whispered as she got out. "And remember… keep a look out for that list I'm sending."

She nodded, then managed to suppress a grumble as she finished getting out. He could tell she didn't *want* to stop here; she *wanted* to take off the rest of her shift, and crawl into the backseat of his car and let him take what was his. He wanted the same… but the pouty look on her face from being teased made it more than worth it to deny himself. He gave her a kiss on the forehead and sent her on her way… And as she left, only the residual scent of her perfume and pussy lingering in his car now… Z-No wondered what the hell possessed him to do something like that. It was out of his usual element but… something about it just seemed right.

Kristina's words circled around in his head as he sat back; *you bring it out of me.*

Apparently, he thought to himself with a sigh, *you're not the only one, Ms. Shank.*

With that, he moved on to enjoy the rest of his day off... then to go prepare the list he'd promised her. He hadn't made a list of kinks in a long time... he wondered if the old one was still accurate.

Chapter 8: Proper Procedure

Showing up a minute or so late to work from lunch was never really considered a big deal. It was easy enough to misread the clock, or to get caught up having to cash your check, and the bosses were fairly understanding about that.

When it came to showing up with slightly disheveled hair and the lingering smell of arousal hanging about your person, however… Kristina somehow doubted her managers would be nearly as understanding, even if she was only 2 minutes late. . Thankfully the uniform she was changing into had pants… but she was still dealing with that strange sort of paranoia one only gets when they perform a slightly sexual act and wonder if other people can tell or notice.

She wondered, as she ran in and grabbed her stuff from her locker so she could change into her work clothes, if she looked as wonderfully wanton as she felt. She gazed at herself in the locker room mirror and thought, based on how decadently dirty she felt after Z-No's words in her ears (and fingers in other places), that she should look much more depraved and filthy than she did in the mirror. She felt as if there were some sort of slutty miasma hanging over her head at this point, like an aura of her own naughty behavior. It lingered in head even if her hair and makeup were all in perfect placement…. And of course, the lack of panties only exacerbated these feelings of pulse-pounding perversion.

Nothing says 'I've been up to no good' like coming back to work without underwear on… she mused as she reported back to her station with a sigh. She still felt the phantom warmth of Z-No's fingers against her clit, and the warmth of his breath against her ear as he gave her commands… it made her shudder a bit even as she was back at the hotel front desk, clocking back in.

"Have fun at lunch?" asked a voice from behind her. Kris turned in shock, relaxing when she saw it was only Rodney, one of her coworker.

"You could say that," she admitted with a shrug of the shoulders and a slight smile. Rodney had worked alongside her for about 4 months now, and she'd noticed him being obscenely helpful and polite when she was around. She wasn't so naïve as to wonder why he was like that with her in particular, but it was always cute how he thought he had a chance to impress her. He was sweet, and not unattractive; he had blonde hair, he was tall, he was fit but not overly muscular. But he was soft… pliable… a natural submissive, even if he himself didn't know it yet. It inspired the dormant dominatrix in her, the side that wanted to use and hurt such fragile, pretty things… but it didn't really inspire her to do much with him at the moment.

It was fun, however, to tease him a little bit from time to time.

"That's what's up!" he said, grinning. "Mine was boring; just ran across the street for a hoagie and chips… but hey, had too much on my plate to take a long break."

"Aw, poor baby!" she said, patting his cheek. "You've been working yourself too hard! Maybe you should take a personal day, call in sick and just relax…"

He'd been working hard, of course, because he'd been picking up some of Kris' extra work. She'd been 'letting' him do a few things for her here and there, at first just to test his submissive nature but… after a while, it was far too convenient not to get the extra down time plus the credit for working harder.

"I'll be just fine!" he said, waving it off. "I would like a day or two off, but then we wouldn't get to hang out. That's no fun either…"

"True," she said with a nod. She could see where he was meekly trying to go with that; see if she wanted to hang out with him without the auspices of working together. He'd been working that angle for so long now it was getting a bit tired… but she didn't mind the attention too much. "Makes me wish I wasn't always so busy these days," was her way around directly saying 'no'.

"I got ya," he said, smile slightly fading. "I mean, I know you got a lot on your plate, too. How's the modeling thing going, by the way? I heard you got a pretty big gig."

"Yeah!" she said, smiling happily. "I'm working with a new company now, and they really seem to be helping me make progress." She placed a hand on his shoulder, beaming at him. "And to think, I wouldn't have had the time to go at all if it weren't for you."

"Hey, just don't forget me when you're a superstar…" he said with a chuckle. "Maybe invite me to a few red carpet things when you blow up?"

"I sure will," she said, giving him a playful shove. "Now go on, cutie-pie… lemme get back to work."

After that, it was just the routine work; checking the schedules of rooms, seeing which needed to be cleaned and rotated out, talking to new guests as they checked in and checking old guests out, marking people down for room service and such… and of course, the best part of any shift at the hotel – standing around at attention while literally nothing remained to be done. She was coming down of her post-orgasmic glow, bored out of her mind, and still had 3 hours left in her shift when her phone buzzed in her back pocket. She let Rodney man the front while she went to the break room to check the incoming message… and sure enough, it was him; Z-No.

"Question:" the text began, "What's your Email address? The list is too long to send via text message. Plus it looks weird on mobile."

She sent it back, along with a winking emoji, and sighed a bit. This was *boring*! She wanted to get on with it already! Part of her could respect the attentiveness and that he didn't wanna go too far too fast with her, but the part of her that had been woefully undersexed and had spent too much time drooling over the idea of being properly owned and dominated was so frustrated she could just scream. She wanted all the fun stuff she read about in erotica stories and fan-fiction: she wanted the degradation, the bondage, the rough sex and romance... and she wanted it now, now, **now**-!

Then she got the email on her phone, and with a sigh pulled up the chart.

Holy-! Well, he certainly is thorough...

There were more kinks listed in the chart than she had even thought were conceivable. She recognized many of the basics, like 'spanking' and 'ball gags' and 'face-fucking'… but some of them she couldn't even pronounce! At least one or two she thought *had* to be made up… but to her relief most of them were in his 'no' category. She wanted to go through and start answering, to get it over with quickly and be closer to the starting point… but then the alarm on her phone buzzed to let her know her 15 minute quick break was over now.

Fuuuuuuuuuu-!

As she went back to her desk, she sent a quick text to Z-No explaining her situation, to which he promptly responded that she had nothing to worry about. "Work is work," he said. "Just complete it when you're free; it's not homework… yet."

The 'yet' part made her roll her eyes a bit... then instantly glad he wasn't there to see said eye roll. Some of the things he said to her reminded her of a certain type of dominant... and regardless of which type he was, most Doms didn't take kindly to their submissive rolling their eyes.

As she stood back at the desk, listening to Rodney prattle on about snowboarding trips he'd taken with his brother and cousin, she thought about that. She'd be working with Z-No, in his civilian persona of Lorenzo... not often, but she *would* be working with him. They'd see each other often... and when she got caught breaking the rules at work...

I bet he'd discipline me right after a photo shoot... she thought, huffing an errant hair out of her face. *Bet he would keep a list of things I did wrong, too... the jerk. Then he'd sit down and make me lay over his knee...*

She was picturing it. She knew better than to let her mind stray in that direction, but the idea was like getting a boulder to the edge of a hill. Her brain could do nothing else but tumble down, down, down that hill… and at the bottom was a delicious and quagmire-like puddle of the filthiest thoughts possible.

She pictured herself being held still by one of his powerful hands while the other began spanking her as he began telling her off about her behavior in that sinisterly calm voice of his. She could practically feel it rumble through her like a cat's purring as he called her out on every indiscretion she'd thought she'd gotten away with, all while the room filled with the resounding 'Swap, Swap, Swap,' sound of her ass bearing the brunt of this punishment.

And the masochist in her was wet. In moments the idea had her so turned on she could feel her heartbeat throbbing between her thighs, thighs she hopelessly pressed closed in a vain attempt to stop the dull ache of need that hummed through her sex.

The catch 22 of being a masochist was that the pain didn't really slow her down from the daydreaming. It was causing her discomfort, yes… but it was the *good* kind, the wonderful kind, the special sweet spot of suffering she always wanted more of…

Wonder if he'd rub my clit while he spanked me… she thought, *Seems like the kind of cruel shit he'd do, just to mess with my head… and he'd be able to do it, too. Most dudes can't find the clit with a road map, and he found it without even looking at my pussy… fuck, that was hot…*

Kris soon found she had to focus part of her energy and thought processes on not touching herself, reminding herself she was still at work. She caught herself shimmying around a bit and huffing, exasperated for no apparent reason, as she spent he full day at work bouncing between fantasies that left her obnoxiously horny, then mildly pissed at herself for getting horny. The vicious cycle she caught herself in made the last 2.5 hours of her shift feel like an eternity.

She could hardly clock out fast enough. The moment her shift was over she headed back to the break room, phone in hand to pull up Uber for a ride home, when she saw she had 6 new message sets. One was a Facebook message from Lisa, asking her if she'd ever been to the art gallery in Uptown. The second was just a standard cluster of notifications from Instagram – likes and comments on her pictures, horny guys in her DMs… the usual fare for 'The Gram'. Twitter was more of the same, with a few retweets for good measure. Then there was a text from her aunt Gina from Virginia, asking if she got the art supplies she'd sent, and another text from her cousin Valerie saying her mom (Aunt Gina) was wondering when she'd come down and visit.

It occurred to Kris she hadn't done any art stuff in a while – she couldn't even remember the last time she sat down with her sketch pad and just went to town drawing out some weird characters or symbols. She sent a message back to Lisa that she'd love to check out the art museum this weekend, provided she didn't have to work. Then she called for her ride and got her bag out of her employee locker.

She felt stupid when she realized her panties still weren't in there, and she was going to have to go home like this: slightly wet, commando under her black work khakis, and pissed about all of it. The horniness has moved around for her now, going from the poignant throbbing in her clit to that dull pulse deep inside her, what she liked to call 'hunger pangs'. She felt ravenous, alright... she no longer wanted to just masturbate, or even get laid: she wanted to get *fucked*. And *properly* fucked at that! She hadn't had a truly satisfying roll in the hay since... since...

*How long **has** it been since the last time I got broken off proper?* She thought this as she got into the backseat of her Uber and took a deep breath. *I haven't even had basic ol' vanilla sex in ages… been at **least** six months. And my last scene was longer than that. It's had to be close to a year since Jeremy and I… god, that's pathetic…*

She spent most of the Uber ride feeling sorry for herself and listening to "Break u Off" by the Roots on Spotify (a song she loved to bits because the combination of that smooth beat and the crooning vocals always made her fantasize), then the last leg of it checking out the chart full of kinks Z-No had sent to avoid thinking about Jeremy – her prior Dominant – and further tormenting herself about the sex and sadism she was not currently able to access. The list did help with that: it was a lot to take in, and so dry and analytical not even Black Thought and Musiq Soulchild combined could keep her arousal going… but once she kind of organized it in her head, it wasn't nearly that bad. She read through the 'favorites' section first, and was relived she liked or loved almost all of them… that she recognized. She put question marks next to any that she didn't know and then moved over to the 'yes' section to do the same. By the time she finished those her ride was over, and as she thanked the driver and made her way up the hill to the townhouse she shared with Jason, she wondered if any of this would be worth anything or mean anything when she was done with it.

Jason was waiting in the main room playing on the Xbox and drinking an Angry Orchid cider. He'd had the day off from work, so of course he'd done what she would've done in his shoes. He'd also ordered pizza, because fuck cooking on a Monday when you didn't even have to work.

Unlike Kris, however, Jason had at least put on pants.

"Yo, J-Man," Kris called out. "I'm stealing your beer, and some pizza. Fight me if you don't like it."

"Battling the undead, Krissy!" he shouted from the Den. "You'll have to wait in line!"

She took a plate with 2 slices of meatlovers' pizza and sat down on the couch a little bit away from Jason, popping the top off her hard cider and groaning out loud.

"Long day, champ?" Jason asked.

"The longest," Kris replied.

"The hotel job still sucks?"

"Of course it still sucks, J-Man."

"Does that one kid who keeps trying to flirt with you still work there?" Jason asked next, not looking away from the screen. He had the disciplined ability to hold a conversation while battling enemies one usually saw in YouTube letsplayers only.

"Yeah... and he's still trying," Kris confirmed with a groan. "And he was the least stressful part of my day."

"Do I even wanna know?"

"No."

"Wanna hop on the Xbox and beat the hell outta some people in another game?"

"God, yes."

"Alright, Slugger..." Jason said with a smirk. "Pick the game so I can whoop your ass in it."

"In your dreams," she shot back, picking up Mortal Kombat.

After a few rounds, a bit of pizza, and a lot of yelling, Kris finally made her way upstairs to finish off her assignment. She even pulled out the laptop to look up some kinks she didn't recognize... like Dacryphilia.

Very, very interesting Dacryphilia was to her… and a quick image search lead her down a little bit of a rabbit hole that took up most of the next hour or so.

Once she was done, she changed that particular kink from a question… to a favorite in all caps.

Chapter 9: Heal Thyself

An undersold part of taking care of one's submissive is taking care of one's self; if the Dominant's mental or physical health falters, they cannot be as effective in providing their submissive's needs, even if those needs are as simple as attention and affection. It wasn't the only reason Lorenzo wanted to see his therapist again, but it was a high-raking reason to be sure.

Taking on a new submissive, even on an experimental basis, is not something to be done lightly. Being a Dominant seems fun, and it certainly can be, but to do it properly requires a lot of energy and time. A true Dom is more than just the person who ties somebody up and gives them a rough and thorough seeing to: they are also equal parts romantic partner, counselor, disciplinarian, and whatever else their submissive partner requires of them.

Being responsible for the well-being of another person is a full time job – it's why licensed caretakers don't work for free, and part of why places like the Dojo exist in the first place: to train prospective and interested Dominants as well as submissives. Z-No made up his mind to go back to attending sessions at the Dojo more regularly, too… but that also was part of why he needed to see his therapist again.

Lorenzo had a full-time job already… and that job alone was already putting a high deal of stress and strain on his psyche. With his current configuration of therapy sessions and medication, he still felt he was barely managing to stay afloat with all the burdens of working with Samuels Photo & Ad… and now he was about to increase his mental workload exponentially by returning to active Dojo duty and taking on Kristina as his submissive.

He explained all of this to Edmund Fisher, his therapist, with only names removed. Edmund was the type of therapist he could discuss such things with, and the kind it took forever to find: open-minded enough not to judge Lorenzo's 'extracurricular' activities, and insightful enough to give him meaningful advice about how to deal with these things. It had taken Lorenzo 6 months of attempts to find Edmund, but since then they'd developed a sort of friendship. He was more comfortable on the plush leather couch in Ed's office than he was in his own home sometimes... maybe because of the smell of old books and scented candles.

So, he sat on said couch and explained everything to Ed, who sat patiently and waited for him to finish rambling before he chimed in with a bit of insight:

"That's heavy shit, man."

"No duh, Ed..." Lorenzo muttered, staring down at his hands rather than looking up. He couldn't look up, because he wanted to stay mad, and Edmund had the kind of face that made him hard to stay mad at: he was black, a bit darker in skin tone than Lorenzo himself, and in his late 40s; he was tall, and had once been athletic judging by his build, but now had a bit of a gut developed now that his metabolism and activity rate were both slowing down; his chest-length black beard was marked with a single streak of gray down the middle that told of his age; and he had wise, kind old eyes that reminded Lorenzo of his grandfather's, behind wide-rimmed glasses that sported gold and faux-wood paneling in places like a 70s Buick. Everything about his appearance was so paternal and warm and full of abundant care, it made it almost impossible for Lorenzo to stay tense and angry around the big bear of a man.

"You're right, you're right…" the elder man said apologetically. "You didn't come to my office today for me to tell you what you already know. I'm sorry."

"Don't… don't apologize…" Z-No said, finally looking up. "It's fine, really. I'm just… I'm tense about it, y'know?"

"Anyone in your situation would be," Ed said, adjusting his glasses. "I mean, if you seemed calm about all of this, I'd ask what you were hiding. Being nervous about a big move like this is natural… healthy even."

"That all sounds nice in theory…" said Z-No, "but it's also a lot to cope with. And you and I both know, dealing with pressure hasn't exactly been my strong suit lately."

"Do we know that?" Ed asked, taking off his glasses slowly. "Son… I remember when you came through my door for the first time. You were… and I'm using the official medical term here… a shit show. You remember that?"

Z-No shrugged. He really didn't remember much of those days clearly… it all felt like one big balled-up haze of panic and depression and psychosis. Any time he tried to call back those memories, they were grainy and out of focus like a badly pirated copy of a movie.

"It wasn't pretty," Ed began, leaning backward in his chair. "You were one of those people who looked like they were barely hanging on. I didn't know if I could help you… or if you even wanted help."

"I'm not sure if I wanted help either…" Z-No admitted, staring down again at his hands. He'd only started going to therapy when his friends had insisted, because at one point they quite literally thought he was dead. He'd taken all his available vacation days, and then spent over a week not leaving the apartment. At the pinnacle of this dark time, he'd wished for death nightly.

"Yes, I saw that too," Ed said. "You were on autopilot – alive but not living. That man? Now that man couldn't handle this. But you are not that man, Z. You are not that man anymore."

Lorenzo looked up from his own hands, raising one eyebrow instinctively as his way of asking 'the fuck you mean?' without the energy of having to use words.

"Z, you chose *life!*" said Edmund, clasping his hands over the younger man's smaller hands. "You made a decision, after everyone stopped forcing you to see me, to keep coming into this office. You made a decision to keep healing. You made a decision to keep yourself going."

Z-No blinked a bit, because honestly he had never seen it that way. He continued to live because he failed to die… and that was that. Had he actually made a decision on the matter at some point and not noticed through the haze?

"Son… I don't tell you this lightly," said Ed, hands still gripping Z-No's. "Most people who've been through what you've been through, at your age? They'd have given up a long time ago. The fact you haven't, means you can survive more than you give yourself credit for."

"So you don't think I'm taking on too much?" the younger man asked.

"I think…" said Ed, slowly releasing his grip and sitting back, "I think you've been playing in the safe and shallow end of the pool. I think you've been doing as little as you could, because you could control it. But now you've grown bored of it."

Lorenzo could only shrug at that, too. He admitted, internally, that he *had* been feeling bored of work, trapped in the monotony of it, and lost without artistic inspiration… maybe the old man was right.

"I think you're ready to try and get back to your old self," Edmund finished with a smile.

"Maybe I am," Z-No replied.

"So dip a toe or two in!" Ed said, clapping his hands. "Go out and experience life again. Have fun! Go out there and live life! Live life, and live life more abundantly!"

"I'll try…" said Z-No with a nervous chuckle. "No promises."

"And just remember, no matter what…" said Edmund, placing one hand on Z-No's hands again. "Whatever you do… I'm proud of you for how far you've come."

As he tried his hardest not to choke up at this, Lorenzo thought how lucky Edmund was to have such a difficult-to-punch face… because part of him was still that angry teenager who wanted to punch him for making him get emotional.

After the revelation he was in fact getting better, and assurances from the in-house psychiatrist he didn't need his medications altered, Lorenzo set off for part two of what was required of him – getting back into the swing of things when it came to the Dojo. After an hour of introspection, a 20 minute drive to the place he once considered a second home was a bit tedious and exhausting in and of itself. But that was part of why he decided to do both the same day in the first place: he had to push those limits into which he'd been self-confined for such a long time if he had any hope of making progress. Work with Samuels Photo & Ad wouldn't be letting up just because he had more to do than work, and so he had to re-familiarize himself with the concept of being tired as all hell and doing what must be done despite that tiredness.

As he got out of his car and parked in small lot designated for the Dojo patrons and members, however, he couldn't help but wondering if this was still too much too fast. It had been over a year since he encountered the woman who nearly destroyed him, who took all sense of self-worth and importance with her when she stomped him out of hope and happiness... and yet he still felt the cold, icy grip of her delicate fingers at his heart strings even in the warm May sunshine of the day.

Best way to break that, he thought, *is to push on despite it.*

And so he walked into the martial arts studio that served as the 'legitimate' housing for the Dojo. Today, he wasn't here for the secretive entrance in the back to the Dungeon proper; however... he was here for the part above ground, the part that was visible.

He was here to get his ass kicked.

Dojo members were not required to participate in martial arts training at their business, nor were they mandated to know any martial arts at all. This was clearly stated on the website, and every form new prospects had to sign to get past the front door. But from its name to the business that served as its more public face, it was undeniable there was martial arts influence involved in the place… and had been from day one. The founding members, the exception being Dante's husband Virgil (who preferred traditional exercising in a regular gym), all practiced some form of martial arts, true: but they'd all studied martial arts before they even met each other. Z-No in particular began studying Hapkido at age 12, which was how he met Dante and Tati in the first place – an interdisciplinary martial arts demonstration in their home town brought the three of them together for the first time, resulting in a friendship that later grew to include the others: Tasha first, since she was Tati's kid sister; Virgil next, because Dante became obsessed with Virgil the day they met and invited him everywhere; and finally Gomez, who arguably got it worst because he had to be evaluated as a potential mate for Tati by not only Tasha but the boys as well.

Then the prior year happened and it was a struggle to even get out of bed, and Lorenzo went from someone who trained at least 3 times a week and did exercises of some sort every day to someone who dragged himself to work and dragged himself into bed, doing little to nothing else for months.

Depression does not really lend itself towards effective martial arts training anyway, so it was probably for the best he withdrew from it rather than trying it and getting injured. Hapkido in particular is a very aggressive martial art, which made it one of the worst things for someone to attempt when their energy reserves were so low that it physically hurt to move. As one might expect, at this stage of the game… Z-No was a bit out of shape and out of practice.

If he was going to do what the lovely Miss Shank asked of him, he had to give it 110% commitment. And in order to give that, he needed to be back in fighting shape again. So, as part of his preparation for the role of Dominant to Kristina… he went back to the locker room, got back into his Gi, and walked in on one of the Dojo's adult Hapkido classes that day.

No time like the present…

Alma was teaching this particular class. She was a relatively new Dojo addition – she hadn't been a confirmed member for more than a month before 'the event' that led to Z-No's temporary retirement – but she'd fast been proving her worth on both sides of the business. When she saw Z-No enter, she smiled and motioned for him to file in with the others.

Not every student at the Black Tiger was a Dojo participant, just like not every Dojo participants was a student at Black Tiger. So that particular connection wasn't mentioned by Alma. She did point out that their 'new student' was actually a 4th Dan Black belt – a rank at which one qualified to become an instructor themselves rather than just attending a class.

"Our guest, Mr. Wallace…" she said, pointing him out to the other students, "is actually as experienced as I am, if not more so. If he would indulge me, I would like to spar with him so you can see what two 4th Dan look like going head to head, and what you may learn if you keep training!"

Oh, for fuck's sakes…

"I'm just here to learn, just like everyone else…" said Z-No, forcing a smile. "I wouldn't want to impose on the instructor."

"It wouldn't be an imposition at all!" said Alma, smiling. "In fact… consider it a direct challenge, Mr. Wallace."

Inwardly, Z-No wanted to scream. Sparring with someone with equal experience but a considerably higher amount of regular practice seemed like the *worst* way to signal his return to the world of martial arts… but it was hard to justify turning down a direct challenge from the instructor, and part of why he was here was to test and push himself.

In for a Penny… he thought to himself, stepping forward with a heavy sigh.

Up close, the juxtaposition was almost comical to Lorenzo. Alma was smaller than he remembered: shorter than him by a head and some change, and about half as wide as him. She was a wiry little thing, with what Lorenzo's uncles would've called a 'high yella' complexion, that – when combined with the relative waviness of her hair – led some to ask her not if she was mixed but what she was mixed with.

When she'd said she wanted to take martial arts because of guys like that, Lorenzo knew she'd get along with everyone in the Dojo just fine.

The sparring wasn't as bad as Z-No had expected it to be: it was worse. Once the bow part was over, he found the true problem with his time away: it had robbed him of his essential speed. His brain, having not become too fried by depression and Xanax to be completely addled, was in fact registering the skirmish properly and coming up with proper responses to Alma's attacks. The problem, however, was that the brain was then forced to rely on his arms and legs to do as they were told with a sense of urgency – something apparently beyond his muscles' ability at this stage. Every time he went to attack it felt like he was stepping through syrup mixed with mud, and blocking was barely any better. Defense was the best he could do… which of course, for someone who'd picked one of the most aggressive martial arts and decided to focus on that one to the point of exclusivity, felt absolutely dreadful.

When Alma finally knocked his feet from under him, Z-No felt almost relieved the whole way down to the canvas. At least it was over. He even went as far as to close his eyes and relax his body as he made his way down to the soft blue matting. The last thought before he felt his body connect with the floor was that the perfume she wore was oddly familiar… and he could still smell it from how close she'd gotten when it came time to take him off balance.

"As you can see, class," he heard Alma saying to the other students, "size is not the matter. So long as you have skill and will, you can take down even the biggest of opponents! Now, split into groups and practice. But first, thank Mr. Wallace for demonstrating."

As the students began to mutter out 'thank you' statements, Z-No finally decided he'd had enough of this an popped up. Part of him was both surprised and pleased he could still get back to his feet in one swift motion from his back – he thought that would've been a lost ability by now.

"No more of that Mr. Wallace crap," he said to the adults there assembled. "Your instructor is Ms. Salazar here; I'm just another student, same as you." He managed a legit smile, and then: "Call me Lorenzo. Most people call me that or 'the training dummy' anyway."

A bit of laughter from the group made Z-No smile a bit wider.

Soon enough, the students began to move to different parts of the training space as Alma gave her sparring partner a playful shove.

"You threw that fight to make me look good, didn't you?!" she accused, giggling slightly as she pushed on his chest.

"I wish I could say that's true," Z-No countered. "The fact is, I'm really just that stiff and out of shape."

"Jeez…" replied Alma with a whistle. "How long you been out of commission?"

"Since I left the Dojo," he told her, smile retreating tactically from his face.

"Christ. It's a wonder you kept up at all."

"I'm aware…" he told her.

"Anyway," Alma said, smiling broadly. "I'm glad to see you're back. I was wondering if you'd ever return…

and none of the old guard told me anything, so I was worried."

"Worry no more," Z-No said, posing for a moment with arms open. "For I am here."

"I can't with you!" she said with a slight giggle. Then she looked at his arms for a bit before re-establishing eye-contact. "You thought about massage, maybe? It might un-stiffen the joints there, get your full range of motion back faster." She paused, looking at his right arm before continuing: "You clearly still remember your moves, and you don't seem that bad out of shape... Looks like all you need would be to loosen up to get your body ready to move fluidly again."

Z-No had been out of the game for quite some time, but he was never exactly slow. He knew that, outside the Dojo job she worked, Alma was a massage therapist. And it didn't exactly take a genius to see where she was attempting to steer the conversation. As if the fact she was wearing perfume while training weren't a big enough hint, this little conversation was the blunt force version of it.

Still, it wasn't the worst idea to get him more limber faster. And he wasn't decidedly committed to Kristina yet…

"I'll keep that in mind," he told her, managing a smile. "But perhaps we should talk about that later, after I see how these regular training sessions will be treating me."

"Fair enough," Alma conceded. "You know your way around the place, I'm sure… just holler if you need anything."

Subtle as a cactus… Lorenzo thought, as he made his way to one of the testing dummies and began working some rudimentary forms out on it. *Besides, how bad could getting back in shape really be?*

That thought haunted the young man as he made his

way home, flopping down on his couch in civilian clothes

and feeling his heartbeat in every muscle of his body. He

felt like he'd been in a cage match with Daredevil, so

thoroughly whooped was his ass. It was easier to count the

places on his body that didn't hurt than the ones that did.

And he was signed up to do this to himself 3 times per

week.

Why am I putting myself through this hell again?

As if in answer to his question, his phone buzzed in

his duffle bag to let him know someone was attempting to

reach him. He reached into the bag without looking down,

eyes still on the ceiling as he fumbled around for the

Android cellular device. When he finally found it, he saw

all his missed messages from the day pop up, beginning

with the most recent:

- One minute ago: Work. Emails about welcoming new employees and some other Lorenzo shit, which Z-No didn't care about right now

- 10 minutes ago (during the drive home): Dojo. Group Chat messages aplenty about life, love, and other such drugs from his comrades there, basically shooting the shit with each other

- 30 minutes ago: Alma.

She'd convinced him to give her his number, then texted him so he could have hers. The whole thing smacked of bad ideas, but at this point he welcomed the idea of her small yet powerful hands working the kinks out of his aching flesh and muscles.

He was envisioning this when he saw the final alert of any substance:

- 50 Minutes ago: Kristina. She'd sent a Snapchat video

Of course, he opened this one first... it seemed just rude not to. And in the video, much to his surprise, was of her in the park nearby where she worked. She was dressed more simply (at this point, he'd only seen her in formal wear – here, she was sporting frayed blue-jeans and a black tanktop), and was wearing far less makeup than the last time he saw her too.

"Hey, it's me..." she said in the video, smiling. "I was out walking my puppy, and I thought of you so... we wanted to say hi!" the last few seconds of the message were her panning over to her dog Rex, who was facing away sniffing a nearby tree, and then back to herself with a bemused shrug. It was so... simple. And that made it stand out to Lorenzo.

Ever since he'd met Kristina, she'd seemed interesting. Beautiful, undeniably... smart, most assuredly… but part of what was interesting about her was what he couldn't see. She seemed the type of woman who was always proper and well-dressed and well mannered… but now, he saw her as uniquely and beautifully human. Just a normal gal having a normal day, sending silly Snapchat messages like some mortal in her plebian clothes…

It was the most attracted to her he'd ever been. And it was what was going to make the next few weeks of hell worth it.

With a long groan and considerable effort, he pushed his way off the couch and back to his feet. He still needed to clean his apartment, get some display images ready for work, and do some photo edits for the Dojo. It was a lot on his plate… probably more than he was equipped to handle.

But he felt good about it. He felt better now than he had in what felt like a lifetime. He was moving forward, getting shit done, and even if it was too much, he could make it fit somehow!

This moment of pride in self and grand realization was interrupted by a loud gurgling of his stomach, reminding him that amidst all these other great plans he would have to eat, too.

Maybe time to start a schedule…

And so he began the process of ordering dinner and typing out a daily planner with Microsoft Excel. The next few weeks were gonna be hell on him… but it'd be worth it.

Chapter 10: Test Drive

Kristina couldn't recall the last time she'd been this excited about spending time with someone other than Lisa.

The munch seemed like a distant memory at this point, and a far different situation. Before then, Z-No was just a fantasy she had and Lorenzo Wallace was just a cute coworker she might let smash because of the forbidden fruit angle. Now they turned out to be one and the same, and she hadn't been able to really handle herself in the 2 weeks leading up to this meeting. Every time he was busy she would find herself pouting, mildly pissed off, and occasionally sending him pictures to make sure he didn't just forget about her. She felt like she had to be getting obnoxious at times, with her need for attention and all...

Then he called her and said the magic words. "I signed up to be a Dominant," he said in that mellow voice of his she loved. "Part of the territory is making sure you get enough attention. That's never going to be something that annoys me, I can assure you."

The words made her melt a bit inside. That softer, more compassionate nature was something that a lot of books and movies left out of the desirable traits for a Dom. He needed to be strict and firm, yes of course… but he also needed to know, in her case, when she needed attention and affection. As far as types of submissives went, she classified as a 'little' – basically, a sub who embodied the phrase "treat her like a princess, fuck her like a slut". She desired the cuddly, soft, affectionate romance, and silly things like coloring together… but she also needed that rougher, almost sinister edge. Something about the same hand that rubbed her back when she needed comfort being the hand that gripped her neck and pinned her to the wall when she needed to be used…

She shivered just from the residual energy of the thought, then looked down at the apartment number in her phone. It matched the door... so here she was. With a deep resigned sigh, she knocked cautiously, still not sure what to expect out of Lorenzo – the man who always seemed to shock her with whatever he had up his sleeves.

She was still shocked when he opened the door sporting a sleeveless red t-shirt, basketball shorts, and a baseball cap on his head. As he welcomed her in, she noted the slight beads of sweat on his arms and neck... he'd been exercising, perhaps? He had that slight, coiled tight tone to him, the kind that wasn't Adonis-like... but it was that strange level between skinny and buff that said someone worked out, but didn't live in or for the gym.

Not that it mattered much to Kris at this point. She was into him already – not much you could do physically to turn her off once she was into you mentally. At this point, muscles were just a plus. A slightly glistening, bitable-looking plus…

She collected herself and headed to the couch, taking a seat and getting herself comfortable. Z-No headed to the kitchen, and proceeded to ask if she wanted anything to eat or drink.

"I got lemonade, sodas, and water," he said as far as drinks, "plus, a little deli meat and cheeses if you're up for a sandwich."

"Just water and I'm good!" Kris assured him, rubbing her hands on her jeans. She'd chosen to go casual today as well, sporting black denim jeans, her favorite boots, and a simple white blouse with all but one button done up to the top. She didn't know what the protocol was for something like this, so she'd wanted to not overshoot it in terms of classiness.

As Z-No returned with two water glasses, he took a seat across from her, getting comfortable as he set his glass and hers on coasters on the coffee table.

"So, you had some extra time…" he said, smiling that slick smile of his. "Did you have any questions about the stuff I showed you?"

"I did at first," Kris said, taking out her phone. "But, since I had the down time, I did some basic Google research. Didn't wanna come in unprepared."

"Sweet," he said, clapping his hands. "That means less work I have to do. Mind if I see your list?"

Kris unlocked her phone and pulled the chart up hesitantly, not sure if she was already about to blow it. There were some on his favorites list that, even when she knew what they were, still fell into her 'maybe' category, plus a few that fell into the 'no' category… and she wasn't sure how well that would go over, or if there was a certain number of his kinks she had to accept if she wanted them to continue. It was that high school second guessing stress all over again, and again she wiped her palms on her jeans when he wasn't looking.

For an unnerving while, he said almost nothing. Then he raised an eyebrow and looked up at her.

"On the kink 'Dacryphilia'," he said, "you marked down 'favorite'. Have you actually done that one before, or were you just interested in it?"

"Well, I've never had the chance to try it, but-!"

"I understand," he interrupted. "Let me double back to that in a moment. How many of the things you marked as favorites of yours have you done?"

She felt a slight chill work its way up her spine. This level of talking was so... proper. It was damn near like he was interviewing her for a job... which Kris realized, mere moments later, he somewhat was. He had an opening for a submissive, and here she was trying to prove herself qualified for the position.

A position that would likely mean me being put into several other positions... she thought. That little silly joke helped steady Kristina's mind, and with a deep breath she began to answer:

"I think most of them. I mean, other than the Dacryphilia one, and the one about candle wax... I can't think of any others I marked down as a fave that I haven't done. I saved most of those for the 'yes' column."

"Makes sense..." he said, smiling again before handing back the phone. "Mind if I ask what made you put those two in the 'favorites' column, then?"

"Well, like I said... I researched them," she replied, finding it a bit difficult to maintain eye contact. She used the water on the table as an excuse, grabbing the glass and taking a sip.

"And?" he asked.

"And… I liked them…" she said, staring down at her water cup. "I liked them a lot. The associated images, when I saw them, both looked messy and pretty at the same time… and I'm a big fan of messy and pretty."

"You don't seem like the type of girl who gets messy," Z-No responded with another raised eyebrow. "I mean, every time I see you, you're so… well, for lack of a better word, put together."

"That's why it's so hot to me, I think…" Kris admitted. "Just… I like the recklessness of it, y'know? I like the idea of me putting all that work in and it being less important than whatever is planned for me, in terms of usage… I like the idea of all that time I spend on hair and makeup and stuff I put in being disregarded, or better yet purposefully destroyed."

She hazarded a look up, to see Z-No smiling again… and biting his lip. Sizing her up.

"I like the way you think, Miss Shank…" he said. He did that thing she'd already seen him do before, and what most guys did: he dropped his voice a few octaves and added a bit of a growl to his voice. Kris loved this voice, but… she didn't love it enough to miss that 'Miss Shank' line he threw out.

"That time, you called me that just to annoy me," she said with a slight sigh.

"You're right," he admitted. "Well, you're partially right. I'm using that because it keeps me from slipping up and calling you baby girl or something of that nature."

You don't have to do that, Kris thought. *Just call me baby girl! Call me baby girl all the time, call me that like it's my real name, call me that till I **forget** my real name..!*

"That brings me to my other big question…" Z-No said next, interrupting her inner monologue. "I identify as more of a 'Caregiver' type of Dominant. That means I'd be looking for more of a 'little' in terms of submissive type. Would you be okay with that?"

*Yes, yes, **god** yes, oh fuck you have no idea-!*

"I… identify as a little, so that's perfect," she said, smiling.

"Like a lock and key…" he said, grinning. "So compatible it's almost scary."

"If that's what scares you," Kris said, the words coming instinctively, "I've got some rom-com movies my friends leant to me? Make you pee your pants."

She was about to be embarrassed before Z-No started laughing… and outright laughing at that, so hard she laughed along as well till both were nearly out of breath.

"Oh god…" Z-No managed, clutching his sides. "I can't even see straight after that one! You shoulda warned me you were this funny!"

"Where's the fun in that?" Kris shot back, her own laughter dying down to a fit of giggles. "I'll have you know I'm full of hidden talents… and trivia. Lots, and lots, of useless trivia."

Eventually the two calmed down fully, and could get back to the matter at hand. Before they officially got into it, Kris paused to observe something:

"I never thought I'd be laughing while talking about weird and kinky sex…" she said, shrugging.

"Some people in the lifestyle take themselves far too seriously," Z-No said. "BDSM isn't all about being serious all the time, y'know… nothing wrong with having fun."

"That's refreshing to know," Kris said with a chuckle, "because if I had to be serious all the time to avoid punishment, you might as well just lock me in spanking position forever.

"You shouldn't joke about that…" Z-No said, picking up his water glass. "With an ass like yours, keeping you bent over for eternity is rather tempting."

"Yes, but then who would feed my pets?" she countered.

"You have pets?" he asked.

"Just two – a mutt named Rex and a roommate named Jason."

This brought out another small fit of laughs from Z-No, which Kris joined in on. After this second little diversion, Z-No chimed back in first.

"I would totally take the dog in," he assured her. "The roommate, though... well, I know a Domme who'd adopt him, provided he doesn't mind getting his testicles stomped on."

"I try not to keep tabs on his sex life," Kris said. "I say try, because sometimes it's unavoidable."

"Ah, say no more:" Z-No said with a sigh. "I've had roommates before too: I know how it goes."

"Alright, then... back to business, I suppose?" she asked, tilting her head. "I mean, do we need to talk about anything else?"

"Kinda..." he said. "I just wanted to let a few tangents happen so you wouldn't be as tense, first." He smiled, chuckling a bit as he put down his water. "I mean, come on! I don't bite... unless you ask very, very nicely and say please."

Kris was honestly a bit surprised she hadn't noticed what he was doing there, but she appreciated the subtle little work he'd been doing to make her more comfortable. It showed he cared... and was even more clever than she'd given him credit for being.

From there, they went on to discuss the terms of the test drive: it would last no less than 90 days, and involve them basically trying out the dynamic of her being his little. He'd assume the Caretaker responsibilities – the same responsibilities as any Dominant, save with a few added caveats of the typical Caretaker nature. There were to be rules, rewards, and punishments they discussed ad laid out... but there was also to be coloring, giant stuffed animals, and maybe a princess crown or two for some roleplaying scenes. Kris insisted on those things specifically. He agreed to care for her in the ways she need and desired, always to the best of his physical abilities, and in exchange Kristina agreed to follow a temporary set of rules for being his submissive. A few of those new rules were as follows:

- No orgasms or masturbation without express permission
- No 'playing' with other people without expressed permission (flirting okay)
- Keep sass, backtalk, and snippy comments to a minimum
- No pouting, especially when given an order
- No negative self-talk
- Always be honest with your Caretaker
- Maintain regular contact with your Caretaker unless it is impossible for some reason

- Safe-word is an all-stop: if you need it, use it – there are no repercussions for using it

- The safe words for now are **red** for 'stop everything' and **mercy** for 'slow down'. After the trial period, if both parties want to continue and move forward, personalized safe words will be chosen, and more rules will be discussed.

Certain rules applied to both of them, like 'maintaining contact' and 'always be honest', but other than that they tried to keep the trial rules simple for the time being. The penalties were also explained simply: sass, snippy comments, and backtalk would result in 5 strikes to her bum per infraction; pouting was the same, with a 5-strike penalty (unless she was pouting when given an order In that case it was 10 strikes); not keeping in contact (unless something unforeseen happened to prevent contact) was 15; orgasms and masturbation without permission were

25 strikes per infraction, plus at least one denied orgasms;

negative self-talk was 40 strikes and a minimum of 5

ruined orgasms; and playing with others without

permission was grounds to terminate the whole

arrangement. Depending on the nature of the lie, the same

could be said for being dishonest – it would be on a case-

by-case basis how that could be handled, but lying about

playing with others was grounds for ending things then and

there.

The lying part went both ways, of course.

Once they typed them all out, Z-No printed them

out and they each signed. Then, after signing her portion,

Kris held up her right hand with her pinkie finger extended.

"Pinky swear!

" she said loudly.

"Beg pardon?"

"Pinky swear," she repeated. "You have to pinky swear to make it official! Otherwise it doesn't count."

Z-No sighed, then managed a smile as he held out his hand and pinky to her.

"I solemnly pinky swear to that which we agreed upon in writing and signed," he said, chuckling a bit as they interlocked fingers.

"Good! Now I can rest easy!"

And with that, and one more bit of laughter, it was done. It was official. It was official and it was real and Kris could hardly believe it. It wasn't everything she wanted, but it was a start. Iwonderful start, and she wasn't sure what to do from this starting point and the uncertainty was as exhilarating as it was terrifying.

He was looking at her. Not the way he normally looked at her. He was looking at her with that same cutting, ravenous shine in his dark-brown eyes that he'd had when she'd first met him outside after the much… the same look he'd had before he kissed her.

"Do you work today?" he asked.

"No, Sir…" she said, clutching the hem of her shirt. "I have the day off from the hotel, and since it's supposed to rain today I didn't take any dog walking appointments."

"Good," he said. "Now, stand up, would you darling?"

"Yes, Sir…" she remarked, standing up on cue."

He stood slowly, walking over to her with that same look in his eyes. Hunger was in his eyes, unbridled… unrestrained. He began to walk around her, and she instinctively turned her head to follow.

"Eyes front, little one."

It was his first order to her, is first official order. She stood as still as she could despite a part of her trembling from being told what to do by this man in that tone. More than the pinky swear, more than the contract, more than any moment before… it meant she was his. And the submissive in her was close to melting based on that alone, before he even deigned to touch her.

"Do you have anything else to do today?" he asked. He was behind her now, but close… and she felt the warmth of his breath on the back of her neck, and the phantom tingle like static electricity as his body was so close to hers she could practically feel them touching already.

"No, Sir…" she whispered, closing her eyes to try and focus on keeping her eyes forward.

"So… you have nowhere to be, and I have a day off…" he said, moving in closer. She felt the shape of his chest against her back, his crotch against her ass, the outline of his dick right up against her ass. "And you've just agreed to be my little toy. However should we pass all this time we have?"

She wasn't sure if the question was rhetorical or not, and the process of thinking about it was made infinitely more difficult when his hand moves up from behind her to caress her neck. The touch was warm and gentle... but with just enough pressure applied to let her know he could press harder, squeeze more, do much worse... or, based on perspective, better.

The song "With Your Permission" began playing on the sound system that before had been just ambient noise to her. She wondered if he'd set the playlist up that way and timed this out, or just switched the songs over while she was distracted... but then he kissed and tauntingly lightly bit the back of her neck, and she didn't care either way anymore. Her body melted back against his, and she let out a small gasp that was almost embarrassingly dainty as her hands reached back and grabbed his thighs for support.

"*Shit*..." She hissed the word through her teeth, then let out a sigh. "Mmm, you're going to make me beg, aren't you?"

"I'm not going to make you do anything..." he replied. "But, if you want something... it would behoove you to speak up."

"Fuck..." she whimpered. He was beginning to sway with her, side-to-side movements matching the rhythm of the music. Instinctively she began to grind herself back against him, as seductively as possible in an effort to draw him in without her needing to speak. But her patience was too thin for that. Eventually, she just began to talk:

"Hurt me," she said, voice trembling slightly with barely restrained lust. "Use me… do what you want with me."

"Was that an order or a request?" he asked, squeezing her neck a bit tighter.

"F-f-… Please, Sir?"

"Please what? Be a big girl, use your words…"

"Please…" she started, swallowing hard. She took her right hand off his thigh, moving it to caress his face and feel the slight roughness of his beard against her palm. "Please… do whatever you want to me. Just… let me feel *you*. Let me feel used by you. Let me feel your power over me… Let me feel you inside me… please?"

"Good girl," he said. Those words made her feel weak again, and a stronger grip on her neck coupled with another bite to the back of her neck made her knees all but buckle against him. She gripped tighter to keep her balance, a soft whine escaping her throat.

She couldn't think of a time she'd wanted anything as badly as she wanted this moment and the moments she was sure would come next.

He ripped her blouse off, a cascade of buttons flying off and clattering on the floor, the combination of the noise and the suddenness of his movement making her gasp. Her breasts were exposed now to the cool air of the room, and the groping of his greedy hands as he palmed and massaged them. One hand went back to her neck, and as if she wasn't desperate to have him… he growled in her ear. Not moaned, not groaned… he *growled* in her ear like some feral beast.

She felt wet enough he could surf into her pussy… and he still wasn't touching it yet.

He didn't have to speak a word to her: he simply spun her around and gave her a stern enough look, and in response she dropped to her knees eagerly, hands gripping at the waistline of his shorts instinctively before he grabbed them and moved them away.

"Hands behind your back, mouth open," he commanded.

Of course she happily sprung to form, as requested.

"Tell me, princess… have you ever had that pretty little throat of yours fucked?" he asked, cupping her chin and bringing her eyes up from the sizable outline of cock in his shorts up to those piercing black spheres he called eyes. "Have you ever had that mouth of yours used like a second pussy, crammed full of dick with the express purpose of being filled and finished off properly?"

She nodded, unsure she had the freedom to answer verbally.

"Good girl, being honest…" he encouraged, rubbing her cheek. "And good girls get a treat. And your treat… is to please me. Understand?"

Again she nodded. She saw him undoing the draw string of his shorts in her peripheral vision, but when she tried to stare down at it her pulled her head back up roughly.

"Eyes up here," came Z-No's next command with that growl coming back into his voice. "Keep those pretty eyes on me. Understand?"

She nodded, focusing as hard as she could on his face even as he lowered those shorts. She felt the heat of his dick bump against her chin as it was finally freed from the confines of his shorts… even though she wanted so badly to take it into her mouth right away. She was no rookie to this, and far from a virgin… she knew to wait for permission.

This was made harder – nearly impossible actually – when he took that heavy, meaty pole of his and began tapping it against her tongue. She could taste him now… that flavor of precum and mild sweat from whatever workout he'd been doing earlier was enough to get her salivating, and she momentarily broke form to try and take more of it into her mouth.

During the moment she was looking down she had to stare at the dick in question: it was big, but not pornstar huge. The width caught her attention first; it looked like she'd have to stretch her jaw just to fit it in. And if it was too big for her mouth…

Her mind was snapped from her mystified awe by a sudden grabbing of her head as he yanked her off his dick.

"Did I give you permission to touch that, little slut?"

"Nnngh! N-no, Sir…" she answered, bottom lip poking out.

"Then why did you do it?"

"I just… I couldn't help it…" she replied, trying her best to look cute. "It just looked so good, and I've wanted it for such a long time…"

"Are you that much of a greedy, cock-starved little fuckdoll you can't resist putting dick in your mouth?" he asked.

"Mmhmm… I'm sorry…" she said next, still pouting.

"Go over to the couch," he growled out next. "Bend over the arm of it and wait for me to deal with you."

Kristina got to her feet in order to follow the order, kicking herself mentally for the inability to restrain her stupid mouth. Her first time and she was already in trouble…

"Who told you to stand up?"

"Sir?" she asked, turning around.

"I told you…" he said, grabbing her neck again, "to go over to the couch. Never did I say anything about getting off your knees, did I?"

He slapped her ass with his free hand, hard, before she could answer. It stung almost right away… and she loved it. The second slap was a bit less direct than the first due to the angle, but it had enough power behind it to hit that sweet spot between pain and pleasure. Even though she knew this was punishment… her body didn't seem to care. Her pussy, specifically, just seemed delighted to be even *close* to where the action was.

"I asked a question, little fuckdoll…" he replied, glaring and slapping her ass again. He punctuated almost every word he said next with a slap to her behind. "Did." **SLAP** "I." **SLAP** "Give." **SLAP** "Permission." **SLAP** "To stand?"

"No!" she yelped out. "No, Sir!"

"Then get back down on your knees, princess," he ordered, releasing her.

She did as she was told, sinking back down onto her knees and crawling over to the couch on all fours. She felt that familiar burning shame of humiliation, washing over and making her skin feel hot despite the chill of the room. She made her way over slowly, a bit unsure… then leaned over the arm of the couch as she was told.

"Good girl…" he responded, petting her head. "Now stay there until I say otherwise.

Kris nodded, internally sighing. She held no delusions about what he was going to get, and what he was going to do with it once he returned. Still, he called her a good girl, and in this current submissive state of mind that was enough to make her smile a little.

Eventually, her mind as distractible as it was in that head space, she began to get bored, idly kicking her legs and humming as she waited. She must have gotten a bit off in her own world, because she didn't realize Z-No was back until she felt one of his hands squeezing her slightly sore ass.

"Are we having fun?" he asked.

"I was just tryin' to behave!" she defended. "You were gone for *ages!*"

"Ages?"

"Yep! Literally ages. I counted."

He chuckled and patted her head again. "You're right, you're right…" he said, smiling. "But I had to get my old gear out. And now, trust me… you have my full attention."

Part of Kris wasn't sure having his full attention was a good thing, considering she was in trouble at the moment and was new to how he dealt with her being in trouble. But before she could really think about it too much, he told her to put her eyes front and her hands behind her back. She felt the familiar sensation of cotton rope wrapping around her wrists and shivered just a bit more, slipping deeper into subspace. She loved cotton rope, and the fact it was him binding her up… the man she'd fantasized about for months on end…

Yes…

He finished the knotting up of her restraints in moments, and she tugged on them experimentally, out of habit. Just as one would expect from a photographer and a rigger at a BDSM dungeon – the rope cuffs were tight enough to have no give for her to slip out, but not so tight that the rope constantly bit into her… unless she moved. She was securely bound up now… at his mercy physically, the same way she'd already been mentally.

Yes…

She was wiggling about a bit when she felt it: that strange but not unfamiliar oblong shape rubbing against her lower thigh before moving up to rest against her ass.

He brought out a paddle… and now was going to begin her punishment.

YES…

Z-No was a firm believer in spanking in layers. He started off spanking her with her jeans still on… and

Kristina was eternally grateful. Those first few strikes, man… they *hurt!* She was still a masochist, so the hurting part was still fun and even arousing for her… but yikes. He hit hard enough to get her right to that edge, the point where the pain stops being arousing and starts just being painful… but never tipping over. It came close though… close enough she began flailing her legs like an obstinate child and whimpering by the second strike.

He held her when she began kicking and asked if that was too hard, and when she shook her head he kissed her forehead.

"You know you can safe-word out and stop me any time, right princess?" he asked her.

"Mmhmm."

"Good girl. Now, you got 3 more." He kissed her forehead again, then rubbed her cheek before getting back into position behind her. "Bet you won't do that one again without permission, will ya?"

"No, Sir…" she said, glad for the 'face forward' order so he couldn't see her pouting. The cognitive part of her brain, such as it was still there, commented on how effective he was. He knew how to go right to that limit of her pain threshold but not pass it, to make sure even through her masochistic love of pain the lesson registered. It was hard enough to make sure she wouldn't make that particular mistake again…

Not for a while, at least.

She took her final 3 slaps to the ass with as much grace and dignity as she could muster, still squirming and yelping a bit. He encouraged her after the slaps were finished, then moved over to kiss her forehead again.

"That's my good girl…" he said, smiling down at her. "Now… would my good girl like a treat?"

Kris nodded, biting her bottom lip. She could still see that thick, veiny, throbbing, precum-drooling dick he had, just in front of her, just out of reach.

"And what does my girl want for her treat?" Z-No asked her.

As if you don't already know… she thought, a slight smirk forming on her lips despite herself. He was making her beg the whole way through, just as she'd thought he would… just as she'd wanted him to. *Fuckin' jerk…*

"Fuck me…" she whispered, wiggling a bit as she spoke. "I don't care which hole you choose… I just want… I need… to feel it inside me. I need you to take me, and take me hard…" then, after a pause: "… please? Sir?"

"You're learning…" he encouraged, rubbing her chin. "Good girl. Now…" he got up on the couch, lining his dick up with her pretty little mouth. "Open up wide for me, princess…"

Thus began the fucking of her throat. She was a bit nervous about it, based on the size of the man's meat in front of her… but at least Z-No wasn't in a hurry. In her experience, most guys weren't up for fucking her face, thinking she was 'too pretty' for it. Those guys tended to fuck her like a delicate flower… which murdered her pain-loving arousal and sent her straight into boredom. The few times she'd found a man who was up for the deed (provided they didn't ruin it by talking too much), they tended to do it with no technique: just a violent set of vigorous rabbit humps as soon as they could, followed shortly thereafter by the guy in question cumming on her face and becoming exhausted from their exertion.

Z-No was more of a realist, it seemed. He pushed his cock into her mouth with authority, but not with speed. He was giving her a few inches at a time, testing out her gag reflex… which made sense to Kris. After all, as large as he was, he'd probably met more than a few women who couldn't fit that entire monstrous thing he called a dick into their mouths. It was rough for Kristina to handle, to be sure… but she wasn't a virgin to blowjobs, nor a quitter. She used every practiced technique she had learned, then leaned forward as much as she could… and on the next push forward, she let him in deep… nice and deep…

She felt accomplished when she looked up and saw a shocked expression across his face. She wished she had a camera, or someone else had a camera nearby and was watching them, just so she could immortalize that moment she first made him make that face forever. She shook him with that little move… and the moment, the second she made him surprised… she felt proud.

It must have showed on her face, because he reached down and patted her head. "Good girl…" he muttered, starting to regain his composure. "Good girl, holy shit…"

She hummed happily around his dick, wiggling her hips a bit in celebration. This celebration was interrupted by a slap to her rear and a growl from Z-No.

"Don't get too excited," he warned. "Keep in mind, you just showed me that your gag reflex is not a concern…"

Her eyes got wide as she realized that… but not in fear this time, no. Instead, her eyes were widened with excitement and anticipation that she might actually get what she wanted.

Bereft of voice due to the current state of her mouth, she instead signaled this joy to her dominant by shaking her rump like a happy dog.

Then Z-No gripped her head, smirked down at Kris, and began to fuck her face in earnest. The movements of his hips were rougher than before, more direct and relentless… now that he knew she could take it. He was, just as he'd mentioned before, 'fucking her mouth like a second pussy'…

And it made her actual pussy wetter.

She liked it better each time it sank in, now she didn't have much choice in the matter. Her hands were still tied up and out of the way, meaning she was mostly useless when it came to her getting away as things got rougher. The only thing holding back the massive shaft of swollen, hot, toffee-colored dick plowing her esophagus, at this point, was Z-No's mercy… such as it was. He popped his heavily veined and meaty cock out of her mouth long enough for her to breathe, for which she was grateful… and impressed he seemed able to use her mouth so ruthlessly while also knowing when to stop and let her get some much-needed oxygen.

Such an observant guy… she thought dreamily, making an effort to keep eye contact with him and not the toned muscles of his stomach. She was getting a bit more weak and dizzy as time went on… and when he finally stopped, she was blinking dumbly for a few moments trying to piece together what had happened.

Did he cum? She asked herself. *Did he just shoot a load down my throat while I was too faded to notice?*

Cognitive functions came back online in her brain and reminded her that no, that wasn't what happened. Even if she'd been teetering on the edge of passing out, a guy like Z-No would've made sure she knew. Besides, something that size swelling up in her mouth the way a man's dick tended to right before their orgasm? She would've remembered something like that.

She was still confused why he'd stopped when the logic of the situation sunk in through her stupor – he wasn't done with her, and his dick was still hard, so…

Oh fuck…

The only logical explanation was right there. She could tell by the way his hips moved and the slight sounds he made while fucking her face that she was doing a good job... so there was only one reason he'd stop.

*Oh, **fuck**...*

As her eyes came back into focus, she saw the final confirmation of her theory; Z-No putting on a condom that somehow managed to fit that behemoth he called a penis.

*Oh, **fuck me**...*

As wet as she was, Kris wasn't sure she was ready for this part. Was she really capable of taking something that big in her pussy? On the one hand, that was half the reason she came here... but on the other hand, how much was too much? Was this too early to let him fuck her? Was this a test? Would she fail or pass if she let him fuck her like this? There were so many thoughts going through her head... and then he was behind her.

She was debating if she wanted to say something now, if she wanted to be "that girl" and tap out before he even got started.... But then she felt something quite unexpected.

She felt his tongue against her clit.

This was one of the last things she expected to happen. Many Doms had rules about oral sex; namely that the dominant partner was always on the receiving end of it and never on the giving end. She didn't know why she'd expected Z-No to be one of those guys... but part of her was happy she was wrong.

Especially when he started licking and sucking her clit while gripping her ass with both hands....

"Uh... I... Oh, fuck..." she whimpered out, unable to resist looking back at him for a moment before moving her eyes back forward. He was good at what he was doing, certainly... the way he alternated between gentle and rougher pressure with his lips tongue, how he switched up between licking her lower lips and sucking her clit… it was clear he knew what he was doing, and was thoroughly enjoying himself. She even heard a few choice moans here and there.

Maybe it was that realization that the Dominant she'd looked up to was enjoying licking her pussy. Maybe it was the fact he was doing it so well. Maybe it was how pent up she'd been, or how long it had been since she last had her pussy eaten, or the fact she hadn't expected it… but within what felt like moments to her, she was inches from cumming. She looked back and pouted, trying to pull away from his skilled tongue.

"S-sir… Can I-? She started, cut off by a sudden slap to her ass and a growl – her punishment for pulling away before he was done. "Fuck!"

She managed to get him to look up at her – that in and of itself a small victory.

"Sir, may I cum?" she asked, shivering slightly in his grip and idly tugging at her restraints.

"Good girl, asking for permission..." he encourages, smiling as he squeezed her ass cheeks. "But no, you may not cum yet."

She started to protest when she heard those words... but then her protests were interrupted when he resumed eating her pussy.

"Oh fuck, oh fuck... nnngh, Sir... Sir that's not... Oh god...."

Her words were a jumble, a random set of thoughts and noises as she struggled to maintain control of herself and not allow herself to cum. There was no sense in asking him to stop, unless she was willing to safeword out of it...

which she bristled at right away. No, no fair... she couldn't wuss out this early, the first thing...

It was easier said than done. Her resolve meant little against the cascading of pleasure from his masterful mouth slurping her sex. She couldn't hold back worth much, despite her best efforts... and in seconds she was trying to squirm away that wonderful wet and terribly torturous tongue of Z-No's, only to have him slap her ass again and pull her back into place.

"Sir! Wait, wait... I can't, Sir... I..." she gasped, hips shaking and eyes starting to water.

"Speak up," he commanded.

"I... I need to cum," she admitted finally, biting her bottom lip.

"Do you, now?" he asked, slapping her ass and squeezing it with one hand. "How badly do you need it, princess? Tell me... be specific."

Kris wanted to scream at him. She wanted to cry, she wanted to pout she wanted to flail her legs and stomp her feet and throw a childish temper tantrum. Making her speak while she was this close to the edge... he really was cruel in a way. Even as the masochist in her thrilled at being hopelessly held at the mercy of someone who (at this moment, anyway) seemed he wouldn't know the word 'compassion' if it were on the side of a train... she was drawn to the pressing and aching current reality of her pussy practically screaming at her that she needed to cum, had to cum, was going to explode if she didn't cum.

"Can I cum?!" she yelped out. "Can I please cum Sir, pretty please? I'll do anything you say, just... nnngha!! I need it, I need it..."

To her surprise, she felt a warm hand rubbing her back next. He leaned over her back and whispered into her ear in a soothing manner, calming her mind if not her pussy.

"Anything I say?" he asked in that rich smooth tone of his.

"Anything, Sir…"

"And if I say you can only cum with my dick in one of your pretty little holes?" he asked next.

YES. Yes, yes, OH GOD, YES! GIVE IT TO MEEEEEEE! Her inner self was screaming, ravenously, in the back of her head, and she foud herself again wriggling her hips and shaking her shapely ass back towards him. She was panting, gasping, whimpering, groaning… she felt so much like a bitch in heat, she should've been wearing a collar.

"Do it Sir…" she rhasped out through ragged breaths. "Please do it Sir…"

She heard a telltale ripping sound, and looked back to see Z-No opening and putting on a condom. She next felt three things at the same time: first, one of Z-No's large, strong hands grabbing a fistful of her hair; second was his teeth biting into the nape of her neck; and third was his cock pushing into her tight, wet, achingly empty pussy, spearing it open and giving her what she desperately craved this whole time.

"Oh shit, oh shit… I can't… Sir, I can't…"

"*Cum,*" he ordered.

Kris wasn't sure what caused her to cum at that moment. Between the denial and final permission, the sensation of being penetrated by the dick of someone she'd fantasized about fucking for over a year, and that gruff masculine voice giving her the order to do it, there were too many factors to choose from. Maybe it was one, maybe all of them… she neither knew or particularly cared. All she could say with any sort of certainty was that she could feel the orgasm roaring forward like a tidal wave surging towards land… just a loud, abrupt rush coming at her with relentless force, followed by a white hot-flash of mind-numbing pleasure that washed away the rest of the world outside. She bucked and shivered wordlessly for a few moments that felt like minutes, then let out a series of audible but nonsensical gibberish as she squirted against his thighs and came herself stupid.

She was still in the haze of her orgasm as she began to feel Z-No's cock still moving inside her, even as she was still overly sensitive from cumming. It sank in, just as his teeth's grip on her neck tightened, that while she had just had an orgasm for the ages… he had taken some time off from receiving pleasure and in a sense was just getting started.

She was in for it.

The size alone was something else; if she wasn't in that pain-pleasure blendin already, she might not have been able to cope with how stretched and full she felt. The tip came to a stop just at the deepest part of her, bumping her cervix as the rest of his shaft spread her walls open around the considerable girth. Then it combined with her still being bound and the heightened sensitivity of an orgasm…. And she was pretty much wrecked. Kris tried, best she could, to beg permission to cum again… and Z-No yanked her face back to look at him.

"Might as well keep cumming 'till you can't cum anymore, little slut…" he hissed down at her with a sinister smirk, "'Cuz I'm not stopping 'till *I'm* done with you."

Those words…they were too much for her brain and body. Everything blurred and melted, as far as her mind was concerned. She felt like she was floating away, somewhere else entirely… and all she could feel was her own juices running down her legs and the glory of being filled and fucked by him. Everything else once again faded away before the orgasmic wave… and the next clear memory she had didn't kick in until Z-No pulled out of her, pulled off the condom, and started cumming on her face.

Perfect.

She lay on her back, clueless as to how or when she'd gotten there, with a faceful of hot seed she endeavored to lick off. Then she sighed and began to collapse. She was only barely cognizant enough to feel Z-No moving her enough to untie her wrists, then gripping her to make sure she was alive.

"You okay, princess?" he asked, his voice showing mild concern.

"Mmhmm…" she muttered out, eyes still hazy. She reached out to him and he embraced her in turn, even kissing her despite the mess she knew her face had to be.

"You did amazing…" he said, smiling. "I'm very proud of you."

She giggled then nuzzled into his neck.

"Cuddles?" she asked, her brain still mildly fried.

"Cuddles," he assured her.

Moments later, they were curled up on his couch and holding each other. And as Z-No fell asleep next to her, Kris sobered up from her orgasm high and felt herself struggling to contain the energy.

WE DID IT! She yelled to herself. *Game, set match victory!!*

And so she drifted off to sleep the way she'd always wanted to… with Z-No embracing her, warm and secure.

And thus began the test drive.

Chapter 11: Swerving

The more time Lorenzo spent with Kristina, the more she made him feel like the old Z-No. The more Lorenzo felt like the old Z-No, the stronger his urges became to punch Zachary in the face.

It wasn't helped by the fact they were closer to being equals now. Someone in management was taking notice of Mr. Wallace's work (as they'd said in emails), and Lorenzo was beginning a slow but steady clamor further up the ladder at Samuels'. This was coming with a slight increase in pay, but… it also meant Zach went from an annoyance he saw around while doing some work here and there to a peer. They were spending more time near each other, more time talking about work… and the more of that happened, the more Z-No started to come out of Lorenzo and begin chomping at the bit to just deck the fucker one time and hand in his 2 weeks.

Of course, you'd have to be insane to do something like that. He had the ideal job – mainly getting paid more than he deserved to do practically nothing. He had time on his hands to do other things, money for rent and bills plus some health insurance, and all those other perks that you get when you reach the top of the ladder.

But every time Zachary walked up to him and started to chat, be it at Z-No's desk or just in the halls, he seriously considered throwing all that away just to shut him the fuck up.

Zachary had the annoying habit of coming to Lorenzo's desk in the middle of the day, right around the time he was trying to enjoy a bit of lunch in peace, and try to discuss things. If they were work-related things, that would be one thing... still obnoxious during lunch, but it'd be something he could deal with it. But instead, he talked about stuff like baseball games he saw because his dad got season tickets, and how he'd gotten his date to give him head in the box office seats.

"You ever get head while watching a live game from the sky box, Lorenz?" he asked, tossing around a baseball as he spoke, causing a repetitive but soft *paf* noise that increased the irritation factor of every word that he uttered.

"Can't say I have," Lorenzo replied, staring at the ball and trying not to think about grabbing it and smashing Zachary's head in with it.

"Tellin' ya, Lorenz;" Zach said, tossing the ball up in the air and catching it now instead of just tossing it hand to hand, "nothing like it. I mean, picture it;" here, Zach paused and held his hands up, as if framing a picture: "You're watching the legends, the types of men you grew up idolizing. I mean, when I was a kid, these dudes were like *gods* to me, right?"

"Uh huh," Z-No replied, tapping the side of his lunch with his fork.

"And now here you sit, in a 400-dollar suit, getting your knob polished… and these champs, these fuckin' *legends*… they're looking up to *you*." He laughed, holding up the ball. "I swear man, it's the power that got me off."

"Right there with ya," Z-No said, trying not to roll his eyes. *Prick wouldn't know what **real** power felt like if it bitch-slapped him…*

"Didn't hurt this girl was fine as hell," Zachary said, smirking as he resumed tossing the ball from hand to hand. "I mean, 19 year old, Irish-Rican mixed broad… she was an 'aspiring model', aka 'livimg with her mommy and works at Denny's', if ya know what I'm talking about." He laughed coldly before continuing. "She had that tight athletic lil' body those types tend to have, but the low self-esteem that lets you treat 'em like shit if you got enough money. Bitch just *reeked* of daddy issues and Vicky Secret perfume. I swear, I could fuck her in the ass if I could figure out what type of cologne her pops wore."

*For the love of all things holy and most things unholy, **shut the fuck up Zachary***.

Mercifully, Zach's watch went off, informing him it was time for him to go work out.

"Ah, fuckin' cardio..." he muttered. "I'm gonna have to boogie."

Oh thank God...

Zachary turned towards the door, then stopped.

"Before I go, though..." he said, tossing the ball up in the air, "you ever hit up that girl from the other week? The model chick with the nice ass?"

She has a name, you pretentious self-important cunt...

"I don't mix work and pleasure, Zach," Z-No responded, lying through his teeth. Of course he wouldn't tell Zach about him and Kris even if they weren't up to outlandish and kinky shenanigans. The guy's mouth was the only thing as big as his ego, and he didn't want to have anything in common with that piece of shit anyway; it might encourage him to talk more. So instead, he told a simple lie and ended it with "Not my style."

"Lame," Zach said with a roll of his eyes. "Maybe I'll take a crack at her, see what happens. Girl like that, she'd definitely be a decent fuck… right?" he stopped at the door again, then continued with: "I admit, haven't fucked a lot of black chicks; no idea how that works out. Do skinny black chicks handle a sausage right or do you have to go for the big ones with the 'ghetto booty'?"

I'm gonna kill him… Z-no thought. He wasn't even angry anymore, it was just a fact. *I'm gonna kill him and burn the body and bury the ashes in the park…*

Zach's watch beeped again.

"Shit, I'm running late!" he said. "Rain check?"

"Sure, Zach," said Z-No. "Can't wait."

The moment he left, Z-No found himself stabbing the lunch he'd brought from home with his fork like it personally offended him. He hated that stupid prick more than he hated the tie he had to wear to work… more than he hated having to make sure pictures submitted by the company conformed to European beauty standards, and that he worked with a company that tended to digitally lighten the skin of women of color and not hire girls his or Kristina's skin tone uless someone recommended them or an activist group came in asking questions… more than he hated not being able to be honest about his lifestyle and his involvement in BDSM. He hated Zachary, he hated the job, he hated the office…

Which of course meant the office was going to intrude more into his life. As he was about to get out his phone and text Kris her next assignment, he got an email alert from work he had to stop and look at:

Company Dinner, this Friday! Formal attire required! Fundraiser for charity! Dates allowed!

Z-No stared at the email and sighed, rolling his eyes to the heavens.

"Oh, sunova bitch…" he grumbled.

"What's the big deal?" Kris asked later when Z-No explained the dinner concept to her. It was about 5 weeks into their little test drive… 3 of which she'd spent coming over to his house as often as possible to cuddle, fuck, get tied up and/or spanked, and make dinner – not an order from Z-No, but because she insisted on it.

"It adds 3 hours outside of work I have to spend with those assholes," Z-No explained, sighing and undoing his tie. "Present company excluded, I like to keep work and anything resembling my personal life as separate as possible. And you, my dear, are one hell of an exception to that rule."

"I'm pretty exceptional, it's true." Kris said with a giggle, currently in the kitchen sporting a maid-style apron and nothing else. "You want a beer or something while I'm in here?"

"Beer's fine, love," he explained, holding the tie up to the light and glaring at it. "I could use the whole 12 pack if I have to go back into this tie on the weekend."

"Let's start with one and see," Kris suggested with a chuckle, handing the cold bottle of Coors original over to him before sitting down next to him with a smile. "You know, I got the same invitation but you don't see me freaking out about it…"

"I'm not freaking out," Z-No countered, "I'm annoyed. When I freak out, you'll be able to tell."

"Either way, why is it a big deal?" Kris asked. "Can't you just, I dunno… ignore it? Or blow it off?"

"Not now that I've been promoted," Z-No said with a sigh as he spun the top off the beer and took a swig. "Plus, when they say the 'dates' are encouraged… they really mean they're mandatory. You can't show up without a Plus One or people start asking questions."

"So… take someone," Kris said with a shrug.

"You'd be okay with that?" he asked.

"Sure," she said, resting her chin on his shoulder. "It's just a distraction trick, after all… I know the difference. But if she gets too friendly and tries to get further than arm candy, I can't promise not to find her later and claw her eyes out... y'know, just so she gets the message that it was wrong. I *totally* wouldn't go further than that."

"That was simultaneously the scariest and hottest thing you've ever said."

"Thank you, Sir!"

"I'll get a date then..." he said, staring at the bottle. "And I suppose you can get one as well. Just know I'll do worse things than gouge out his eyes if he gets fresh. On to other subjects, though... has my little girl been doing her homework?"

Kris nodded, getting off the couch and walking over in front of him.

"Turn around and show me," he said, managing a slight smirk.

Kris did as she was told, albeit slowly and a bit nervously. She leaned forward a bit, hands on the coffee table for support, as she displayed her 'homework' to her new Dominant caregiver. Her bare backside exposed that her tight little ass was plugged, sporting a silicone princess plug with a dark blue jewel adorning it. The pussy beneath this little jewel was almost as shiny, wet with her juices already.

"Good girl…" he encouraged, gripping her ass with one hand. "And you've been doing this all week?"

"Mmhmm…" she said, looking back at him. "At least 2 hours a day, just like you said. I've been keeping it cleaned up back there, too…"

"That's my girl," he encouraged, with a playful slap to her rear. "I bet that ass is clean enough to eat off… but we'll go find that out later. For now… turn around and tell me how it feels being plugged so much?"

Kris spun as she was told, hands clasped in front of her as she began speaking.

"At first, it kinda hurt…" she admitted, staring down at her hands. "It wasn't the first time I had a thing in there but… it was the biggest thing. And…"

"Eyes forward," he said sternly. "Look up at me and continue."

"Sorry, Sir…" she said, sighing and forcing herself to make eye contact. "Well, after the first time, it started to feel a bit weird. Not bad, not really good. Just weird. Then it started to feel dirty… which of course made my princess place all wet and messy… and then I started to like it more."

"I see…" Z-No said, sitting back a bit on the couch with one hand still gripping his beer. "So, tell me princess… have you ever had your tight little cunt fucked with something like that shoved in your tight little asshole?"

Kris shook her head, looking down at her hands again.

"I've read about it..." she said. "And I looked it up online, with pictures. They were... it looked so intense. And it made me very excited... I wanted to play, but I was good."

"I'm sure you were," Z-No replied, standing up and cupping her chin in his hand again. "Also, you know why people use these on princesses, right?"

"No, sir..." she said, still trying to look away a bit. "I've heard different reasons though."

"Men like me..." he began, smirking at her, "use them to train our princesses' tight little assholes so they'll spread wide enough to take dick. It's part of making you the multi-purpose fuckdoll you were meant to be. Now, doesn't that sound like fun, little one?"

Kris nodded, leaning her head into his palm. He felt the warmth of her cheek in his hand, and for a moment stared into her soft, doe-like brown eyes – so wide and gentle it was almost impossible to believe a masochist who got off on verbal degradation and mild to moderate verbal abuse was behind them.

Z-No felt a deep affection for her at moments like this; these silent, soft moments where she was so serene and at peace in his hands, at his mercy. It was so enthralling to see how much she trusted him, and drew him closer to her.

Part of him wondered how deranged he had to be to see someone so beautiful, so soft and kind, and know she trusted him… and then to be able to hurt her relentlessly the way he did.

Then he remembered how much she enjoyed the crueler sides of his nature, and it felt more justified. That's one of those things about BDSM relationships like this; she gave his sadistic side focus and meaning – a purpose. Just as he gave her masochistic side a release and a safe place to be explored… she gave him the same for his sadistic side. She was his shelter, a safe haven for him to be both sides of himself.

He realized then that he was falling for her. He might have already fallen for her and not noticed. And that was terrifying after his previous experiences with love. He noticed the hand that was cupping her cheek was shaking… and he pulled it back a bit.

"Are… are you okay?" Kris asked him, reaching out to him.

"Yeah, just fine…" he replied, forcing a smile. "Must be a bit chilly in here, that's all." Z-No took a step back from her outstretched hand, grabbing his beer and taking a swig. "I come from a long line of southern folks, y'know. We get cold pretty easily, my whole family does. At least on my Dad's side-!"

You're rambling! Z-No screamed at himself. *You're panicking, you're rambling, shut up shut up* **shut up!**

It was too late; it was already happening. He felt the trademark feelings of a panic attack rushing to meet him; he was clammy and hot all at once, his heart rate was so rapid and loud he could feel it in his ears, the world was turning into a bunch of white-hot noise combined with blurring colors.

*No, no, **NOT FUCKING NOW STOP STOP STOP PLEASE FUCKING-***

There was a flash of clear thought where Lorenzo thought to run towards the bathroom and grab whatever

Xanax he had left in the medicine cabinet… and then that was the last thought he had that was anything close to clear.

He took two steps, gasped for air, attempted to speak words… and then, the world went black.

Chapter 12: Coming Cleaning

Lorenzo had been experiencing panic attacks off and on since he hit high school. The intensity of them varied based on a number of factors, like what caused them or where he was at the time. Once, during a particularly bad one in 9th grade, he freaked out and accidentally shoulder checked another student into a wall so hard he chipped 2 of the poor guy's teeth, shortly before bolting out of the academic building and hid out in the locker room for almost 2 hours. Senior year he abruptly left a bonfire he was attending with some friends and was found on a construction site, miles away and hours later, with a torn ankle ligament and no logical explanation of what happened. Freshman year of college, he rambled to the young woman he was dating at the time for ten minutes. When she said he wasn't making any sense, he stopped mid-sentence and sprinted away, running until he threw up.

Every single time he had a panic attack was the same; he just ran. He ran from whatever was freaking him out, whatever was making him feel that white-hot hum and that crushing tension in his chest… and eventually, he was fine again. It just needed to be run out of his system.

Sophomore year was the first time he couldn't run fast enough or far enough. He remembered being at a friend's apartment for a party, and then the world spun… and he couldn't get outside to the door… and then he woke up to a crowd of people standing around him with varying levels of concern.

He'd gone home about a week later, and told his mother about what happened. She made him see a shrink, and thus began his regular use of and reliance upon Xanax. He lied about it constantly, hid it better than most kids hi their weed, and told practically no one anything about his problems with anxiety. He joked to one of his few friends that did know about his condition that he'd rather die than let someone know he had to be on meds to keep from running away or passing out.

Then something happened. 'The cur' happened. She'd found out about his condition, and come in like some sort of guardian angel… a beautiful older woman who offered to make everything alright when he came to a new city and knew almost no one else. She was his Domme, his center, his salvation…

Or at least, that's what he thought she was, once upon a time.

He hated himself for having trusted her… and he hated himself for even now, as he blacked out, imagining her laying next to him, stroking his hair and cheek and soothing him and…

Wait. Part of that wasn't imagined. Someone was next to him, stroking his hair and cheek.

He bolted upright, eyes bucked open as he scanned around frantically... and they came into focus on Kris. He panted a bit, before feeling one of her small, soft hands on his bare chest easing him back down. He was on his couch... and his shirt was cut down the middle.

"Shhh, it's alright..." she said, her other hand still rubbing his head. "You're at your house, you're safe... it's okay."

"God... what happened?" he asked, rubbing his face for a moment. "Did I just... fall asleep? Was it like, just a bad dream or something?"

"Not exactly..." Kris said, tilting her head. "We were talking, and you started to look nervous... then you collapsed." She reached over to the side of the couch, pulling a wash cloth out of warm water and placing it onto his forehead. "Luckily, I've seen panic attacks before and I knew what to do about one... but man, you're heavier than you look." She paused and chuckled, placing one hand on the side of his neck. "Whoever said muscle weighs more than fat was *not* kidding, lemme tell ya…"

Z-No groaned audibly. This was just another nightmare he'd had; Kris, the woman he was starting to care for so much, seeing him like this. Nothing ruined the whole image of being a Dom and in control of all things like having to be literally carried by your submissive.

"God… I'm sorry…" he muttered, covering his face with one hand. "Last thing I wanted was for you to see me like that…"

"You're lucky I did," she shot back, "or you would've fallen and cracked that beautiful face of yours." She smiled warmly, then kissed his forehead. "Besides, it's nothing to apologize about; people have panic attacks every day."

"I'm supposed to be a Dom," he said, rubbing his eyes a bit. "Showing that kind of weakness, for someone like me, is-."

"Human," Kris interrupted, taking her hand off of his neck and placing it on his chest. "It's human, that's all it is. You're a person, and people have problems and issues. People struggle, people fail, people need help and support. It's nothing more catastrophic than that."

Z-No blinked a bit, confused by all of this kindness.

"You're not grossed out by it?" he asked.

"Why would I be?" she asked. "Like I said, you're just a human. You're not a god or some unreal being... you're a man. That's more than enough, at least for me."

He looked up at her face, and it occurred to her that she meant that. It was sinking in, however slowly, that she was serious about all of that stuff about not caring if he was human ad flawed.

Before he knew it, he was choking up. And a few moments later, despite himself, outright tears ran down his face. This only served to make him feel worse about the whole thing, his stomach churning and his entire face hot with embarrassment.

"Did… did I say something wrong?" Kris asked. The warmth of her hand on his chest was comforting, as was her gentle tone… and that only served to make Lorenzo feel worse about choking up in front of her. Being consoled by someone wasn't his thing… it wasn't how things were supposed to go. But here he was…

"No… you didn't do anything wrong," he said after a pause, disgusted by the way his voice was cracking now as he spoke. "It's just… I didn't expect… I wasn't…"

He sat up, covering his face with his hands. It hurt.

It's over now… the wicked depressed thoughts inside his head told him. *She's seen the weakness. She'll either leave or exploit it. She'll bring you down… she'll rip you apart. Just like-!*

She held him close to her and began rubbing his head, humming gently. And suddenly he felt like the depressed thoughts, though still there, weren't quite as loud anymore. Usually it would escalate and escalate, until he couldn't think or speak. But this time, instead, he just… he felt them. They were still there… but they were manageable. He still felt sad, very sad… but he didn't feel like it was out of his control.

He felt sad… but functional. He wasn't paralyzed, he was still alive. So he hugged Kristina back, tightly as he could.

"I can't sing, so… this is the best I got in terms of soothing," she said with an awkward chuckle.

"It's perfect," he said, voice evening out a bit. He held her like he was scared she'd float away, like this might somehow turn out to still be a dream. The fact she'd stayed around for this part of himself… for Lorenzo the scared and weak and vulnerable… it meant all the world to him and then some.

A few more moments passed like that, just the two of them holding each other and rocking gently. Finally, Z-No gently nudged his way loose, hands on her shoulders.

"I think I'm okay," he assured her. "I need to sit up for a bit."

She acquiesced to this by moving over on the couch to let him sit up, but kept one hand on his back ever so gently. On the table was a glass of water… which he picked up with both hands, glad they weren't shaking.

"So, you really carried me all the way to the couch?"

"Mostly dragged," she admitted. "Like I said, you are *heavy*."

"Well, either way… thanks." He held the glass still, then looked over at her. "You really fuck with me, don't you?"

"The long way,' she replied, smiling and rubbing his back. "Lorenzo… I've been about you since I found out about you. I read everything associated with you, I checked out all your photos and stuff… I wanted to know everything there was to know about you. Then I met you in person…"

"… and you realized your mistake?"

"No self-depreciating humor after you just fainted, asshole," she warned with a playful shove. "Like I was saying… I met you and you were so… different from what I expected. You were sweet, and funny… you were kind, and smart… and you still had that Z-No edge like I wanted.

You weren't like I daydreamed you would be; you were better." She paused, then kissed him on the cheek. "And you think I'm gonna let that go just because you're not 100% perfect? You *must* be crazy."

"Keep talking like that," Z-No said while setting his glass down, "and I'll never let go of you. I get attached to people who are this kind to me."

"Good," she said. "I mean, that's the point, right? Besides, I'm already pretty attached to you."

"So, we can just attach ourselves to each other?"

"I think that's what the mortals call a 'relationship', Z," she said with a giggle.

"Ah yes, the relationship; I've heard tales of them, from the olden days…"

"You are older than me, so I don't doubt that…"

"By like, 5 years!"

"Yeah, whatever you have to tell yourself, cradle-robber."

"Grave-digger."

"Asshole!"

They laughed a bit, then Z-No took another sip of his water. He stared at his reflected eyes in the surface, saw the redness around them.

"When I was in high-school," he said, "people used to tell me I looked like a demon when my eyes were red. I scared people back then. But really, they were just red because of allergies. And because I spent a lot of time crying. Crying about the fact my parents were getting a divorce, crying about the fact I wasn't normal, crying about the way other kids treated me... I was just sad and nervous, all the time. My mom swore I'd eventually just get over it... but instead it got worse."

From there, he told her everything… everything minus a few bits. He told her about his parents and their rocky, verbal abuse-laden relationship that lasted until he was a senior in high school. He told her about how he was always nervous as a kid thanks to all the yelling, was always nervous he'd do something wrong. He even told her about his first few panic attacks.

"Later on," he explained, "when I got to college… I found out it was a medical issue and not just me being weird. I started taking the pills and focusing, and for a while life was good. I was keeping pace with the rest of the world, out living life and having fun… then last year, something happened and that wasn't enough. I kinda fell apart. That's when I stepped away from everything… from the Dojo, from art, from the world. I just kinda… fell into my day job and never came up for air. I've been more or less a broken toy ever since…" he trailed off. He couldn't tell her about the cur, not yet. Hell, he hadn't even said her name out loud since the incident… so he just let the words hang in the air, unable to continue them.

"… and you thought," Kris began, taking her hand off his shoulder and turning her whole body towards Lorenzo now, "that because you were a 'broken toy' as you put it… I would lose interest in you and just leave you alone? You thought I would abandon you because you weren't 'normal' or something?"

Lorenzo nodded, unable to look up at her for long. He instead focused on the reflection he saw in the glass of water; those same dead, bloody red eyes as before he was invited back to the Dojo, when he'd lost all interests in life and run out of joy and zeal in his spirit. Now here he was, feeling that same way again… preparing for her and all that energy he'd gained back to be gone.

It's going back to the cold, he said. *I'll go back to the pills and the chemical drain and the monotonous hum… and eventually, I'll just forget about it all. I'll forget…*

He felt warmth, abruptly – Kris' hand over his, contrasting with the chill of the glass.

"Look at me… please?" she asked him.

He sighed and slowly, nervously, turned to do so. He felt he owed her that much: the right to look him in the eye before she left.

"What made you think I was normal?" she asked. "I mean seriously; what in the world made you think *any*thing about me was normal?"

Lorenzo blinked, as if unable to process the question.

"I'm get turned on by degradation," she said, chuckling softly. "I have a best friend who does coke and runs from cops. I online stalked a guy from a BDSM dungeon website for almost 2 years before I got up the courage to even talk to him! What part of that is normal?"

He had no answer, so he just stared at her. The warmth of her hands was making the water less noticeable.

"I'm not... I'm not going to abandon you," she said, staring down at his hands. "I didn't do all of this, I didn't come all this way... just to leave it alone the first time things got hard. I don't want perfect, or normal. I want you... even if it's temporary. Even if after the test drive you decide you're done with me."

There was a pause, and Lorenzo heard a sniffle, and realized she was starting to tear up.

"Don't start that, or I'll start up again too..." he warned, managing a soft little grin.

"It's your fault… being all honest and emotional…" she said, taking one hand off of his to rub her eyes. "I wasn't prepared to have emotions like this today, damn it."

"I know, I know…" he said. He put the glass down, wiping the condensation off his hands. The water was basically room temperature now anyway. "Hey, your turn now; look up here, at me."

She managed it, still wiping away at the corners of her eyes.

"Unless something completely insane happens in the next week or so…" he said, taking both her hands as he turned to face her, "I'm not going anywhere. I'm doing the rest of the days mostly as a formality at this point. I can't see me letting you go unless you ask me to."

Kris smiled at him, a single tear running its way down her right cheek.

"You mean that?" she asked.

"Yep."

"Good, then… can we do something else?" she grinned a bit, pausing to take an errant strand of hair and brush it out of her face. "Because right now… my emotions are all sore, and I'm really tired."

"We can… cuddle and watch Netflix," Z-No suggested.

"Can I pick the movie?"

"A movie? Why not a show?"

"I kinda have a movie in mind already," she admitted.

"Does it involve goofy dialog and bad CGI?"

"You know me all too well, Sir."

He kissed her forehead, then handed her the remote. Moments later they were watching a cheesy sci-fi movie together, until Kristina fell asleep in his arms. He felt the warmth radiating off her, and the soft noises she made as she slept reverberated through his chest like a kitten purring or a car engine turning over.

"I'm gonna end up falling for you hard, ain't I sweetie?" he asked her softly, mostly just talking to himself. "Oh well... I guess there's worse ways to die..."

And with that, he drifted off to sleep holding onto her, arms firmly wrapped around her, as the TV droned on about killer lizards.

Chapter 13: The Mixer

Kris wasn't quite sure what she'd managed to get herself into at this point.

She meant what she said... at least she did when she said it, she meant it. She meant everything she'd said about it not being a big deal to her that Z-No... no, Lorenzo, important to use his real name for this... that Lorenzo had anxiety issues and depression. She'd meant that... at the time. But when she thought about it... was she really?

She hadn't told Lorenzo about her own depression issues - how she was on antidepressants like Prozac and Zoloft since she was in middle school, how she'd sunk into a worse depression after her mother walked out on her and her dad, how she'd lost jobs and friends when she was a wounded soul... but it was there, rattling around in her brain from the moment she left his apartment and well into the next day. She took the day off, curling up on her bed with her laptop by the bedside and her phone in her hand, texting people to avoid talking and sending emails about work. It was all she could do to get up from her bed and get the Chinese food she'd ordered. And she hated days like this more now that she thought about Lorenzo.

What if I have a day like this when he needs me? She thought signing and sitting on the couch to watch anime in her shorts and an overlong t-shit. *What if one day he reaches out and I'm too tired to grab his hand?*

She sat on the couch and watched a scene in the anime where a character fell to the ground, frozen, and shattered. She couldn't help but think about when Lorenzo had collapsed in front of her… and how terrified she'd been to do the wrong thing. She felt so scared she thought *she* was going to have an anxiety attack… and she still wasn't sure if she did the right thing or just got lucky and Lorenzo would have recovered anyway.

The what-ifs of the situation were crushing her, until she heard the familiar buzz of her phone and looked down at the table. 'Z-No' popped up on the screen, his name adorned with little hearts. Thankfully it was a text, not a call... so she picked it up and looked.

"Hey, hun..." the text began. "Sorry about yesterday. Thanks for sticking around long enough to, y'know... save my life and shit." The text included an emoji, the 'nervous sweat-drop' emoji – a rare thing from him.

"No need for thanks," she sent back, meaning those words at least. "I'm just glad you're okay." Then, in a second message: "Are you still okay?"

"Yeah, I'm right as rain," he sent back, along with a smile emoji. The next text picked up, saying: "I spoke to my doctor over the phone. I have an appointment for next week to get my medicine readjusted."

"So you have to wait a whole week to get your medication adjusted?" she replied. "Boo! That's shitty!"

"It's probably for the best," he said. "After all, the mixer is coming up tomorrow. Last thing I want is to be on some new meds while trying to deal with assholes from work I don't like anyway.

"Fair," Kristina sent back. "I personally wouldn't even go, all things considered…"

"Not an option," Lorenzo replied. "The job demands I be there, so be there I will. Be there I must."

"Speak like Yoda, you will?" she sent back, along with a wink emoji.

"Wise in the ways of the force, you are," he replied.

"Trained by a Jedi I was!" she shot back.

"But resist the dark side you did not," he replied, along with a smirking emoji.

Kris couldn't help but grin. It felt good to see he was back to his old self.

"Breaking character…" she sent back, "… as far as the mixer goes, I have a question: what's our protocol for something like this? Like, are we supposed to avoid each other?"

"That would raise suspicion," he said. "We should just act like normal coworkers would at a boring work mixer; say hi, make small-talk, and do the same to everyone else we're stuck hanging around with."

"That sounds sucky," Kris said, sending a pout emoji. "I don't wanna act like I'm bored with you! Though to be fair, my date will be boring so I won't be too far out of my acting range."

"Clever girl," he sent back. "Mine will be someone you've already met from the Dojo. Remember the Fairy Queen?"

"Titania?" she asked.

"One and the same."

"No fair!" she said next. "Your date is pretty and interesting. I'll be stuck with milk-toast boy all night!"

"I'm sorry, sweetie…" he said. "To make it up to you… how about we play a game at the gallery?"

"I like games!" she sent back, with a big beaming grin image.

"Splendid. This game is called, 'last one standing'. Basically, throughout the night we flirt with each other, via phone only, and play with each other's emotions… and the first one to give in because of how horny they are loses."

"Sounds fun!" Kris replied quickly. She was already starting to feel a bit better. "What do I get when I win?"

"*If* you win…" Z-No sent back, "you'll get one play session with no orgasm denial. I'll make you cum as many times as you can stand, no restrictions or edging."

"Oooh! That's a good prize!" Kris replied, wiggling excitedly in her seat. "But… what if I lose? Hypothetically, of course, since I'm gonna win and always win cuz I'm the princess."

"I get to pick one of three punishment games to play with you later on that night," the next message she received read, punctuated by a devilish grin. It was clear Lorenzo was feeling better, and back to his old Z-No self.

"That's no good…" Kris said. "I guess it's a good thing I won't lose then!"

"Admire your confidence, I do," said Z-No.

"Flatter me, you mustn't!" she sent back, chuckling. "Grow too proud I will!"

"Take you down many pegs, Master Yoda will," Z-No sent back, with a grin. This was followed by a second message: "Do you think they make punishment paddles that look like lightsabers?"

"I would be sincerely surprised if they didn't," Kris said. "But if they do, I've never seen one."

"I'll look that up right now," he sent. "By the way, if I find it? I'm getting the purple blade saber like Windu had."

"Will it say B.A.M.F. on the hilt?!" she asked excitedly.

"… Is it odd that you knowing that reference turns me on?" he asked.

"Nope. I'm pretty amazing."

"Yes you are," he said. "For now… I gotta get some rest. Have you been doing your training today?"

Kris gulped a bit, then looked down at her lap. She had taken a complete day off, meaning she hadn't done any of her tasks assigned for the day. She wasn't sure how much trouble she would get into for not doing her work... but then she remembered yesterday.

He didn't lie to me, even about that... she said, sighing. *I have to tell him the truth.*

And so she told him everything... or the beginnings of everything. She admitted to having depression first, and that she still struggled with it some days... and between that and everything that had happened the day before, she hadn't felt up to doing her assignment. She still apologized for missing an assignment, and fully expected some form of punishment for it... but the response text showed Z-No could still surprise her.

"Next time you have a day like that," his next message read, "let me know right away. I'll try to do something sweet to help you feel a bit better."

Kris blinked at the message, then blinked.

"So, I'm not in trouble, Sir?" she asked.

"Not at all, little one," he sent back. "On the contrary… I'm going to be sending you a gift to help you feel better."

Kris was still staring at her phone in a bit of disbelief, when another message from Z-No popped up:

"Thank you for being honest with me, sweetie. I know it can't have been easy."

"Well, you started the honesty train," she replied. "That made it easier."

"Well, in that case… glad I could be of help," he replied. "For now, get some rest and enjoy your day off. That's an executive order."

"Sir, yes Sir!" she said. "And… thank you."

"No problem. Get some rest, take your medicine, and take care of my princess or I'm kicking your ass." This sentence was punctuated by a heart, and Kris couldn't help but think about how heartwarming it was… in a strangely sick way.

Maybe this can work… she thought, sighing and setting her phone down. *I mean, I'm a mess… but at least I'm a mess with someone who has to know I'm a mess and doesn't mind anyway… And isn't that what love is?*

She was about to set her phone down, when another text disturbed her train of thought. She looked down to see who it was.

Well, hello Rodney…

She'd chosen Rodney as her date, of course. He was a safe, fun, submissive bet… and besides, he deserved something for all the times he'd put up with her shit. She saw the message from him and it was a picture of him wearing his suit he planned on wearing for the night.

"I clean up nice, don't I?" the text said attached to the picture.

She had to admit he looked nice… but it also looked like he was buying or at least tailoring a new suit for the occasion of taking her to this little mixer. He was so excited… so hopeful.

Oh, you sweet, sweet summer child… she said, laughing inwardly. Something about the power she could inflict over certain men always made her feel better… like recharging a battery, it just brought her back from death and put her into peak performance. Somewhere deep down, she almost felt bad for using Rodney the way she did… but she also knew he loved it, and was grateful for the chance to be used. So what was the harm?

She got off the couch, shaking herself a bit to get the circulation back in her limbs. It was time to get geared up for the mixer. And as she made her way upstairs, playing 'Use me Up' by Bill Withers… it was hard not to be a little pumped about spending time with Z-no *and* using the likes of Rodney for other amusement.

She opened the doors to her closet, shimmying her hips as she hummed along to the dulcet tones of Withers. She'd be using one man and being used by another… just the most delicious of set-ups.

About an hour later, a delivery man arrived with flowers from Z-No… along with a note reminding her he cared for her and to get better soon. It was the little gestures like those that surprised her, and warmed her; he had to be going through hell, but he was still thinking of her.

This meant, of course, she had to thank him properly… and thankfully, she knew just how to do that.

The day of the mixer arrived, and Kris walked in on the arms of the well-dressed and ecstatic Rodney. He was, as her father would've said, 'happier than a hog in shit'… and why wouldn't he be? She was looking great, dressed to the 9s in a floor-length black ball gown that hugged every curve, with a diamond-cut window that showed off her toned stomach. The cut in the abdomen was almost long enough to kiss the cleavage-exposing V in the top part of the dress, that showed off the twins in (almost) all their splendor, oiled up just enough to be practically impossible to miss… with a few flecks of glitter in there for good measure. Her makeup had been professionally done, as had her hair for the evening… all coming together to make her look like a young Ertha Kitt decided to rock shoulder-length cornrows and poured her fine ass self out of the silver screen and into the world of color TV. She loved the vintage look.

More than that look, she loved the looks of the other people in attendance. Men where almost drooling as she walked by, their women cut their eyes at her like daggers, and all she could think about was how good it felt to make this many rich white people uncomfortable at the same time.

A few women were also checking out Rodney… which was only fair. The boy was pretty… and he made for great arm candy. But he was little else, beyond that… which Kris thought was a shame. He had a pretty smile, lovely eyes, clear skin and (from what she could tell) decently sized piece of hardware in his slacks… but he had all the personality of dry wheat toast.

Maybe I could whore him out to lonely rich housewives… she though, giggling to herself as she imagined a confused Rodney being yanked into the home of some bitterly undersexed soccer mom. *Oh, but that would be mean… plus knowing him, he'd try to stay and cuddle afterward.*

It was as she was toying with this idea she was one of those sights that made her blood run cold; Z-No and Titania, the Fairy Queen.

She'd remembered when Lorenzo told her he would be bringing Titania as his date… but she hadn't really been prepared for what that would mean. The Titania she was thinking about was the one from her classes at the dojo, who though gorgeous didn't seem the type to dress up for shit like this… but much to Kristina's surprise and chagrin, she'd found the energy to not just show up but *show out*. She had on a smart dark-blue number that showed off her hips, her ass, and much larger tits just enough to tow the imagined line between acceptable and slutty… she had a gorgeous smile and miraculously pretty eyes…. She had the hair of a goddess and the smile one only saw in toothpaste commercials.

Plus her thighs and ass were just amazing.

If I wasn't bi before…

Holy hell, she, she was gorgeous. Titania was always a beautiful lady, but she'd always seen her in Dungeon gear… other than when she saw her briefly at the munch and dressed down in Civilian clothes at the classroom. She'd always seemed standoffish, imposing and mildly terrifying… but now she was all that with her lovely face exposed and killer figure exposed in a designer dress and a pair of heels that could slit a man's throat.

Kris found her wasn't she if she wanted to be her or wanted to be fucked by her. Both? Probably both.

She was also surprised by how clean and professional Z-No looked in his suit. Sure, she'd seen him dressed up before, on their first little date… but that was nothing. Here he was in an ink-black suit that fit like he'd been poured into it, dressed like something from a spy movie… and between the two of them, the figure they cut was like something Kris would dream of.

And here she was with bland ol' Rodney… at least the boy'd cleaned up nicely.

She was forced, over the course of the evening, to speak to several people she didn't know and others she wished not to know. Zachary Samuels was chief among those people in the latter category; she hadn't forgotten his creepy behavior previously, even if he seemed to think she had. They exchanged pleasantries, she introduced him to Rodney, and once the two upper-middle class white boys began chatting about the fact they'd joined the same fraternity in undergrad (always an uncomfortable topic for

Kristina because of personal bad experiences with Caucasian frat bros), she waited for an opportunity to slip away.

Sure enough, Rodney began speaking of the great past time known as golf and the pair became engrossed in the topic. While they chattered away about different types of grass, Kris politely made her exit, heading towards the punch bowl while furiously texting Lorenzo:

"Zachary is here," she said. "Ugh, can feel my skin trying to crawl away…"

"He's the boss' son, love…" he sent back. "Of course he's here. He hasn't been overtly creepy to you again, has he?"

"Other than staring at my boobs like a hungry infant?" she asked. "No. Not overtly. I left him with my 'date' talking about golf."

"So you bought yourself 15 minutes. Clever."

"Only 15?!" she protested, going up to the bar and getting a drink. "Just kill me now…"

"I'd rather kill him," replied Lorenzo. "He already annoys me and I've no interest in necrophilia."

She giggled aloud at the text, much to the annoyance of the bartender, then covered her mouth in embarrassment.

The bartender, another black woman, gave her a slight smile of sisterly synchronicity. "Get it in, sis," she told Kristina, winking before passing her the first drink she'd ordered; a water, as a palate cleanser.

"It's nice to know I'm spared death due to my sex appeal…" she sent back, teasing.

"I'd miss your witty banter as well…" he replied a few moments later, "but I'd be lying if I said I wouldn't shed a single tear at the thought of losing access to that sweet, sweet ass of yours."

The bartender came back with her drink, as requested: a special little cocktail she'd discovered online called 'sex on the grass'. It was like the infamous sex on the beach, but with vodka, Midori Melon instead of cranberry juice, and Lime SoCo. In other words, it was sweet, sinister, and dangerous… exactly how Kris was feeling tonight. And after a sip to see it was made to her liking, she gave a slight grin as she looked down at her phone.

"Speaking of my sweet, sweet ass…"

She looked around, and the moment no one was paying close enough attention she switched over to Snapchat, slid the phone down… and discretely took a picture of her panties under the dress. They were sheer enough to be see-through… see-through enough to show off the outline of the princess plug she was wearing in her tight back door.

She sent it quickly, then began to look around to see if she could spot Z-No in the crowd and catch his reaction… right when Zachary sat next to her.

"Oh, hey!" she said, forcing a smile and setting her phone on the bar screen-side down.

Remember, he's the boss' son, she reminded herself.

"I hate to see a pretty woman ordering her own drinks…" Zachary said with a smile. "Wouldn't that be something your date should be doing?"

"Oh, Rodney?" she asked with a dismissive wave. "He's not really that much for drinking. Besides, he needs to stay sober enough to drive, so…"

"I see…" said Zachary. "Still, I feel that should be the role of a gentleman to order a lovely lady's drinks. In fact… allow me." He snapped his fingers at the bartender without looking at her, ordering the poor gal around with a hand gesture. It was an obvious attempt to impress her with his power over people… but as someone who'd worked behind a bar before, she was just put off by his flagrant disregard for others.

"I… already has a drink," she said. "I barely started this one, and they're really strong."

"This thing?" he said dismissively. "Looks like something you'd find in a lunchables' container." He took a straw from beside the bar and helped himself to a sip without asking her, smacking his lips and rolling his eyes. "And it just tastes like fruit and sugar…"

As he ordered himself and Kristina each a Manhattan, the two black women shared another sisterly synchronistic moment of revulsion – just enough of a glance to exchange an understanding that 'fuck this guy' was indeed the thing they both were thinking.

Kris started to tell him about the ingredients. She started to warn him about the mix of dark and light liquor, and the fact there were 4 types of alcohol overall… but instead, still reeling in revulsion from the blatant violation of her space that was taking some of her drink without consent, she decided to do the world a public service. She decided to keep him talking… and drinking… for the good of society.

And maybe, perhaps, she would get a bit of a laugh in herself but… that was an aside.

"Maybe I'm just a lightweight…" she admitted, stirring her own drink and looking at it. "I don't really drink much these days… what with working here and my other jobs, I have to keep in shape and awake."

"Other jobs?" Zachary said incredulously, knocking back his own drink in a few quick gulps to seem 'more manly'. "You mean jobs as in plural? Jeez, how much are we paying you?"

The bratty boy he was, Zachary soon snapped his fingers at the bartender to bring him another drink. Kris just hoped the poor woman behind the bar could see what the ruse was…

"I mean, you guys pay me fine…" Kris said, smiling slightly. "But y'know… city living isn't the cheapest thing in the world these days."

"Whatever we're paying ya, it's not enough if you gotta work more than one extra job," Zachary asserted. "I tell ya what; I'll talk to my dad, see what we can do about that."

Kris was going to interject, but the bartender came back by with another sex on the grass for Zachary, informing him she'd made this one a bit stronger before taking a quick moment to smile at Kris before going back to bartending.

"Of course, maybe you should be talking to Lorenzo about that instead of me…" Zachary said, taking a large gulp of his drink. "Dude just got promoted a week or so ago. Plus, I know for a fact he likes you."

You don't know shit, Kris thought.

"Well, I wouldn't want to move my career forward with any undo favors like that…" Kris said. "I mean, it's nice to be offered, and thought about, but… that sort of 'quid pro quo' thing always comes back and bites you."

"Nonsense!" Zachary said, already a bit loud. "It's just a…. a sort of 'mutually beneficial arrangement'. You scratch my back, I scratch yours… everybody gets their 'itch' taken care of."

He started to put his arm around her, a move that Kris had seen so many guys use on her at this point she didn't even need to think in order to dodge it by turning and raising her glass.

"Well, then a toast…" she said, smiling, "to everybody getting what they want, and what they deserve."

"Here, here!" chimed in Zachary, raising his own glass to hers. He knocked the rest back in one gulp, then spun to the bar. "And while we're at it, let's get a real drink! That's the second one and I hardly feel anything!"

As he was saying this, his speech was already slurring… but Kris didn't want to rain on his parade. Besides, she was on the bottom of her drink anyway.

"I suppose a Tom Collins wouldn't hurt," she said in a coy, faux-shy way.

"A whiskey woman!" Zachary laughed. "I knew I liked you for a reason. Lorenz? Lorenz has good taste in womens, man. Good taste in womens."

She let him order the drink, then thankfully was saved by a buzz on her phone.

"Ah, looks like my date's gotten himself lost…" she said, sighing. "Rain check?"

"I gotcha," he said. "Don't worry about me lil' lady. I'll be just fiiiiiiine."

"Me, worry about you? Wouldn't dream of it, Mr. Samuels," Kris said, grinning.

She walked away to find 'Rodney', not upset at all that the message that had pulled her away wasn't from Rodney after all, but Lorenzo.

"I almost opened that in public…" he said, complete with a laughing emoji. "You're a naughty little girl, aren't you?"

"Correction, Sir; I'm YOUR naughty little girl," she sent back, grinning. "Such a shame you have a date tonight… or we could… nevermind."

She sent the message and grinned a bit. Was it petty and messy of her to do so? Of course it was. But that was part of what made it so gosh darn fun.

She went back to Rodney, who was indeed standing by himself looking awkward, and walked him around to see some more of the people and the things hanging around. The mixer was being held in the office, of course… but she'd never explored it this much. There was so much interesting art on the walls… it made her curious, and a bit inspired.

She stopped for a moment to take in some of the art, just in time to see a message from Z-No.

"My date is more interest in your date than she is in me," he sent back. "She said he looks like a perfect new pixie and she would like to break him in... unless you're already claiming dibs on him, of course."

"I mean... I'm flattered she'd ask," she said, "but I've never been all that interested in Rodney – not in that capacity or any other. In fact, he's all hers... it'd give me more time with you."

"This is very true..." Lorenzo said. "That might not be a good idea, though, given our current surroundings."

Kristina sipped her drink as she headed out of the party into the hall, smacking her lips. She was a bit upset, sure... but then she remembered that idea she had when she first got interested in Lorenzo, before she knew he was Z-No. She'd thought about tempting him out of his professional persona, and drawing the animal out of him, even before she knew how much she adored said animal.

Now she had a chance to get that fantasy fulfilled too. All it would take was a little bit of perseverance.

"So I shouldn't tell you how I'm drinking whiskey, which always makes me horny?" Kris asked in her next text.

"Probably not," he replied.

"So I shouldn't tell you that I just humiliated Zachary, which also made me horny?"

"Also probably a bad idea."

"So I shouldn't go to the bathroom and take my panties off and wait for you to come find me?"

"Also not the best idea…" he sent back.

"Well…" she sent back, finishing off her drink, "I just finished my third whiskey drink, and I'm headed to the bathroom to take off my panties… despite your orders. So I guess you'll just have to find and punish me… won't you, Sir?"

Silence and more silence… and then, after so long Kris thought she might have crossed the line:

"Wait 15 minutes," he responded. "I'll be right there to deal with you."

Victory!

Kris could barely contain her excitement… especially having recently polished off her Tom Collins. She felt flushed and happy, and horny… so she was especially nice to Rodney as she sent him a text saying she would be indisposed for a bit, and he should make new friends. The poor guy deserved that, at the very least… he really was a trooper.

Maybe Titania would put him to good use... that might be nice...

As she stepped back into the hall to pass a bit more time at the party, Kristina noticed a clattering crashing noise, followed by a bit of strange yelling. Kris quickly turned, along with several other people, to see a staggering drunk Zachary having knocked over a waiter and currently screaming and yelling at as many people as were around him.

"Boy, someone can't hold their liquor..." Rodney said from nearby, one eyebrow raised. "What is *with* that guy?"

"Not sure..." Kris said, chuckling slightly. "But whoever he is, he's quite the mess. Probably needs someone to take him home, poor thing..."

Rodney gave Kris a look, as if he was aware she knew more than she was saying. He looked like he was gonna ask her what she meant by her text message… but then, Zachary swung at a random gent and inadvertently knocked over a hapless lady. In the midst of the scene being created by the young Mr. Samuels slamming people around and screaming about how important he was, Kris dismissed herself to head on to the bathroom. The combination of devious mirth from being responsible for that shit show everyone was watching combined with the intense pending tingle of impending office sex made it hard for her to resist skipping.

She did actually manage to keep it together, right up until the point she got around the corner and out of sight of the main party. It was dark, since this hallway was clearly not meant to be used as part of the evening's festivities… and with her heart already hammering, she felt it kick into overdrive as a strong hand grabbed her wrist before leading her into one of the restrooms.

She was half-terrified for a few moments, even though the most rational part of her whiskey-saturated mind knew who it was leading her away by scent and the feel of that hand alone. As many times as she'd held it, or been held by it, or been spanked by it these past few days... there was only one person it could be.

Still, her breathing relaxed by quite a bit once she turned the lights on and realized it was indeed Z-No. She started to speak, to say something coy or clever... but she didn't really have much time before he dragged her into one of the stalls and pressed her up against it, his other hand on her throat while one still held her hand... though it was now pinning said hand above her head.

"Panties, off..." he growled softly at her, his lips brushing hers as she spoke. "**Now**."

"Yes, Fucking, Sir..." she whispered out, trying hard not to pout already. If she hadn't already been a little wet, she was now… practically slip-and-slide wet. She could practically taste him already from this distance, and that more feral dominant side of him… always did something to her. Something wonderful. And now, here she was… just buzzed enough to be naughty, about to get fucked by the man himself in a public bathroom like a filthy little slut should be…

"I need my other hand for that part, though…" she said.

"Right… uh… sorry…" he said, releasing it and letting up on her neck a bit. A nervous chuckle escaped, and for a moment she saw Lorenzo and not Z-No… just like her fantasy where the two began to blur. It made her happier than words could express that the two of them were the same… because it meant she could have both to herself.

There was a moment of giggling between the two of them, like horny teenagers… and then she yanked her panties down and handed them over. He stuffed them into her mouth, returning his grip on her throat to its original tightness as he kissed her forehead and undid her pants.

"I already figured trying to keep you quiet was pointless any other way…" he said, still grinning. "My little noise-maker…"

Fuuuuuuuuck…

His left hand slid between her thighs, rubbing her pussy as he held her pressed against the bathroom wall.

"You're already wet, little one…" he hissed, his smirk becoming a bit more devious. "Was it that exciting, walking around with your pretty little ass plugged?"

Kris nodded, mostly because she couldn't really talk with her own panties stuffed in between her lips. She could taste her own juices in the fabric, her tongue flopping around instinctively against it as she felt him handling her pussy while choking her.

This is so bad... she thought to herself. *I'm going to make noise, I'm gonna cum, we're gonna get caught...*

Her pussy didn't seem to get the memo. On the contrary, she felt hotter than ever...

She was still thinking this as she watched Z-No pull his fingers away from her drenched sex and lick her nectar from his fingers before undoing his pants. Her heartbeat was up by the back of her throat, putting it literally in her Dominant's hands, and she felt a strange electric shill as she realized what was about to happen.

This is stupid... she thought. *So stupid, so stupid, so, **so** stupid... So whyyyyyy do I want it more than words can say?!*

She moved her legs up onto the toilet behind Z-No to get her hips up enough and line them up enough to grant him access.

It occurred to her, albeit briefly, that this was about to be the first time that the two of them had sex without a rubber in the way. There was a moment of trepidation about that, a second where, even though they'd both been tested and spoken to each other about it before… she was a bit scared of the ramifications of this moment. They were about to cross a major boundary in their dynamic.

But then the head pressed against her lower lips, and she didn't care. On the contrary, she just pushed herself forward and pulled him in closer.

Put it in, put it in, please put in SiiiiiiAAAH! FUCK YES!

It felt too close to perfect. It felt better than she expected. It felt messy and raw, pure and real… and she groaned out loudly into the gag around her mouth in bliss and pleasure. She wasn't sure if she was allowed to cum, if she had to ask, or anything… and she didn't really care at this point.

She felt his hands on her ass, his teeth against the nape of her neck, and she was clutching the back of his head and holding onto his hair as he stuffed himself into her waiting and wet little pussy relentlessly.

"You like being my dirty little slut?" he growled into her ear.

She mumbled out a 'yes, Sir' through the gag. She was starting to drool all over her own tits… and didn't care. She just wanted more, more… *more…* and she locked her arms around him, trying to get closer so she could get exactly the 'more' she craved.

"You wanna cum for me, princess?"

She nodded furiously. Maybe it was the alcohol, maybe it was the situation, but… she felt nightmarishly close to cumming already.

She locked her legs around his hips, part of her subconsciously scared he might pull out and not let her cum. But as she bucked her hips against his, and took that thick dick of his deeper into her… he pressed his lips against her left ear, and snarled out the following words:

"Cum for Daddy, you filthy cunt…"

She'd never felt so grateful to have permission to cum. And cum she did… as loudly as she could through the gag, with a furious bucking of hips and a slight kicking of her legs.

Just as things were starting to get good, Z-No's phone began to ring and he stopped.

"Shit," he hissed. "That's the high-priority ringtone..."

Kris took the gag out of her mouth slowly, sighing. "Just answer, I'll be fine,"

He opened up the phone, placing it to his ear. Before he could even say hello, Kris could hear someone on the other line yelling.

"Yes sir..." he said. "No, I understand... I'll deal with it Monday but... Well, because I'm preoccupied, that's why."

Feeling a bit risky, Kris snuck a kiss to his neck at that point. He suppressed a groan of pleasure, then smirked and rolled his eyes at her before holding up a hand to keep her silent and away from his sensitive spots.

"No, I understand sir..." he said. "I'll deal with it later. You too." And with that, he hung the phone up.

"Good news?" Kris asked.

"Well, Zachary almost got himself arrested for assault…" Z-No replied, chuckling. "So, it's bad news for the company but great news for me."

"So…" she paused, pointing down at her dress and the spot where they were connected. "We gonna finish this off or?"

"Oh! Fuck, you're right…" he said, laughing slightly. "Actually… we may have to take it home. The building's about to be evacuated in 5… 4… 3… 2…"

As if on cue, the fire alarm sounded and the sprinklers began spraying.

"How did you know?!" asked Kris, yelling to be heard over the fire alarms and rushing water.

"Same protocol we use any time the Golden Boy Zach makes an ass of himself…" Z-No said with a grin.

"Distract the public and run like hell. Except... I can't exactly just walk out the bathroom with you in tow."

"So we wait for everyone else to evacuate?" Kris asked.

"That or go on unemployment together!" he responded with a laugh. "I swear, only you could get me in situations like this..."

This was one of those unique moments and times... the kind you didn't see or have often in life. The moment where she was holding onto someone who cared deeply for her, laughing together mid-coitus while water poured over their bodies... it was wonderful. She kissed him and held onto his face and hair, slowly grinding herself against him a bit more.

She hadn't told a man she loved him in years... and that was deliberate. She didn't really feel she needed to, until now... and part of her still thought it was just the combination of alcohol and sex that was making her willing to say it. She only said it softly, even then, while kissing him and half-hoping the sound of the alarms and makeshift rain from the sprinklers would drown out her confessional.

Something about the way he kissed her next, however, made her fairly certain he knew. And she wasn't that upset about it... how could she be, really?

As the crowd died down and they made their escape through the back way and Z-No took out his phone, trying to get them an Uber before anyone could see them, Kristina couldn't help but think that this was the most fun she'd ever had at a place she worked... or at a job-related event... or any time she was with a guy.

She kissed his cheek, then sent a text to Rodney, apologizing for leaving him hanging and hoping he got out okay.

"Oh, I'm fine!" Rodney replied. "I met a nice woman named Tasha, and she offered me a ride home!"

Oh, Rodney… you poor, lucky bastard….

She almost wanted to warn him… but then their ride arrived, and she couldn't really care less. Rodney was a big boy… he would be fine, right?

Besides, she had a night of sex with Z-No to look forward to… and she still had a princess plug shoved up her tight little ass…

Chapter 14: Catching Up

Z-No wasn't sure how much longer he could deal with this. The longer he spent working with the Dojo, and the more he spent time with Kristina, the more insufferable and infuriating he found the people at the office. This could partially be blamed on the fact he was having more fun outside, making the job just a distraction from sex and fun times with his friends…. And part of it could be blamed on the current readjustment of his medicine.

After the panic attack he'd had, everyone in his life who knew about it insisted he check back in with his doctor about his medication for the anxiety. His doctor had decided he did need to try a new balance, so they lowered his monthly marijuana allotment and put him back on a small dose of Xanax.

The good news was that it was working... kind of.
He wasn't feeling nervous or anxious anymore... but
instead he was feeling angry. Irritability, as he knew, was a
common side-effect of smoking less weed... but even with
that to account for it, he could almost swear that Zachary in
particular was getting more and more annoying by the day.
Even after making an ass of himself at the mixer, the Son
of Samuels was the same creepy and misogynistic prick
he'd always been, strolling about the office and completely
unflappable.

*Must be nice to have a guaranteed job no matter
how bad you suck...* he thought to himself, reviewing an
email he was sending for common mistakes using
Grammerly.

He was getting his work done at a healthy clip...
work he'd stayed well after hours to complete. He was the
only person in the building, at first... then the shadow fell

over his desk to let him know that Zachary had wandered
in.

Oh, goddamn it, not this shit…

"Hey, Lorenz! You got a sec?"

"Of course, Zach…" he said, pushing back from his
laptop. "What can I do for ya?"

"Lorenzo, please! We're friends, remember?" he
said, tossing that ball up in the air as per usual. "It's not
about what you can do for me… but it's about what I can
do for you!"

Oh, this should be good.

"I'm listening…" Lorenzo said, knitting his hands
together.

"Well, I was thinking about that actually…" he said,
taking a seat on the edge of Lorenzo's desk. "I mean, I was
just in my office talking to myself and I said 'Self? What

can *we* do to help out our bestest best pal, Lorenzo? And you know, I thought hard and long about it, but… I couldn't come up with anything at first. But then! Then it hit me…"

"Uh huh…"

"Why don't I set him up on a date!"

"… No." Lorenzo said the words coldly, distinctly, succinctly. He would normally entertain the thought, or at least pretend to entertain it… but today, he was in no mood for this shit. He couldn't keep playing the games, or dealing with the politics. He just wanted to get his job done and go back home, where Kris and his friends would be waiting on him.

"Ah, c'mon Lorenz my man! It's not like…!"

"No, Zachary… No."

"Dude, you haven't even heard what my plan is!" he complained.

"I don't really want to," Lorenzo countered. "Whatever you've got going, I'm guessing it entails you needing a fourth for a double date?"

"Hot Polish twins," Zachary confirmed with a nod.

"And I would do this for you why exactly?" Lorenzo asked.

"Oh, I dunno…" Zach said, starring at his toy ball. "Maybe so I don't expose that you've been doinking some local talent by the name of Kristina Shank?"

Lorenzo felt his entire body tense up. Instinctively, his hands balled up into fists and his lips pulled back from his teeth. He felt like a cornered animal, and for a split second he felt that rush… the flooding of blood into his face and creating a buzzing hum in his ears. The world was hot and he tasted copper… but he managed to take a deep breath and dial it back just a bit.

"Excuse me," he managed, getting up from his desk and plastering on a smile. "You're going to have to repeat that last part. I think I misheard you… what did you say?"

"Did you think I didn't know?" Zachary said, scoffing. "You, usually a quiet little beta male around the office… suddenly your works getting better, you're working out, you're speaking up, and Dad's talking about promoting you? I knew something had to be up. So… I had a P.I. I hire sometimes tail you after work."

Oh no, oh fuck no…

"Well, at first, I didn't find anything interesting…" Zachary said. "I noticed you were going to a martial arts gym downtown, and I thought you were just getting your swell on and that was what made your nuts drop. But then, well… you brought her to your apartment through the front

382

entrance after the office mixer, bro. Rookie mistake my man... rookie mistake."

Lorenzo's right arm tightened again. He had indeed been training at the Dojo, and even though he didn't feel quite up to par just yet... he was getting back into his original fighting shape. He knew he had the strike speed and physical strength for it now... one punch would be all it took. A single blow, one strike to the jaw, and that bitch-made daddy's boy would fold like a stack of cards.

He knew this would be a terrible idea... but like so many terrible ideas recently, it was just so, *so* appealing at the same time. It took a conscious effort just to unfurl his fist and go with talking instead of action.

"So you're threatening me..." he said to Zach, tilting his head, "by saying you'll expose me for doing what you've been doing for years?"

"I don't play fair, what can I say?" Zachary replied with a shrug. "Besides, no one ever has evidence of *me* doing anything against the rules…"

"Just the women you've screwed around the office," Lorenzo countered.

"Women who will never speak up," Zachary shot back with a laugh. "Oh, you think I would keep them around if they didn't know how to shut the fuck up?"

"And you think you can keep them all quiet, huh?" Lorenzo said. He realized somewhere inside his head that the fog he usually felt before a panic attacks was… different this time. He was feeling a strange new warmth coming from somewhere inside him… but it wasn't the kind that usually made him pass out. He felt something surging inside him… like a rush from too much coffee. He felt live… giddy…

It occurred to him he was smiling. It might have been the first time he ever smiled a genuine smile in this office other than the day he met Kristina.

"I doubt you can find a single bitch in this office," Zachary began, sneering slightly at Lorenzo, "who won't jump when I snap my fingers. And any former employees? Who cares what they think? I can just say they're bitter because they got fired."

"You really think so?" asked Lorenzo. The smile was spreading now, as was the giddy, bouncing feeling. "Because I have friends, if you'll recall... friends in the press, friends with long reach, friends who would snap up a story like that. And you've seen the news, Zach... you know if I get one 'bitch' to roll..." he paused, holding up his hand and making a slow circle with his finger: "it's like shoving a snowball down a hill. Sure it starts off small and slow... but it gets bigger, and bigger... picking up stuff along the way, gaining mass and speed... until you got a full fucking avalanche headed down towards ya'. Now, does that sound fun to you, Zach?"

It was about the moment he said this it occurred to Lorenzo he had been walking towards Zachary the entire time he was speaking, and had now backed him against one of the walls of the office. He didn't even remember getting up… but it felt right. It felt like what Z-No would do, and he was (for better or for worse) Z-No again. The normally composed little fuck Zach, as an added bonus, was looking nervous… and that giddy feeling wasn't leaving.

"I don't like being threatened, Zachary…" Lorenzo said, keeping his voice low and nasty. "I don't like blackmail, or insinuations of threats. They make me feel like someone pulling a loaded gun on me. You ever been held at gunpoint, Zachary?"

Zachary stammered and shook his head, and Lorenzo laughed.

"Silly me, of course you haven't…" Lorenzo said, adjusting the other man's tie. "You're not the type. You don't have the stones for that. We both know it. But anyway… the thing about someone pulling a gun on you is… you know, in that moment, that fucker can end your life from across the room. So you have nothing to lose by attempting to defend yourself. Worst case scenario, you die anyway. Best case, you get them first." Lorenzo laughed again, then took a step back. "Oh, but I'm rambling, Zach. The point I'm trying to make here is…"

Lorenzo then stopped, picking up a picture form his desk. It was a picture of his family, before the divorce: his mom, his dad, his baby sister, all smiling and pretending to be happy. Good days. Better days. Simpler days. He turned his back to Zachary, rubbing the edges of the picture… and for a moment, he felt a slight sense of calm. His mind quieted, and he realized what this situation could mean. He had to choose his next words carefully… very much so.

Any slip of the tongue could be disastrous… so he took a breath and ordered his next thoughts

"The point is… don't ever pull a gun on me unless you're willing to use it," he said, setting the picture down gingerly. "I have lived my whole life being threatened by things, and by people, scarier than you will ever be. I've lost time, love, money, and health to things you couldn't comprehend. But I've gotten them all back. And I'm not letting you, or anyone else, take anything from me again."

He stopped, turned around, and smiled.

"With that being said, I'll be respectfully declining your offer but hope we can still be friends. Now, if you'd be so kind as to walk on out? I have more work to do."

Zachary stood for a moment, even as Lorenzo walked over to his desk and took a seat in front of his computer.

"Sack of steel ya got there, Lorenz…" he said, sighing out a long breath. "You really grew a pair since you started getting laid on the reg."

"I assure you, Zachary, I've always had a pair…" said Lorenzo. "I've just stopped tucking them in to protect your little feelings." He stopped typing his email, looking up at the other man. Strange how, even when seated, he felt bigger than him at this moment. "I'm done being a whipping boy. My momma didn't name me Kunta nor Toby, and I refused to be treated like a slave on the plantation."

"So you think threatening the boss' son is smart?!" he asked.

"Nope…" said Lorenzo, leaning back in his chair. "See, this isn't a threat, it's just a wager. I've been nothing before; I've been bottom of the barrel, in fact." He sat straight up in his chair, smiling a broad, crazy smile at

Zachary across the room. "I can go back to that… as much as it might pain me to do so… and I can survive there. I can build myself back to where I am now from the ground up if need be, and I know I can because I did it before. But you? You have *far* farther to fall from than I do."

Silence, then Zachary asked the obvious question:

"What?"

"Think about it, Zach…" Lorenzo said, hands knitted together on his desk again. "You fuck up and get exposed, why… it tanks your whole company. The brand your father built for you, all squandered… the ship goes down in flames with you as the last man on the helm. And you think old man Samuels will be forgiving of you destroying his life's work because you couldn't keep your dick in your pants?"

Zachary gulped, hard.

"I lose this wager of ours, and I lose a job I already hate," Lorenzo continued. "You lose this wager, you stand to lose your legacy, your family… your everything. So no, it's not me threatening the boss' son. It's a game of poker between two grown men… and you tipped your hand early." He placed his hands, palm-side up, on his desk, lifting the left one first. "I'm not betting with anything I can't earn back with a little spit and elbow grease. You, on the other hand?" he raised his right hand higher, then shook his head. "You're all in, buddy. Even if we both lose, I win."

Zachary turned red as a beet, then began to fume a bit.

"Don't think this is the last of our conversation," he growled at Lorenzo.

"I hope it is, for your sake," the other man said, smiling brazenly. "Now… if you'd be so kind as to fuck all the way off?"

Zachary stormed off, and Lorenzo laughed a bit to himself, before holding his head. He wasn't sure what had gotten into him right there, but as good as it had all felt… he was mostly playing with bluster and knew it from the word 'go'. In one conversation he'd made an enemy of the second most powerful individual in the whole damn building… and he wasn't sure why he'd done that.

He sighed a moment, then sent Tati a text message saying he needed to talk to her. He checked in with Kristina for the moment, and let her know nothing of the current situation at work. Then, last but not least, he grabbed the flask he kept in his desk – the one with a built-in cigarette case - and headed out to the parking lot 'for a quick smoke'… i.e., to check and see if his car had any sort of tracking devices on it.

Corporate espionage is for the fuckin' birds… he thought as he angrily stormed out to the garage.

A few hours later, as his work was finally finished, Lorenzo checked his car again. Clearly whoever Zachary had spying on him knew that he knew about the trackers by now, and was planning for that… which meant any advantage he'd had was lost by his frantic decision to go out earlier in the evening and check his car. He'd found no tracking device the first time, but nervous instinct wouldn't let him get in the vehicle without checking it again.

He didn't see anything again… but he still didn't trust the car. So instead, he uninstalled Uber, used his own cell data rather than company WiFi to install Lyft, and called for a ride instead. Halfway back to his house, he had the driver stop and let him out, at which point he hit up a nearby food truck for a stress snack of tacos and Pepsi. It occurred to him, as he marched down the street stuffing taco into his face that this was an insane amount of work for one to undergo when just being followed by a private investigator… but still, he was unable to stop himself. The confident buzz from earlier was gone, replaced only with the anxious hum and that unique drive that told him quite simply and in no uncertain terms that his best bet was to run and run far away. So that's what he did: he ran.

He really walked, because a black man running draws too much attention in crowded cities at night, but the spirit of the thing was still there.

He was about 5 miles outside his usual route home when he realized he was in the wind, twirling his proverbial thumbs, and no one had a clue where he was in case something happened. It was also here that he recognized the signs for the gallery, the same gallery where *Mermaid under Glass* stood haunting and taunting him, and where he'd last met with Tati. He felt safe sending her a message:

the point at which Zachary would've had him tailed was long after the initial meeting with Tati, and since then he'd never met with her anywhere but the Dojo.

He was also fairly certain anyone who'd been tailing him was confused and lost by now from all the changing of direction and random stopping he'd done, along with running some crossing lights and other such tactics. It was better than nothing at the very least.

He broke a few more laws of pedestrian traffic, almost getting hit a few times as he made a roundabout way into the gallery. He made his way in and paid cash to enter, not bothering to use his old membership I.D. lest it be traced somehow.

And then he just sat. He found an exhibit he liked – a painting of crows flocking away from a farmhouse at twilight – and sat staring at it dumbly for a while. Time passed around him, he knew that much... but he couldn't tell if it was hours or minutes. Here, in this mostly quiet place that smelled softly of cleaning supplies and old art supplies, time meant almost nothing. He could pass days here in solitude if the place didn't close… and even with the loathsome inclusion of what he considered his worst work on the walls, this gallery was one of the only places he never felt panic.

Tati took a seat next to him, without saying a word at first.

"I'm sorry-," he started, but she placed a hand on his knee.

"Don't apologize," she said sternly. "You did what you were supposed to do, what I was hoping you would do; you lived your life, you became a free man, and you had fun. The only person with something to apologize for is that bastard who's trying to ruin things."

He wanted to hug her. He wanted more than anything to fling his arms around Tati and cry like a baby, to hold her like a child would their mother. He wanted comfort, and to be told things were okay, so badly he was shaking.

But he couldn't allow himself to break down here in the gallery so instead he just nodded and shook.

"Gomez is already running counter measures," she said, smiling. "Virgil is helping him, which is in and of itself a funny sight to behold... but between the two of them, we'll get somewhere. As for the problem itself... well. I'm sure we'll come up with something."

"What do I do in the meantime?" Lorenzo asked. He felt lost just saying those words... vulnerable and soft. He couldn't even look her in the eyes as he said them, for fear he might tear up.

"In the meantime, you go home," said Tati, patting him on the shoulder as she did so. "You go back to your apartment, you get some rest, and you relax."

"But he's had this guy follow me for god-knows-how-long," Z-No replied. "He knows where my house is by now..."

"And he's being paid to stalk you, not kill you," Tati reminded him. "Besides, in about an hour or so, we'll know who he is, and he'll have more important things to deal with than chasing you down."

"You guys really shouldn't go through this much trouble to help me..." he replied, finally able to look up only to have Tati cut him a cold, ruthless glare.

"You're family, Lorenzo..." she said, her scowl remaining as she jabbed a finger into the side of his head. "How many times to I have to say that before it sinks into that thick skull of yours?"

He put his head back down and sighed.

"I just don't want anyone else getting mixed up in all this mess…" he said. "Just because you guys are willing to help me in a time like this, doesn't mean you should have to."

Tati's expression softened, and she patted him on the back.

"We know we don't have to do anything," she reminded him. "We do this because we want to… because we want to and because we can. If one of us were having problems, you'd help out wouldn't you?"

"Of course."

"Then let us help you." With that, Tati kissed his forehead and patted his back gently.

Z-No felt like he was going to weep.

For a few moments, the two simply sat together in silence. Z-No stared at his hands for a bit, then over at the painting, letting himself get engrossed in the rich mixture of black and purple and blue the painting was using to convey sunset and time passage. He couldn't help but to compare it to *Mermaid under Glass,* and the things he hated about it, as he tried to focus himself back on the moment as it sat and the myriad tasks at hand.

Finally, Tati spoke:

"Have you spoken to the girl yet?" she asked. "Miss Shank, I mean… Your girl?"

Lorenzo sat up a bit, shocked.

"How did you know about Kristina?" he asked. As far as he knew, he'd only told Tasha about her, and had been keeping this whole thing a secret.

"Please," Tati said, "don't insult me. I noticed her the moment she came to the munch... pretty women like her don't get by me often. When I saw her leave to go after you, and then noticed the changes in your behavior, I put two and two together."

"We really did a shit job of keeping it quiet..."he admitted, letting out a soft chuckle.

"Yes, you did..." she replied, rubbing his back. "But you shouldn't have had to hide it in the first place, is the reason. You two weren't doing anything wrong... don't let that fucknugget you work for twist your mind about it."

"Easier said than done," Lorenzo replied to her, staring back at his hands.

"I know," said Tati. "But for now, worry about that later. For now, it's important to let her know what's going on so she's not blindsided. Besides... we have resources, but we don't really have enough to protect both of you."

Lorenzo let those words sink in. Of course, it was up to him to protect Kristina. She was, unofficial status or not, his submissive… and as her caretaker, it fell on him to take care of her. That was his job, his goal, and his purpose… and with that in mind, he abruptly got to his feet.

"I'm going to deal with this…" he said. "I'll handle Zachary with my bare hands if I have to, but I *will* deal with this. He's not hurting Kristina because he's got an axe to grind with me."

He got to his feet and he felt it again: the spinning sensation, like the world was rushing around him in a whirlpool of colors and light. He could hear his own heartbeat in his ears. It felt a bit different… a ball of angry heat rather than the cool waters of despair… but it was still the same feeling every time before his anxiety overtook him and he collapsed.

Useless, he told himself. *You're so fucking **useless!***

"Calm yourself," Tati ordered, gripping his hand. "You're no good to her or anyone else if you fly off the handle. For now, just call her and let her know what's going on. Take it one step at a time, and deal with the smallest things first."

Lorenzo was abruptly aware how hard he was breathing. He was getting himself wound tightly about this issue, and he needed to deal with things in smaller doses. He sat down slowly, and it occurred to him now how tired he really was. It was like he'd run a marathon.

"You're right…" he said. "You're right. Sorry."

"You're doing what you think is right, Z…" she said. "Stop apologizing and take it apart. Remember: how do we eat an elephant? One bite a time, that's how."

Lorenzo sighed, then nodded… and as he stared down at his phone, Kristina's contact pulled up, he thought about what to say and how. After a few moments, he typed

up the words 'we have a situation' and pressed 'send'.

He could only hope this didn't make her think less

of him…

Chapter 15: Getting Even

Kristina didn't get mad often. She got mildly annoyed, and acted more annoyed than she really was for the sake of entertaining people and making jokes. But she seldom felt really angry, because few things were ever worth getting angry about in her opinion.

This, however? This was well worth getting upset about.

The idea of that creep Zachary threatening Lorenzo was enough to send her into full-on rage mode, stomping around her apartment.

*That bastard… how **dare** he..!*

When she got the texts from Lorenzo explaining what was happening, her initial reaction was to be concerned… but then she realized what this meant from another perspective. The Samuels group was just a gig to Kristina… but for Lorenzo, this was his career that Zachary was threatening to destroy. And that snapped her from self-preservation mode where she worried about her own future to a defensive stance over Lorenzo. Things weren't official between them – there were still a few days left in the 'test drive' – but she'd already said the L word. She'd already fallen for him. Lorenzo was hers… and no one threatened one of hers.

She did a bit of stomping around to burn off some anger and bile she felt about this recent turn of events, and eventually took a deep breath before going to her phone and scrolling to Lisa's number.

"We got us a live one," she sent. "Zachary Samuels. Get me everything you can find about this fucker."

"What makes you think I can find *anything* about him, Kris?" Lisa sent back.

"He has a penchant for drugs, manipulating young women, and is a rich snobby white kid who loves abusing his power gained via 'Daddy's Money'," Kris replied. "I'm certain you can locate something."

"Ah…" Lisa replied. "So he'd probably run in some of my old circles… Well, lemme do some asking around, see what crawls up out the sewers."

"I'd appreciate it," said Kris. "Consider it a personal fucking favor."

"Two questions, before I begin:" her best friend asked in her next text, "What did he do, and do you have a picture of him so I can find him easier?"

"He's threatening Z-No," Kris said. "And actually… let me get one."

She pulled up the Samuels company home page, and began browsing around. Sure enough, there was the

smug little mug of Zachary Samuels on one of the pages…
a page Kris took a screenshot of and sent to Lisa.

"Oh… oh that is just perfect…" Lisa replied.
"Bitch, I don't have to do a single bit of research. I know
that little fucker personally."

"Why am I not surprised or disappointed?"

"Because you know I've done worse things than
hang with trash like him and you're my best friend and
don't judge me?"

"I'm not sure if I'm judging you or not…" Kris
said. "Just tell me you didn't fuck him."

"Do you *really* think my standards are that low?"

"Joey Casavedis," Kris replied.

"That was my birthday!"

"*Billy* Casavedis," Kris retorted.

"It was *his* birthday!"

"Cameron Albertson?" Kris asked.

"If we count every time I fucked an insufferable puissant rich boy while I was stoned, we would be here all night Kris…" Lisa retaliated. "Let's just retire my hoe stories for now, and get back to how I know the creep in question."

"Fair, fair…" Kris said with a sigh. "I just wanted the distraction, that's all. I'm just so fucking mad!"

"Well, this should make you happy…" Lisa said. "You'll never guess how I met that schlock piece of trash. The name of the place alone should be enough to bury the creepy bastard for a long, long time."

"You have my attention…" Kris said with a smile.

She knew it was coming, it was only a matter of time. The moment Z-No had let her know what Zachary had threatened to do to him, she knew he would come after her. And sure enough, she got a text message from an unfamiliar number, claiming to be Zachary needing to "speak" with her.

Predictable.

She feigned ignorance the whole way through the conversation, asking him why he wasn't calling her from a work number and what this sudden need to talk to her was about. Zachary, in a moment of restraint that almost surprised her, said he couldn't talk about it now and they'd best meet in person, somewhere away from the office.

Kris, in response, suggested a coffee shop she used to frequent back when she was in her hipster phase at the end of high school. The place was popular, populated, and well lit – three things that would help if the bastard tried to pull a fast one.

She also texted the address of the place to Lorenzo and Lisa. There'd be at least 2 people who'd know where she was going and what was happening should it all go awry.

Just as she'd hoped, Zachary agreed to the meeting place. He either didn't know the location or was just arrogant enough to think it didn't matter, which was a win in Kris' eyes either way the cookie crumbled. So, with that figured out she decided it was about time to prepare for combat.

It says a lot about a woman when she has a playlist on her phone called 'WARPATH' - and Kristina Shaw had that playlist since she was a middle-school. She'd been adding to it her entire life, it seemed... but it always contained one song. And as the playlist kicked in, she heard the distinctive and familiar kick-drum and guitar intro of "Mama's Broken Heart" by Miranda Lambert. She tapped her foot to it for a bit as she went into her closet, and began getting out her battle gear. It might seem odd to some that she even had that… but she was the type of young woman who was taught as a child a proper lady prepares for everything… including unpleasantness like having to possibly kill a man for trying to blackmail you and the man you cared for.

She had set everything up for this: she'd picked out a sweater and pants that were comfortable enough to move in, just in case things got directly and old-school fisticuffs physical. She'd also picked this outfit out for the reason that it was tight enough to make it look like she'd have nothing on her… but in reality, there was enough room in these clothes to hide a small arsenal of petite, pretty, and potent little pieces of hardware. She'd actually counted it out and routinely adjusted her gear accordingly. But with these two pieces of clothing, she had enough space to hide

two knives (long but with thin blades, they held up against

her waistline right behind her belt buckle), a knuckle duster

(just large enough for her dainty hands, which fit inside her

large belt buckle itself), a pair of covered razor blades (in

the bra, mostly in case she needed to cut some restraints off

and her knives got found and taken), and a small Tazer

masquerading as a lighter in her left pocket. This was

before she put on her boots (steel-toed with space for one

small knife in each), or her jacket (small bottles of mace in

each side pocket, big girl Tazer in the inside pocket). If that

prick Zachary or anyone he hired laid a single finger on her

or Lorenzo, they'd lose a whole hand.

As she got all geared up for this, she stared in the

mirror to make sure none of it was obvious. Then, it was

off to the races... so to speak.

She hopped public transit most of the way to the

coffee shop, then got out approximately a block away. A lot

could happen within that block, she knew… so she kept her hands on the bottles of mace in her jacket pockets. Thankfully, no one really seemed to be looking at her the whole time… but that didn't rule out people coming from behind her. She took one hand out of the jacket to check her phone, to see two texts had arrived: one from Lisa, and one from Lorenzo.

"I can see you, babe," Lisa's read. "Anything happens, I got your back. Me and 5 little friends." This message was followed by a gun emoji, which made Kris roll her eyes a bit.

Really, Lisa? You brought a gun with you? Jesus…

"I'm parked across the street from the coffee shop," read Lorenzo's message. "I'm with a couple pals from the Dojo. We've got the place pretty well covered but I still don't like you going in alone."

She wanted to reply, to let him know she was alright and to put his mind at ease… but that would require she take her eyes off the people around her for too long. She had to stay alert. Sharp. Tactical.

She made it to the shop without incident. Only there, once she'd gotten a corner booth and put her back to the wall, did she text both her best friend and Lorenzo back to let them know she was safe.

She then put her phone on mute and tucked it away safely in her purse, before taking a deep breath inward and waiting.

She knew what was coming. That didn't make it any easier to deal with it when Zachary Samuels sat down across from her at the booth.

"Mr. Samuels," she said, forcing a smile. "To what do I owe the pleasure?"

"Don't get too excited, lil' missy…" Zachary replied with a slight sneer. "You don't know why I'm here yet."

Oh yes I do, you smug sunova..!

"Enlighten me, then," she said, still fake smiling. "What brings you all the way out here to meet with lil' ol' me?"

"Well, it's about a mutual friend of ours…" Zachary said, pausing to grab a waitress by the wrist and demand two cups of coffee – one black with sugar, presumably his… and one with cream and sugar and other extras, presumably hers.

Kristina debated cutting the meeting short right now and just gutting him for daring to assume he knew what type of coffee she liked… but that would be rude.

"I uh… don't recall telling you how I take my coffee…" Kris said, still trying to be pleasant.

"I can guess…" Zachary said with a shit-eating grin. "Most models, they eat healthy and starve themselves to be pretty… so they splurge on the coffee calories." He chuckled, then shrugged his shoulders. "But then, I suppose you might take your coffee like you take your men; black, strong, and a little bit bitter if I'm not mistaken?"

"I'm not following you," Kris said, tilting her head.

"I'm fairly sure you are…" Zachary said. "I mean you and Lorenzo Wallace, from the company. I know you two have been seeing each other outside of work."

"Oh, do you, now?" Kris said, twirling a bit of hair around her left finger. "I guess the 'bitter' part was what threw me. See, Mr. Wallace is many things… but bitter?" she shook her head, making a 'tsk, tsk, tsk,' sound with her tongue. "Never that. He's sweet as honey… at least to me."

"So you admit it?" Zachary asked, chuckling.

"I did no such thing," Kristina said with the same smile as she kept twirling her hair. "I simply said Mr. Wallace is a sweet guy. But I'm not seeing him. What even lead you to believe that?"

"I have a professional investigator," Zachary said, his voice lowered and his tone slightly gruffer, "with pictures of you two that say otherwise."

"So you paid a man to follow Mr. Wallace around?" Kristina asked, eyes wide. "Maybe *you're* the one who takes his coffee strong, black and sweet…"

As expected, that got a bit of a rise from him. A clatter of dishes as in he hit the table so hard most of the coffee shop turned in their direction…which of course had been part of Kristina's plan. Now people had seen them here together, in case Zachary started trying to get cute.

To make things even better, this little outburst had been triggered to happen right as the poor waitress came over with their drinks. She immediately cast Kristina a 'are you okay?' glance, showing she was willing to call someone else in if need be.

You may have money, Mr. Samuels… she thought, suppressing a sinister smile, *but I've got allies all around me you can't even see.* She nodded to the waitress, cast a look from her back to Zachary, then let the other young lady set down their coffee. She knew things would probably get hairy sooner than later… in fact she was counting on it.

As he calmed himself down, Zachary adjusted his tie and sat back in his chair before clearing his throat and continuing onward.

"You seem a bit cavalier for someone who's just been told she was caught fucking a coworker," he said, still huffing and red in the face from earlier. "You do realize what that could do to your reputation, right? I mean, Lorenzo is somewhat established in this town… he's got a reputation, he could survive this. But you? You're a freshman model with no rep of worth yet. A mark on your record saying you got fired for fucking a superior, you'll never work in this town again! Hell, most other places won't touch you either; you'd be classified as a 'distraction'."

The sneer on his face returned as he said this; that trademarked sickening grin of his that spread like his face splitting open. He was so sure, of confident of himself…

It made what Kris had planned that much sweeter.

"So… you're here to extort something out of me, I'm guessing?" she asked. "I mean, I'm only guessing but… considering you haven't gone through the proper channels to have me fired, you must want something. Either that or this whole story about pictures is bullshit."

"You're a smart one, Ms. Shank…" Zachary said, still smirking smugly. "I see why our Lorenzo takes such a shine to you."

"Allegedly," Kristina said with a roll of her eyes.

"Right, right… allegedly," Zachary said with a chuckle. "Well since we're working with alleged and hypothetical situations, let's do one more. Hypothetically, I've got all this evidence that could tank your career. Hypothetically, I could just report you to my dad right now and destroy your hopes and dreams." He sprinkled some sugar into his coffee for emphasis. "Or, if you wanted to avoid that fate, you could hypothetically do something for me. I might have a hypothetical proposition for you."

Of course you would, you slimy degenerate fuck… Kris thought, giving him the once-over.

"Whatever could I do for the likes of you, then?"

"All you have to do is say Lorenzo Wallace came onto you," Zachary said, waving his hands in the air. "Just walk into my dad's office, say he tried to… I dunno, grab your tits or something, after your first photo shoot with our company."

If only…

"Make it sound bad…" Zachary continued. "Like, really bad. Then say I stepped in to stop it. I'll corroborate the whole thing, you keep your job, and Lorenzo is gone. Everybody wins."

Kristina stared down at the drink he'd so boldly ordered for her. She could dump the whole thing in his lap and walk away, she realized. She could throw it into his face, or crack the mug over his head… but as badly as she wanted to do all the above, she restrained herself. She didn't even want to touch that drink anyway.

"So you're asking me to lie…" she said inquisitively, "so you can get Lorenzo fired… or else you're gonna get *me* fired?"

"Hey, I'm not gonna get you fired…" Zachary said, with shrugged shoulders. "The pictures my P.I. took are gonna get you fired. I just happened to receive them and might just happen to turn them in."

"Like you just happened to hire a man to stalk at least one of your employees?" Kristina asked.

"I prefer to think of it as a 'wellness check'," Zachary retorted, slurping some of his coffee loudly. "I was simply concerned for my dear friend and coworker…"

"I find that hard to believe…" Kristina replied, staring back down at the coffee on the table. The drink she hadn't ordered was sitting there, getting cold… and she wondered why he'd picked that out for her. They'd only met a handful of times, if that. They'd only run into each other a few times since she started working with his father's company. How could he possibly be arrogant enough to think he knew what kind of coffee she liked?

"Believe what you want…" Zachary began.

"I believe I'm being extorted, then," said Kristina. "And if I am… I don't feel bad for returning the favor." She paused to reach into her purse, and get out a piece of paper she'd printed out after Lisa explained how she knew the charming young Mr. Samuels. She slid the paper over, grinning, and let Zach pick it up and look it over.

Zachary took one look at the paper, instantly paled, and crumpled it up while nervously staring around the restaurant to see if anyone else had noticed it.

"Destroy that copy if you want, Mr. Samuels…" Kristina retorted, a slight smile creeping at the edge of her lips despite herself. "I have the original digitally backed up, and a friend of mine has access to it. So we can print thousands of them."

"You self-righteous, smug little bi-!"

"And, I know you're a man fond of making threats and upping antes, so I'll one-up you right now:" Kris said, the smile on her face spreading. "If you, or someone you 'happen to hire', touches one little hair on my pretty little head, or threatens me again... my friend, the one you don't know about and can't find? She'll leak that picture everywhere in this city, and everywhere on the internet. It'll be like the liberation of France."

Zachary seemed a bit... off-color. He wasn't quite pale, because he was too angry... and he wasn't red, because he was too afraid. He was just the wrong shade of white, not his usual shade, and that's all Kristina could confirm. All she needed to confirm, really... it made her happy to see him nervously sweat it out.

"Remember when we were talking earlier, Mr. Samuels, about who could survive what?" she asked, grinning openly now. "Well, I'll concede you had a point about me being outed as dating a photographer being a hard scandal to recover from. But it's doable... I mean, people do it all the time. But something like that? Something like these pictures? Oh, dear... I don't know if *anyone* could come back from that!"

Zachary blinked for a moment, then tilted his head at her as if he were just seeing her for the first time.

"What did you just say?" he asked, in an almost droning tone. It was like a robot in the movies whose processor had malfunctioned.

"I said..." Kristina replied, one hand under the table and in her jacket pocket, "I'd have a much easier time recovering from my fall than you would from yours. Hell, I already started as a nobody, like you said… I can go back to square one from square two, no problem."

Zachary made a sick wheezing sound. It was almost a cough but wasn't. It took Kristina to put a finger on what it sounded like… what it was supposed to be:

Laughter.

"Y-you sound… you sound just like him…" he said, still making that unhealthy wheezing sound. "Your smug little boyfriend said that same shit to me the other day when I confronted him." Another wheeze where a laugh would normal is. "You guys fuck so much that his persona's already rubbing off on you?"

"What can I say?" Kristina said, fingering the mace in her pocket. "He's a good influence. Only natural to want to mimic his strength, isn't it? I mean… look how shook he's got you."

Kristina wasn't sure what part of this sentence pushed Zachary Samuels over the edge. She wasn't sure, at that time or any time after, if what she said was the correct thing. But she knew two things with certainty: one, it felt good to say those things; and two, it was at that moment Zachary lost all semblance of composure and lunged for her like a rabid dog, flipping the table as he did so.

Kris had already expected this of course. In a single smooth and fluid motion she slid to the side, and got to her feet at the same time she pulled her mace out of her pocket. He was just turning towards her, just seeing the canister in her hand, when she let loose with it and coated his face.

He screamed. He let out a sound like a wounded animal, and began pawing at the air for her wildly. Most of the noises he made weren't words, let alone human, but she could distinctly make out things like 'kill you' a few times over.

Kris didn't even bother with her duster, or her knives, of the other can of mace. She just waited for an opening, adjusted the palm of her hand accordingly... and with a single swing, caught the rabid animal once known as Zachary Samuels squarely in the throat.

As the man collapsed before her, clutching his throat and gasping, Kristina noted the one thing she'd been hoping for was there; cameras. Most people in the vicinity had their camera phones out, recording the entire thing with whispers to one another and baited breath. Once Zachary fell to his knees though, she heard a strange whooping sound of joy, before another black woman in the restaurant, a stranger to her, stood up and just walked over to hug her.

People all over the restaurant were chanting and clapping, making Kris feel like she'd just won some sort of gladiator-like public fight. She felt overwhelmed by the rush of it, the thrill... and she hugged the other woman back.

Somewhere amidst the swirling haze of hugs and cheers, she heard someone – maybe the waitress? – saying the police were on their way. This, as irony would have it, would be the moment Kristina Shank would remember she still had a small arsenal of weapons on her person and (regardless of who'd attacked first) she was still black.

The woman hugging her, breaking the hug for a moment, began asking questions.

"Who was that, sis?" she asked Kristina, as if they'd known each other their whole lives. "He your ex boyfriend or something? Is he a stalker? I had a stalker before, they are *crazy*…"

"No…." Kristina said, sighing. The adrenaline was wearing off, and she was out of breath. "No, he… he's my boss, kinda."

"Shit, girl!" the other black woman said. "Well, good news is, with all these cameras you won't need a job. You can sue that sumbitch for every penny he ever had."

"Right... right. Say, uh... what's your name?"

"Angelina."

"Okay, Angelina... my name is Kris and... well, this is gonna sound crazy but-!"

"You need me to hide some shit?" Angelina asked with a smile.

"How did you know?"

"Girl, you were meeting with an unhinged white man!" Angelina said with a laugh. "If you *didn't* have more weapons on you, I woulda been more concerned. Now c'mon... start crying, we headed to the bathroom."

And so Kris pantomimed fake tears as Angelina moved her through the crowd to the restrooms. As she went in, and began handing over to this new lady every weapon she had (save the razor blades in her bra… there was trust and then there was foolishness), she couldn't help but admire how composed Angelina was about all of this.

"None of this freaks you out?" she asked the other woman.

"Girl, please!" Angelina said, rolling her eyes. "I'm the oldest of 5 sisters, and I taught the other 4 how to shoot. This is nothing I ain't seen before."

"Wow… thanks."

"Any time. Now, give me your number… I'll get this shit back to you when the cops are done."

And so the exchange of numbers commenced, and moments later Kristina was outside, walking up to a uniformed police officer.

"We've already seen video of the man in question attempting to assault you, ma'am…" the officer said. "We'll check you for injuries, take your statement, then you're free to go."

"Thank you, officer…" she said, smiling shyly and meekly as possible.

"No problem, ma'am." He paused, then lowered his voice and said "between you and me? I hope my daughter learns to fight like you."

And so, true to their word, Kristina was briefly questioned and then let go. Zachary was still belligerent and hostile… plus he had a small baggie of some drug on him, so he was off to jail on principle alone.

Kristina felt relieved, like some giant weight was off her chest. And then… well, then she saw Lorenzo and Lisa both standing outside waiting for her.

She ran up and hugged both her favorite people, and began to explain everything.

Chapter 16: Loose Ends

There's awkward Monday morning conversation, then there's coming in to work the day after your secret girlfriend (who's technically not your girlfriend) beats your boss' son like a rented mule, and then gets him arrested.

Lorenzo didn't know if they made a word for how fucked this situation was.

He was proud of Kristina for defending herself... and he'd told her as much. Part of him, a very large part of him, also had to admit he felt a sort of giddy joy watching the smug little prick that was Zachary Samuels being carted away in handcuffs. But that didn't mean the next day at work would be any easier. There would be a mess and a half when he got in, and he knew this as he sat in the parking lot at work, listening to Red Hot Moon by the Transplants.

For starters, there were a good number of people at the coffee shop that day… and almost all of them had their cameras out when the fight started. There was little chance it wasn't on social media (he hadn't dared to check twitter or anywhere else). There was no denying that Kristina was there when it all went down. And between the cameras and the cops who would probably tell the head Samuels everything, there was no way to avoid the revelation that Lorenzo was there as well.

Wouldn't be hard to piece together why… which was the exact thing Lorenzo had wanted to avoid.

Now here he was, getting ready to go back into work less than 24 hours after being seen with the woman he wasn't supposed to be dating, after she beat *and* embarrassed the boss' only baby boy. And the Samuels family had long money – money long enough that Zachary was probably already out of jail by now.

Z-No was sitting in his car chiefing out a one-hitter as he thought of all this. He was also on a Xanax and a half, which was a bit more than he was supposed to take on any given day at one time. But considering the situation as it stood… he felt bending the rules a tad was called for, if not outright justified. Even with the mixture of marijuana and the pills in his system, he felt the tension and unease in his stomach. Even the bumping of his music couldn't drown out the rush of his own blood in his ears. For a moment, he reclined his seat and tried to focus on something else… anything else. Then the alarm clock on his smart watch went off, letting him know he had all of 10 minutes to get inside before he was considered 'late'.

Thus begins the last day of the rest of my life… he thought as he sat up, spraying himself down with cologne and putting drops in his eyes to prevent looking and smelling too much like a pot head.

Then, it was out of his car and off to the office, to face whatever music was playing there.

Everyone in the actual office seemed rather calm, when he first walked in. Business as usual, with the normal chit chat and people buzzing around. That made Lorenzo all the more nervous, as he couldn't be sure if the people milling around were actually stealing glances at him and whispering about him or if that was just his paranoia… or the ganja in his bloodstream.

Maybe all of the above?

He almost went to his old cubicle, purely on auto-pilot, before he remembered he had to go and face the music. He began walking towards the conference rooms, still trying to sort things out in his head… and right there, in front of his door, was the man himself.

Walter Samuels II, Zachary's father, stood in front of Lorenzo's office. He was a stout older man, but tall as all hell – at least 6 inches taller than Lorenzo. Even in his $6,000 suits, you could tell that at one time this was a man who worked out, and worked hard, and could crush most normal men like a grape if he wanted. He way balding at the top, what hair he had left collected around the sides and back of his head like a wreath of silver.

He always reminded Lorenzo of a Roman emperor from the cartoons.

Walter heard the steps coming his way and turned towards their source, spotting the shorter of the two and smiling. "Just the man I wanted to see," he said, in a deep mellow tone with a twang of Southern accent.

"Me, sir?"

"Lorenzo, my boy…" said Walter, placing one of those melon-crushers he called hands on Z-No's shoulder, "we both know you're clever. Don't try to play dumb at this point. It don't suit ya."

"Uh… what would I be playing dumb about?" Lorenzo asked. If there was one thing he learned as a kid, and if there was one thing he remembered from his time before this job when he had not-so-regular run-ins with the local P.D., it was to deny everything until you were accused of something. No sense confessing to shit they didn't even know about yet.

"Why don't we discuss it in my office?" he asked, walking that way. "Like the hair, by the by… what made you grow it out?"

"Felt like a change was in order," Lorenzo said, forcing a slight smile.

"Maybe you're right," the older man said.

If that's not code for 'you're fired!', thought Lorenzo, *then I don't know what is…*

He still followed Walter to his office. He'd seen the old guy make his way up the stairs and into that mahogany door so many times he couldn't count them all – the window of his office was set up in such a way it could be seen from the main floor where Z-No worked before his promotion, and there was a bit of 1-way glass up there that said old man Samuels could see *you* too. But this? This was his first time actually in the office of the Boss. And it was swanky.

The place was decked out in the most expensive way possible. Everything was leather or wood, and smelled like the inside of a well-treated Cadillac. The walls were lined with achievements and awards, as well as photos of Samuels in his younger days. Of course, there were also a few photos of Zachary up there with his father...

"Come, sit!" said Wallace, taking his own seat behind the desk. "Would you care for a drink? I've brought bourbon."

"Bit early for me, sir…" Lorenzo replied, taking one of the seats in front of the grand and ornate structure that old man called a desk. "But thank you for the offer."

The old man nodded, then poured two glasses anyway, before passing one across the desk to Lorenzo.

"You're gonna want a drink for this, son…" he said.

Lorenzo accepted the glass, setting it on a coaster for the time being. Mixing the liquor with the current chemical cocktail in his bloodstream seemed like a bad idea.

"I spoke to Zachary this morning…" Walter said. "Around 2 AM, I got that damn call. He's in jail… but I'd assume you already know that."

"I'm not sure what you mean by that," Lorenzo replied.

"Oh, stow the shit son… the boy already told me everything," Walter snapped, glaring at him as he took a sip of his whiskey. "You know he can't keep his damn mouth shut."

"So… what did he tell you?" asked Lorenzo. He felt the slight panic bubbling up, but he was medicated enough to keep it down for the time being.

"Well, for starters," said Walter, "he told me you were dating someone in the office. One of the new models."

Lorenzo swallowed hard, but didn't answer.

"I don't know if there's any truth to that particular accusation," the older man repeated. "It would seem a bit convenient he got arrested meeting up with the same woman he's accusing you of humping behind all our backs, but… then you have to wonder why she was there in the first place."

"It all does seem rather murky, sir…" Lorenzo agreed with a nod, staring down at the bourbon in the glass for a moment. Beads of condensation were forming on the outside of it, like sweat on a warm summer day, and it made the younger man wonder if he too were sweating. He felt like he might be: he was in a stuffy suit, sitting in an equally stuffy office, as one of the only African Americans at this firm speaking to his white boss about how said boss' white son ended up in jail. If anything could make someone sweat, it was a situation like this one.

"Regardless of what happened, or didn't happen, with you and that girl…" Walter interrupted, holding up his hand, "it doesn't really mean much to the cops at this point. When I spoke to the people in the jail, they told me they had video of Zachary attempting to assault the poor thing in broad daylight. So that's an open and shut case if ever there was one." The old man grumbled a bit, staring at the glass of whiskey in his hand. "To make it worse, the damn fool had cocaine in his system when they arrested him… and since he drove his car to their little pow-wow, that's operating a motor vehicle under the influence of narcotics, along with attempted assault, causing a public disturbance, making criminal threats…"

"Quite the uh, laundry list of charges, sir…" Lorenzo said matter-of-factly.

"No shit," said Walter as he took another pull of the amber liquid down his throat. "And that's not even all the charges yet. Since he was arrested, the car was impounded… and thoroughly searched. They found more coke, a handgun, and his phone. The later of those they're getting a court order to go through… and I'm sure nothing they find in there will do him any favors."

He had a gun with him that day?! Lorenzo thought. *Christ on a Kendo Stick…*

"Even if the girl doesn't press charges for the assault," continued Walter, "We're looking at a lengthy and expensive battle to get him out of this little hole he dug himself. And personally, I'm not sure I want to spend the money." He stood up, walking over to his window. "The video the cops have is all over the internet... I've seen it 15 times at least. It's a P.R. disaster. Hell, I came in early and unplugged my phone because it was ringing off the hook with reporters asking for a statement. Frankly, I'm inclined to let the boy sit and stew. Maybe he'll learn his lesson if Daddy doesn't bail him out on this one."

There was a long, uncomfortable pause after that... just Walter Samuels staring down at the main floor and Lorenzo glancing between the old man and his own drink. Minutes passed, but... he said nothing else

*He wants **you** to say something, you dumb fuck...*

"Sir, if I might?" Lorenzo asked, standing up to join him.

"You may…"

"Well, with all due respect, sir…" Lorenzo began, clearing his throat, "he's still your son. And Zachary may be big, but I don't think he's cut out to wait in jail for a trial. Lots of dangerous, mean people in those cells… no telling what'll happen to him. Especially when it leaks out he's in there for attacking a woman: they don't exactly cotton to that in the big house."

"You seem to know a lot about jail, son…" Walter said, turning his head to face the younger man.

"I have an uncle who's a predicate felon," Lorenzo admitted. "Guy spent so much time in and out of jail that when I was a kid I just thought that was his house."

"I see…"

"Anyway, letting Zachary stay in jail might get a message across to the press," Lorenzo said, hands slipping into his pockets so the boss couldn't see how badly his palms were sweating, "but it sends that message at the potential cost of your son's health. What I would do, instead? I would have someone write up a press release about how you condemn his actions, and have it read the day you get him out. Say in the interview that you know your son needs help, and you're committed to getting him the treatment you didn't know until now that he needed." Lorenzo paused, then shrugged. "Put him in a rehab facility, out of state. That gives the whole thing time to blow over, and it plays well to the public and the jury."

Walter gave Lorenzo a strange stare of disbelief and amazement.

"That's the most clever thing I've heard all day…" said the elder of the two.

"Well, I work for one of the best marketing and P.R. firms in the country…" Lorenzo said with a smile. "Some of it was bound to rub off on me eventually."

Walter chuckled a bit at that line, which made Lorenzo smile a bit more.

"Seems like a lot of trouble to go through for someone who was threatening you…" the older man said at last.

"Clearly," said Lorenzo, "he wasn't in his right mind when he did that. And me? I'm all about forgiveness… moving forward. That's all I've ever wanted to do."

Walter let out a deep sigh at that, followed by a whistle, before patting Lorenzo on the back.

"Men like you, son…" he said with a smile. "This world could use more of 'em. And so could this company, quite frankly... let me make some calls, then we'll talk about your future... say over lunch? I know this wonderful little place uptown.

"Sounds like a winner to me, sir..." Lorenzo replied, smiling as he was ushered out of the office. "But, uh, before I go... about those accusations Zachary was making..."

"Boy, forget about that!" Walter said with a laugh. "Between you, me, and the fence post... we all know that son of mine was sticking his dick in anything that stood still long enough... hypothetically, of course." He winked, then slapped Lorenzo on the back again. "So let's say that, hypothetically... there was some sort of relationship between you and that young lady. Based on your work around here, then... it might be easy enough to let something like go unnoticed. Provided you can hypothetically keep your own mouth shut about it, of course."

"My lips are sealed…" Lorenzo assured him, pantomiming the zipping of his lips for emphasis. Then he 'unzipped' them and added: "Hypothetically."

And just like that… the meeting was over. Lorenzo was a free man, and had miraculously managed to skirt away from being in trouble for all the shenanigans he'd been inadvertently involved in these past few weeks. He'd essentially set his boss' son up to get his ass kicked by his secret girlfriend… and now he was getting a promotion out of all of it.

The corporate world is weird as shit.

There was a moment or two where he sat at his desk, unable to comprehend that he wasn't about to get fired. Then his phone began to buzz in his pocket, prompting him to pull it out so he could check it.

10 Unread Messages, his phone told him.

Holy fuck...

First 5 were from Tasha and other members of the Dojo... and all of them were words of encouragement. Gomez was reminding him that he still worked at a law firm, and if he got fired to speak to him immediately. Dante was promising to bring down a media shit storm, Vergil was passively hinting he knew someone who could make sure Zachary never left jail alive, and Tasha... Tasha was offering her services as a drinking partner.

It was nice, knowing the family still had his back like that.

The next 2 texts were from Tati, explaining that she was already preparing some back up plans for him and assuring if he fell, he wouldn't fall far. 2 more were from Kristina saying she supported him no matter what, and asking where he wanted to meet for dinner tonight.

The last one was from a number he didn't have saved in his phone, and it simply said 'hi.'

"Hello?" Lorenzo sent back. "Who is this?"

"Oh, silly me," the sender replied. "I forgot, this is a new phone number. But still, I'm surprised you didn't guess who I was yet."

"This isn't a good time for games," Lorenzo sent back. "Tell me who you are or I'm blocking this number."

"My, my... you've gotten quite feisty since last we met, haven't you Kuro?"

Lorenzo stared at the words in that message like they were a death threat. Only one person... one woman... ever called him by that alias. The nameless one... the cur herself.

"How did you get this number?" he sent back, a mixture of fear and anger making his hands shake.

"Silly boy…" the next reply read. "It's me we're talking about here. I always know where to find my little Kuro. Besides, you're nowhere near as difficult to find as you might think."

Lorenzo felt himself panting a bit, sweating nervously again as he stared at that message.

I always know where to find my little Kuro…

Why was she reaching out now?! Why was she back?!

"What do you want?" was the question he settled on asking instead.

"Such a cruel boy…" the unknown number replied, followed by a pouting emoji. "I just heard little whispers my Kuro was in trouble. So, I thought I'd offer to help…

after all, it sounded like my sweet little pet had gotten himself in over his head."

"I'm not your boy," he replied immediately, instinctively, repulsed by her use of the words. "I'm not your pet, your 'Kuro'... I'm nothing of yours. Nothing of me belongs to you, and I do not need your help."

"My, my... someone seems to think he's grown now..."

"My family has my back," he sent back, "just like they had my back when you broke me. I do not need you. Stay. Away."

"I will... for now..." the next message said. "But don't think I'm not keeping an eye on you. And by the way... cute little tagalong you picked up recently. It's nice to see you still have exquisite tastes, at least."

Lorenzo's blood ran cold. She knew about Kristina... which meant she had to have been following him for a while now. Someone was probably talking to her, as well... And all of this was bad fucking news.

He blocked the number, deleted the texts, and threw his phone into a drawer in his desk. He had to change his number when he got home... not that it would stop her.

I always know where to find my little Kuro...

He rested his head in his hands, taking a deep breath in as tried to hold himself together. He just took a massive step forward... which meant there had to be another, equally massive, setback for him to deal with. It was the way of his life... he could never keep a good thing going, without something going wrong. Why was it always like this?! Why was there always a down side whenever anything good happened in his life?!

After a few moments, he was finally able to drag himself back to his work. But it was a slog to get through the rest of the day. He was exhausted... all the ups and downs of this day were starting to take a toll on his mind and his energy levels.

He wanted to ignore everything else, but a buzz from his phone drew his attention and he finally looked down in the drawer at it.

It was a Snapchat message from Kristina. He was almost scared to open it... but when he finally did, he couldn't help but smile. Kris was recording herself bouncing around and smiling, wearing a cute purple dress. She'd even added a filter full of sparkly bubbles and cheery music as she held up a piece sign to the screen.

It was those little moments that seemed to make everything better. And it made getting through the rest of the day a possibility.

He managed to make it through at least till lunch. Then, during lunch, he went to his little hidden smoke spot in the office, lit up a joint, and told the rest of his little extended family everything. Everything except for the call from the cur.

That could wait…

Chapter 17: Meeting the Family

Tati had always known about them.

Kristina had always known that Tati had known. She had the look of a woman who just knew things. She possessed the sort of aura that made you feel she looked through you rather than at you… like she could peer into your mind and see everything in there. She was the type you couldn't keep any secrets from.

Still, it wasn't like Kristina just accepted that this woman knew about her supposedly clandestine relationship. She'd thought she put a lot of work into hiding their relationship, and whatever subconscious threads that told her this woman knew about their relationship were just her imagination running wild. It still unnerved her when Tati told her, in no uncertain terms, she already knew about Kristina's relationship with Lorenzo.

"How did you know?" she asked.

"Lorenzo is a shitty liar," Tati said. "And you aren't any better."

"I wasn't lying…" Kris countered. "I didn't know you guys, so I didn't feel right speaking up."

"That's fair," said Tasha. "We aren't always the easiest people in the world to get to know."

They had brought Kristina downtown for lunch, these two. They brought her, of course, to discuss the current and ongoing madness revolving around herself, Lorenzo, Zachary Samuels, and all other fuckery of that nature.

"I thought that was by design," Kris said, hazarding a smile.

Neither woman smiled back, so she let the smile die before looking down at her hands.

"Usually, members introduce their new submissives and play partners around the Dojo after a while…" Tati said. She was pausing to speak between sips of green tea and bites of the healthiest salad Kristina had ever seen. It made her feel unhealthy just staring at the mass of green shit on her plate.

"Though, with Lorenzo… there's a reason why he didn't," Tasha said. She was, in contrast to Tati, munching down on a pulled pork sandwich that looked as delicious as it was sloppy. She ate with no real worries, pausing every so often to wipe her lip… usually when Tati gave her a death glare. "We let it slide because he's a bit of a… special circumstance."

It occurred to Kristina that both these women could kick her ass, and were both beautiful in completely different ways from her, and from each other. They were both, she noted, beautiful in ways she didn't consider herself to be. Tati, on the one hand, was lean and fit…

sculpted and sharp like a well-balanced blade. She looked like a woman who'd be perfectly at home doing ballet… not exactly the build Kristina had. Tasha, on the other hand… Tasha was 'slim thick'. She had weight to her, but weight in all the 'right' places – ass, thighs, hips, and tits. She had a balance to her. She had a healthy, heart radiance to her. She looked like she was taking good care of herself but still plush and soft enough to grab anywhere and be pleasing.

Kristina fell somewhere between these two women in terms of what made them beautiful. But they were both, undeniably, very beautiful. And here she was, middle-rung between two women who'd both known Z-No much longer than she had. And they both called him a 'unique circumstance' or a 'special situation'.

She wondered which of them had fucked him first. She'd no doubt, in that doubt-filled mind of hers, they'd both fucked him and both had done a better job than she had. She just didn't know the order.

"I think he's special too, y'know…" she managed after a pause. She'd chosen to sip on a smoothie and chomp on a light club sandwich. Again, middle rung.

"That's not what we meant…" Tati explained, dabbing lightly at the corners of her mouth. "You see… about a year ago, something happened to our boy Lorenzo."

"Some*one* happened to him," Tasha corrected, bit of sandwich still stuffed in her craw. "Someone whose name I can't even mention without getting sick these days." She glared at Kristina, then looked away. "She damn near broke him entirely."

"What happened?" Kristina asked, obviously concerned.

"Well, dear..." said Tati first. "Lorenzo wasn't always a Dominant. In fact... when he first came to our circle, he was... a pet."

"He was younger then, of course..." interrupted Tasha, having finally swallowed her food. "He had a bigger smile, too. He was jut... bright then. I don't think I remember many times he wasn't smiling back in those days."

"Then the cur broke him down," Tati finished. "She went against everything the Dojo teaches about Safe, Sane, and Consensual BDSM. She hurt Lorenzo.... And she hurt him badly."

Kris blinked a bit, both curious and frustrated at the vagueness at the same time.

"So... are you going to tell me what she did?" she asked, hopeful tone in her voice.

"That's something Lorenzo will have to go over with you…" said Tasha. "We can't break his trust like that. We're just telling you part of the reason Lorenzo isn't… always on point… is because of what that cur did to him."

"We're also letting you know that, if you two move onward and become something to each other…" Tati added, "You'll be held to the same standards we'd hold any member. Which means if you ever do to him what the cur did to him…"

"We'll do to you what we did to the cur," finished Tasha.

"And what did you do to the cur?" Kris asked.

"Nothing," said Tasha with a smile. "Nothing at all."

"Noting that can be linked back to us," Tati chimed in with a matching smile.

"Okay…" said Kristina, tilting her head a bit. She could see the two were clearly sisters. "For what it's worth, I have no intentions on hurting anyone ever… especially Lorenzo. And if I ever hurt him accidentally, make sure you know… I'll probably be more distraught than you can imagine."

"Good," both sisters said at once.

"Now, I have a question…" Kristina asked, hands folded in front of her. She paused, took in a deep breath, and then asked:

"What's a cur, anyway?"

Vague threats aside, Kristina actually had to say she liked Tati and Tasha. They were both very nice once they were more relaxed around her, and they even could be charming and clever. Tati was more of a motherly figure; a smart, shrewd woman with a way of grinning that said she knew far more than she would ever let on. Tasha, on the other had… Tasha was just fun, in a big sister sort of way. She seemed like the type of woman who was just affable and hilarious, up for mischief and trouble. If they'd met under different circumstances, Kristina could've seen the two of them becoming fast friends. Even now, she hoped that would end up being the case.

After the three of them ate together, Kristina headed home thinking about the discussion they'd had. Whatever had happened with this woman they only referred to as 'the cur'… it had been bad. She'd seen Lorenzo's panic attacks firsthand… and if this woman had anything to do with those, she already hated her.

As she took the long ride home in the back of an Uber, she wondered who the cur was… what she was like. She had to be curious about the kind of woman who could entrance a man who'd so entranced her… and she was.

Was she pretty? Was she anything like Kristina herself? One would assume she had to be if the same man was attracted to both of them, right?

She was still thinking about this, along with other things, when her phone began to sing out the song 'Papi Pacify' by FKA Twigs. Only one person that could be…

"Hello, Sir…" she said in her most sensual voice. "How did negotiations with the bosses go today?"

"Swimmingly, actually…" he said softly into the phone. "It just occurred to me, though… You made a request of me when we first met, and I have yet to fulfill it. Are you free tonight?"

"I can always clear some time for you, Sir…" she said, grinning to herself. "When and where?"

"I've rented a little space for us…" he replied. "I'll send you the address when I get home. Meet me there around 7:30… I have to prep the place and myself."

"That sounds… promising…' Kristina said, instinctively toying with the hem of her skirt. "Should I wear anything fancy?"

"You can if you'd like…" Z-No responded. "Just know whatever you put on, it may end up getting ripped off your pretty brown flesh by the end of the night. Except your panties… Those will probably end up stuffed in your mouth to stifle your cute little screams.

"You're such a romantic, Sir…" she said, grinning widely. "I love it when you say such sweet things."

"Hey, you are what you eat…" he told her. "And I've eaten your pussy more than a few times at this point."

"You're the worst…" she said with a giggle.

"And you love me for it," he said with a chuckle.

"I absolutely *adore* you for it," she corrected him. "I'm on the way home now… I'll be sure to pick out something nice."

"Looking forward to it…" he said. Then the call ended and Kristina snapped back to reality, realizing she was still in her Uber and still on the way home.

I bet the guy took the long way while I was distracted… she thought crossly to herself. *Stupid Kristina, very stupid…*

Back at home, Kristina went through another epidemic of mild panic as she tried to pick something to wear for such an occasion. She always struggled with orders like the ones she'd just been given – getting fancy enough to be seen as sexy, but not so fancy it would hurt her heart (or wallet) should the clothes she was wearing be ripped off. That was… well, complicated put it mildly. They were almost conflicting ideals in her head. So, eventually she settled on it; a TJ Max black dress that looked more expensive than it truly was and hugged her curves like she was poured into it, showing off just enough cleavage and tight enough on the chest that she had no need for a bra. She put on her favorite black lace panties, with an 'easy access' slit down the middle… and a pair of her favorite black heels to match the whole ensemble.

She had learned to go simple on the earrings when meeting with Z-No; she almost inevitably would end up taking them off, and they tended to get in the way. She'd lost one out of her favorite pair, and almost felt like she was going to lose an ear, when the overly ornamental piece of jewelry got snagged in a restraint she was tied in. She'd never screamed the word 'RED' that loud in her life… and after a bit of panic and a lot of laughter, she and Lorenzo had an unspoken rule about the ear jewelry being minimalist from there out.

He'd replaced the missing earring, though… which she always thought was sweet of him.

Soon enough, Kristina was in an Uber and soon after that same Uber pulled up in front of a strange-looking building. The place looked almost abandoned, and she felt trepidation as she walked up to the front door. She called Lorenzo to tell him he was outside… and the front door swung open, revealing the man himself, dressed down in just a t-shirt and some rather beat-down looking work jeans. The boots he had on were in similar condition… covered in so many different types and colors of paint she couldn't rightfully tell what color they were originally.

"Come in," he said with a smirk. "I just got done setting things up.

Kristina stepped in, still filled with bundles of nervous energy... but she noticed there was no sign of decay. The building was actually well lit, at least on this floor... and there was music playing. Some things were set up as well, including an easel, a tarp, some unlit candles... and a bag full of what she could only assume were Lorenzo's favorite goodies.

"What... what is all of this?" she asked, looking back to him with a bit of bewilderment in her large brown eyes.

"It's an art studio..." Z-No said with a smirk. "Well, a studio space that's for rent. People with art projects that require silence and space rent these little units out all the time, all over town; dance and theater troupes use these as rehearsal spaces, a few struggling artists film their first music videos here... and of course, every so often you get your average brooding artist like yours truly."

"I would've never known this was here…" she replied, looking around in wonder. "Have you used this before?"

"All the time, when I was painting more and working less," Z-No admitted sheepishly. "There's like, 10 of these units all scattered throughout town, and I used to reserve this one at least once a month." He held out a single hand, rubbing fingers across a spot on the wall. "Every time I had a bad week, I'd reserve this place for the weekend. Then I'd get a 5th of whiskey, throw on my party pants-," he paused here, patting his right leg to show off the jeans he was in, "and I'd get to work. I jammed out, I made a mess, I slapped images onto canvas, and woke up the next day to do it all over again." He sighed as he remembered it. "Picasso woulda been proud."

"Sounds like you really knew how to throw down back in the day," said Kris. "I bet you made some fantastic paintings."

"Most of it wasn't worth writing home about," Z-No said with a shrug. "After a while, you get too tipsy to make effective art and you're just rocking out the sorrows of the week. But I guess some of them turned out alright..."

"Bet money you're being modest..." Kris said, rolling her eyes. "So... not that I'm complaining to get to know more about you, but... why are we here?"

Z-No turned back to her, and smiled.

"You said you wanted me to take pictures of you when we first met, remember?" he said. "At the munch, you said you wanted me to take the type of pictures of you that I take at the Dojo. What, did you think I forgot?"

"To be honest..." Kris said, smiling sheepishly, "I was the one who forgot. But I'm glad you didn't." She walked up to him and took one of his hands in both of hers, before standing on tip-toe to kiss him on the cheek. "So... what's with the candles and stuff?"

"You put wax play down as a must-try," Z-No said with a raised eyebrow. "Don't tell me you forgot that, too?"

"I did?" Kris said, this time in an exaggerated manner. "I certainly don't recall *that*…" she put her finger to her chin, tapping it as if she were deeply pondering the entire situation. "Nope! Don't recall saying that at all!"

"So you say…" replied Z-No in a gruff, grumbling tone. "Let me put it like this, then…"

He placed his hand under her chin and brought her face up to look at him. Kristina's heart always fluttered when he did this. It looked so sweet and romantic but had his hand in perfect position to grip her neck and force her to the ground any time he wished to remind her who was truly in charge… and the not knowing which he would choose was the part that really got her blood pumping.

"I want to cover you in hot wax," said Z-No, "while you are bound and gagged and helpless. Then, using the wax I will make art that I will take pictures of… and then paint over the wax and take pictures of that as well. It's a little technique I learned… but you're always free to say no, princess."

She felt a cool chill running down her spine that she wanted to blame on the air conditioned room… but she knew it was more to do with the way he talked to her. He could command her, he often did… but he let her choose things like this. She was going down a spiral staircase of debauchery, holding his hand all the way… but even when he assured her it was alright, the choice to go further down was always her own.

It was wonderful.

"I want whatever you want, Sir…" she said, her hands still on his as she brought that palm up to her face and began to rub it against her cheek. "Whatever you think will make the pictures best… I trust you. You've always known how to capture my good side…"

He kissed her forehead then smiled at her.

"You're such a good doll," he said to her." Now, let's start with some before pictures…"

He led her to the Tarp and positioned her in a few 'service' poses first, fully clothed: including but not limited to 'Wait' (chest out, hands behind back while standing with feet shoulder-length apart), 'Wall' (hands on the wall, ass out, head lowered with feet shoulder length apart), and 'Humble' (on knees, feet and face flat, arms as far in front of you as they can reach). It was almost like Yoga… almost. Main differences for Kristina were that she had never been in a Yoga session that was this sexually charged… and she'd never wanted to fuck a Yoga instructor.

Once the pictures were taken, Z-No proceeded to restrain her. He first put a pair of large cuffs around her thighs, securely… then attached each of them to a harness, keeping her legs spread no matter how she might try to close them. He then placed a cuff on each of her wrists, securing that to her thighs, making her hands useless as well. And they she lay before him… head on the tarp, ass in the air, still dressed up.

She could feel her heart hammering as if it were trying to escape her ribcage.

"You're wearing those to our little date?" Z-No asked, in a way that let her know he was talking about her panties. Of course he could see them, in this position… wasn't really much she could do to cover herself at this point.

"Well…" Kristina began, only to hear his belt hit the tarp behind her.

"Yes or no will do, baby girl…" he responded coldly.

"Yes, Sir."

"Panties with an opening like that…" Z-No said behind her. "And you're already visibly wet…"

She could hear him walking behind her, back and forth like some apex predator picking an angle to attack its prey.

"How badly did you wanna get fucked, little doll?" he asked.

"Very badly, Sir…" she said, holding her head up as much as she could. "I'm such a bad girl… such a naughty little fucking hole… I just…"

The belt came down on the tarp again and she silenced herself.

"That will do," he said.

The next thing Kristina was privy to was Z-No putting a ball gag in her mouth. She had a love-hate relationship with being gagged – on the one hand, she loved it because it meant she didn't have to try to be quiet... but on the other hand, she didn't get to talk as much as she liked. It limited what dialogue she could add...

Then again, it registered with her that that was the point... and the fact he had that level of command with her made her giddy as well.

Then the blindfold came over her eyes. This was where things got more intense and a bit scary for her still. She couldn't tell what he was going to do next with any sort of certainty now... and fully restrained, all she could really do was wait. The idea sent a bit of a thrill into her, enhanced by the new location and the almost public nature of it.

Then Lorenzo turned the volume up on his wireless speakers, and Kristina was basically in absolute darkness now. The pulsing rhythms of the music he was playing would drown out his steps... So she had no idea where he was coming from and when.

The tension built, and soon enough she was nervous. She began to wiggle a bit in her restraints, partially to wordlessly display her nervousness at this and partially to see if she could entice contract of some kind... any kind.

The strike to her ass that earned her was actually a relief in comparison. The sting of his belt was almost as comforting as a caress, confirmation he was still there and watching her... and aside from the masochistic part of her that always enjoyed the pain, something in her was legitimately happy to have her behind slapped by his belt like that. It put her mind at ease.

She was realizing how fucked up that was when she abruptly felt a slight chill across her backside, near her spine. Something metal, sliding up the back of her dress....

A knife?

She realized whatever this was, it was cutting off her dress. Probably scissors... and she was grateful she hadn't picked her favorite dress for this evening.

Two more snips, one to each shoulder, and the deed was done. She felt the fabric fall loosely off her frame, and she was exposed... naked save for the panties she had on that hid literally nothing.

She was bare, on the floor of an industrial-looking building, at the mercy of a man she'd known for only a few brief weeks... this was insane. *She* was insane. What if he snapped? What if he was doing all this just to kill her?! What if-!

"Calm down, Princess…" she heard next, his voice in her ear. "I'm right here. Are you okay? Do you need me to stop? Do you need me to let you lose?"

The concern in his voice was something Kristina could feel as much as hear. He was so kind… so understanding at moments like this she almost forgot he was a sadist. As he rubbed her back and checked on her condition, she thought the term 'Caretaker' Dom had never applied more to a man she'd met. She felt so cared for, even at this moment.

She shook her head and did her best to mumble out the words 'I'm Okay!' around the gag… to which Z-No smiled and patted her on the back.

"Good girl. Now comes the part where I hurt you with the wax," said Z-No. "And I want to be clear… this isn't a punishment. This isn't because you've misbehaved or done something naughty… this is because I enjoy it.

And because I know my little pain slut enjoys it too…
doesn't she?"

She couldn't even mumble up an answer before she
felt one of his hands between her thighs, tauntingly rubbing
her achingly underutilized pussy. She groaned low and loud
at the attention, so grateful for it to happen at this point she
almost wet in relief.

"Look how wet just the mention of me hurting you
gets your little cunt…" he growled into her ear. "You
messy, filthy little girl… you're looking forward to me
hurting you, aren't you?"

She nodded, enthusiastically. There was no playing
coy in her current position and condition; she was already
wet enough to start a water park ride, and she really didn't
want to do anything that might prompt him to make her
wait. She needed pleasure, pain, tongue, dick, release…
him. She needed him, and she knew it. She needed him to

hurt her, to hold her… to please her and punish her… she needed to be led by the same hand that wrapped around her throat. She needed a night like this.

She wasn't quite sure what she mumbled out next. She was ambiguous with the noises because she herself wasn't sure what she wanted to say. She wanted so many things, she wanted him to do so many things to her, that the words she spoke could've been 'use me' 'bruise me', 'hurt me', or 'fuck me'.

What she made clear, however, was the last word: 'Sir'.

She felt the wax between her shoulders first. It was hot enough to shock, but not to burn badly. She knew that certain types of candles were made and sold just for such play… but it still was new to her. The heat juxtaposed with the chill of the room to create a strange sensation that was like numbing her before she felt the pleasant throbbing warmth that mixed her pain and pleasure lines so, so well… she loved it.

As she reveled in the dull throbbing of it, she felt another set of drops begin at her left shoulder. It was sinking in now that part of the buildup was because she had no idea where the wax would be coming from next, so her body was unable to prepare for it.

Z-No, you evil fucking genius…

She yelped as more wax was added, seemingly sporadically, to different spots along her back with the music around them blaring loudly. She felt her body relax after each long pause, her mind slipping into that strange subtle sub space. She was comfortable… wet… enraptured.

The drops of wax spread from place to place… then there was his warm breath in her ear as he told her to be still. She loved that voice, and she nodded to the order. She held herself as still as she could for him… knowing he was taking pictures she wouldn't get to see was harder on her than the wax had been! But soon, she knew... soon he would be done.

She could hardly feel the paintbrush strokes through the wax; they were too mild, and her back too covered for them to register much. She only knew he was doing it by the occasional tickle of cool paint and horse hair on bare flesh, and his occasional insistence she hold still. The slow process, along with her curiosity, made waiting that much worse for poor Kris.

She didn't expect him to roll her over onto her back when he was done, but that's what he did. And now there was wax dripping onto her front: onto her neck, her stomach, her breasts and nipples... she could feel it splashing down on her. It felt better on this side from some reason... maybe the sensuality of it? Maybe because she knew he was looking at her face while he tormented her? Maybe it was because the wax on her nipples was providing some stimulation to a part of her that was more geared towards it?

Kristina didn't know. She didn't much care, either. She was wet, she was pulsing with need, she was raising her hips and chest to the wax as she groaned out primal noises of pleasure and pain and need... always the need, more the need.

Libido is dumb, a wise person once told her. Libido is dumb and simply wants what it wants the moment it wants it. It is a stupid, greedy, and childish part of us all... and Kris couldn't agree with that statement more as the wax continued to pour. Her libido remained greedy, remained unsatisfied, even as the mix of pain and pleasure washed over the rest of her body. The throb, the ache between her thighs persisted, humming away with its redundant and repetitive message:

Fuck me.

As the music played and her body felt like she was melting into a warm soak and drifted away in the waves she was dragged back by the steady pulse of her pussy, still calling:

Fuck me...

She wanted it to stop... but the wax kept getting close and pulling away. After being denied stimuli over and over, it only screamed louder:

Fuck me!

The moments where Z-No took pictures or began painting were the worst. There was no other stimulation to distract her, and so Kris had nothing to focus on. Nothing existed for her but the dumb yet resilient rhythm between her thighs. She began to mutter the calling to herself, over and over... until Z-No took the gag out to check on her.

"Fuck me…" she groaned out, hips lifting and dropping as she repeated the words. "Please, fuck me. You said I was a good girl… I need it… I need it so bad, Sir… Please, just… just for a moment?"

Silence. Silence and then the sound of a zipper…

Oh thank god, fucking finally!

She felt like she could count the number of attoseconds between that sound of the zipper coming down and the head of that familiar, thick, heavy dick of his slapping against her clit. She wiggled her hips enthusiastically, ass jiggling as she tried to push herself back to take that dick into her needy little hole as soon as possible.

This was rewarded with a familiar grip; his powerful hand squeezing her slender neck.

"Did I tell you to fucking move?" he snarled above her.

She whimpered and went still as she could, trying not to beg too pathetically. She didn't seem to realize how, given her current situation, pathetic begging was the exact order of the day.

"Mmm, I love when you beg little fuck toy..." he growled, open palms slapping down on her ass 3 more times in quick succession. "Beg more, pretty fucking doll... beg more."

Kristina was in the midst of trying to organize words to describe how badly she wanted to be fucked when she felt warm wax returning to her chest, the sudden warmth a shock that made her buck her shoulders and hips because that was all she could move.

This was unfair. This was cruel and unusual punishment. This was downright nasty. And she loved it.

She loved how he seemed to know where that sweet spot was for her between pain and pleasure. She loved how he made her walk it like a tight rope over and over. She loved how relentless he could be, how diabolical… how she couldn't cute her way out of being of service to his sadistic side. He hurt her the way only someone with his type of mental lien could; he hurt her *because* she was pretty. He stroked her ego as he demeaned her, because he made sure she knew he was breaking her down because he loved to destroy beautiful things.

His brand of sadism fit her brand of masochism like a key sliding into a well-oiled lock. Every rough edge of him fit a groove inside her mind perfectly, pushing all the right buttons with just the right amount of pressure to pop her open before him. And god help her… she was open for him now.

He held her at the precipice of denial longer than she thought she could wait without going mad. She felt herself shiver and thrash a bit harder at her restraints… she heard herself sob… and she knew that nothing was outside the realm of possibility now. He could tell her to kill someone in exchange for getting the dick she so craved at this moment, and unless it was someone she loved there would be no hesitation before she did them in and positioned herself to be fucked. And when she finally formed the words to beg… and the head pressed in…

"D… Ugh!! Sir…!!" she squealed.

"Shut that pretty fuckin' mouth…" he growled back, one hand over her lip. "You wanna cum, you cum on my dick. That's how a good girl cums; with a dick in one of her holes." He growled again, and she could tell he was close to her face now. "You gonna cum on my dick, baby girl?"

Kristina nodded. She was barely holding the orgasm back at this point... and barely wasn't gonna cut it much longer because of her current condition.

"Cum for me."

Those words reverberated in her head, shook her body to its core, just as she felt herself speared open and shoved down, pounded and used to the fullest extent by that dick she was already growing to adore. She convulsed, and dug her fingernails into the tarp as hard as she could. She started to cum... then she moved her head away.

"You look up at me," came the order, followed by a grip of his hand on her neck. She couldn't see past the blindfold but she still turned her head towards the man in question.

"That face when you cum belongs to me..." he snarled. "That pretty fucking face? That face is *mine* you

filthy little slut. Now show me that pretty face and fuckin'
cum for me."

He wasn't going hardcore on her, she noted. He
wasn't pounding her relentlessly… but neither was he
making love to her. He was fucking her at the pace he felt
appropriate… though his stroke game was impeccable. He
knew his angles… like a pool player, he just adjusted his
hip movements while he was up on top to make it register
in those spots that let her know he was at least thinking of
her… before he just started stroking and using her pussy as
something he intended to cum in. The switch-up in motions
happened just enough she knew they were coming, but not
enough she knew when.

Every time he hit that perfect angle for her… every
time he stuck in just deep enough and just right… she
thought about the lock registering its perfect key. Just a
distinct image from back at some point in school where
they used an x-ray diagram to show how keys worked…

and she thought of that perfect fit as she came, and came, groaning into his hand, eyes rolling back behind the blindfold as tears of grand relief streamed down her cheeks.

Time soon became infinite for Kristina. She didn't know how long she'd been detting dicked down, but she knew she wanted more. It could last months, weeks, forever... all she wanted was more. She didn't care how long they'd been going at it until she felt the signs that he was cumming. Despite her infatuation and his prowess, Z-No was still Lorenzo and Lorenzo was still human. She had been with enough men to know the changes in stroke pattern, the twitching of his cock, and the slight groans could mean nothing else.

She didn't think of it... she didn't really think anything. She just nipped at the hand over her mouth until he removed it, and the moment she could speak she leaned up and began to beg:

"Cum in me…"

She got a good enough hold on the floor she could thrust her hips back. There was an advantage and she was pressing it… if for no other reason than she wanted to win at some part of this.

"Gimme that cum, Sir… please flood my pussy… reward me…"

She wished she could lock her legs around him, that she could grab him and dig her nails into his back, that she could hold him in and make him stay close to her until her pussy milked him dry and every last drop of his seed pumped into her. Of course, in her current condition she could do literally none of those things… which was its own layer of hell since she couldn't ensure she got what she wanted. All she could do was buck and beg, beg and buck… and she knew that was what he wanted.

All she could do was hope she begged well enough

to get what she wanted… and a long, rumbling growl

punctuated by a final thrust and the distinctive feel of his

manhood pulsing inside her said yes, she would. She felt

the relief and success, the validation and pleasure of

knowing she could make him cum like this. She felt like

she'd done well and was being summarily rewarded… and

as she felt the strange sensation that was the man atop her

trying not to cum, she did the one thing she could to get just

what she needed:

"Cum in me, Daddy…" she whispered, licking her

lips. "Cum inside your tight little princess… Please?"

Z-No made a noise above her, almost as if her was

in pain… and then she felt the throbbing, the twitching, the

warm rich seed pouring out of him. She felt their bodies

synching up; each pump of his dick inside her matching the

contractions of her climaxing walls. He pushed it out, she

drew it in… and finally, she had what she so desperately wanted.

Yesssssss!!!

She was barely cognizant as she felt him slide out, only able to offer feeble protests of pouts and puppy-like whines at the lack of his body heat on top of as well as within her sore and well-used body. But it felt nice to feel the mobility return to her limbs again… that sort of dull pins-and-needles feeling as blood was able to pump more adequately and reawakened her muscles.

"Are you alright?" Z-No asked, rubbing her left shoulder gently. "I wasn't too rough, was I?"

"No… you were perfect…" she said, smiling and taking off her blindfold herself. "God… it drove me fucking crazy. But in the good way, y'know… like, I was just perfectly into that head space, and it was… wow."

"I'll take 'wow' as a compliment…" he said, smiling. She could see some mixture of color on his bare chest, sticky with the wax he'd poured on her.

Realization kicked back in as she saw that mix of colors, and she attempted to hop up… only to lose balance and have Z-No get up and rush over to catch her.

"What the hell are you doing?!" he asked, seeming more worried than angry as he held her shoulders.

"Sorry, I just… well…" she paused, trying to figure out the words for a moment before asking, "Can I see a mirror?"

"Mirror… right…" Z-No said, rubbing his forehead. "God, I almost forgot. Let me take a few final pictures…"

The last pictures were, for symmetry's sake, Kristina in the same poses as before but now mostly naked and covered in wax. Z-No then sat down on the floor to look over the pictures he'd taken.

"You can come look, if you want…" he encouraged her.

So look she did. She leaned her weary head on the shoulder of the man and watched as Lorenzo scrolled through the pictures of her… starting with the before pictures. She loved how he took pictures of her… he always captured her at all these angles, to make her look absolutely perfect in almost any lighting.

The 'during' pictures were equally beautiful, if not more so. She loved the lewdness, the depravity, the anticipation that came with these pictures. She looked at each of the pictures of her, knowing what was happening next but wanting to see it play out. The photos told the tale. Pictures of her bound and in her dress first, of course; pictures of the scissors he'd used and a close-up on them cutting into the fabric of her dress, followed; one last

picture of a shoulder strap, moments before it was clipped,

the moment it was caught in the jaws of the scissors framed

beautifully against her rich brown flesh; pictures of her

bound and now naked except her panties, taken from many

angles; pictures of the candles being lit, then of the wax as

it was poured onto her; pictures of the patterns the wax and

paint made across her body, which she had to marvel at

once she could see the painting he'd made on her back that

looked like a starry night sky; then pictures of her front,

looking like a sunrise.

She stared at this, then looked over at Z-No… and

nipped at his neck hard enough he let out a surprised noise.

She giggled and threw her arms around him, then

stared back at the touch screen pictures.

"You're still my favorite photographer…" she said softly, kissing his cheek. "Every photo you take of me is like a painting you'd see in a gallery."

"Fairly easy to take good pictures," said Z-No, looking back over his shoulder at her with a wistful smile, "when you understand the subject matter." He paused for a moment, then slowly got to his feet. "I say we call that the only scene for the night… because I don't do bondage impaired and I don't feel like spending the rest of this night sober."

"Fair enough," said Kris.

Z-No walked to his bag, procuring his flask he kept a few rolled joints in, along with a small bottle of Birddog Rye Whiskey and two shot glasses.

"You came prepared…" she said with a giggle.

"I didn't bring food," he admitted. "But we can order pizza."

"I don't think *I* can," Kris countered. "My voice is a bit raspy, because *someone* made me beg like a pathetic bitch all night."

"Was it anyone I know?" Z-No asked as he poured them each a shot.

"Fuck you," she sneered back.

"I would've thought that you'd have had enough of that by now…" he countered, getting one of the joints out of the 'secret' compartment on his flask and lighting it on one of the play candles.

"For the time being…" she countered. "But I'm rather insatiable… as you well know."

"Indeed," he countered. "Well, for now… here's to a successful scene and aftercare done Lorenzo Wallace style."

They took a few shots and a few tokes each as they discussed the scene; mostly what went right on Kris' end, and where Lorenzo felt like he could do better. Once the 'debriefing', as Kristina called it, was over… they just lay on the tarp together, staring up at the ceiling. Paint was up there too somehow, making the black wood look like a fantasy version of the night sky with rainbow-colored stars. Kris stared up at it, then blew out a small puff of smoke, joint still in hand.

"You know," said Z-No calmly, "this was the last day of our 'trial run'."

"I wasn't counting the days…" Kristina said, not willing to look over. "I just kinda hoped it would last forever."

"Yeah…" he laughed. "I kinda was too…" He then paused, and sat up. "But hey… the whole point was to figure out if we liked it enough to go for something permanent, right?"

"Very true," Kris said, passing him the j.

"So…" he said, letting the word linger as he hit the weed.

"So?" she repeated.

"So, do you wanna go permanent or..?"

"Are you kidding?" she laughed, sitting up. "Good luck getting rid of me."

Z-No chuckled a bit, then choked on the weed smoke.

"Oooh, a choker? Can I reconsider that answer?" she asked teasingly.

"Fuck you," he retorted as he caught his breath.

"Promise?"

"I'd say it's pretty much a guarantee."

"Good."

And with that, they spent the rest of the night in the gallery space. Z-No had brought a sleeping bag for them to share… and as she drifted off to sleep, Kristina wondered when, if ever, she should ask about 'the cur'.

Then a sleeping Z-No growled playfully in her ear and ground himself against her, and she felt his warm breath on the nape of her neck.

Fuuuuuuck… thought Kris, grinding back against a definitively growing bulge she felt twitching against her backside.

It could most definitely wait.

Chapter 18: Pomp and Ceremony

There hadn't been a collaring ceremony at the Dojo in quite some time. The last one was when Dante proposed to Vergil, and the pair got married a few months later. Ever since then, there hadn't really been a need for one; most new people came to the Dojo as couples already, after all, and all the original members (save Z-No) were already in relationships.

Needless to say, this was a cause for celebration. Tasha and Tati squealed like schoolgirls when Lorenzo told them the news, and Gomez clapped his massive hands together so hard it sounded like a clap of thunder. Vergil, being Vergil, immediately jumped up and hugged Z-No...

while Dante just shook his head and said it was 'about damn time'.

The staff at the relatively nice restaurant where Z-No met them all to make this announcement seemed a bit nervous. This was, after all, a relatively large group of mostly black people making noise and celebrating… that tended to make the lily-white staff at places like this obscenely nervous.

Not that anyone at the table cared…

"We have to get the Dojo ready!" Tati said, hands over her mouth. "We have to clean it up, and get decorations, and a caterer who doesn't talk too much, and… and..!"

"Sis, calm down…" Tasha said, cutting back into her stake. "If worse comes to worse, I'll cater the damn thing."

Every head at the table (save Kristina's) turned to eye Tasha incredulously.

"Not me personally," Tasha clarified. "Fuck you think? I got peoples for that, though.. one of my little friends, he owns a little catering company." She took a bite of her steak, then laughed. "Y'all know Tasha don't cook for shit!"

"We know," said Gomez in his usual gruff manner. "Seriously though, congrats lil' brush. I'll get the ball rolling, and we'll have everything lookin' spick and span for the day of."

"I'll do the décor!" said Vergil, raising his hand. "Ooh, we'll do streamers, candles, maybe some little table pieces…"

"Love, calm yourself…" said Dante. "We don't want a repeat of Jessica's wedding."

"Jessica's wedding was a smash and you know it," Vergil shot back, arms folded.

"It went 33 grand over budget!" countered Dante.

As the two of them argued, and everyone else began to go over what they needed to do and when, Kristina looked over at Z-No with a mild bit of concern.

"Should I be nervous?" she said. "Because I'm a bit nervous…"

"It's fine, hun…" Z-No told her, squeezing her hand. "They're just excited, that's all. This is a big deal… for all of us."

"I wasn't expecting it to be this much," she admitted, shrugging her shoulders. "I guess I forgot what a big deal you are to everyone. I mean, you're a big deal to me… but that's another story."

"Flattery gets you nowhere…" he reminded her. "You've already got me."

"It's truuuue," she insisted, poking out her lips.

"And that's 5 later for pouting…" he reminded her.

"No fair…" she said, still pouting.

"Ten," he said.

"Buh… but..!"

"Yes, right on your butt. Now be a big girl…"

The others looked over, all eying Z-No and Kristina with mild amounts of interest.

"I would hope you'd save some for the collaring ceremony…" said Dante. "It's been ages since I got to watch you spank a sub."

"Oh we will… don't worry," said Z-No. "But in the meantime… we have to go get ready. For now, let's shoot for next week as the date?"

The rest of the team agreed, and after a few more moments of excited chatter they started to let them leave. Tati, Vergil, and Tasha stopped Kris on the way out to discuss flowers and such, while Dante and Gomez started to discuss other things with Z-No for a bit. And after that, Kristina and Z-No went to their respective homes, in different rides to avoid suspicion from others since the issue with Zachary wasn't quite resolved yet.

At home, Z-No took a bit of time to work on a more personalized and permanent version of his contract with Kristina. He had most of the wording memorized, of course… what needed to be there and so on was mostly self-explanatory too. But he still wanted to make sure it was perfect. He cross-checked it online, and with Gomez the next day, just to make sure every I was dotted and t was crossed on his end of the equation.

He got it done fairly early on into the week, to make sure he had time to run it by Kristina. He met with her at the art gallery, where *Mermaid under Glass* was still displayed, just to hand her a manila envelope that contained within it the contract for her submission.

"I really wish we didn't have to sneak around like this," she said, looking over the paperwork. She was dressed to be low-key at this little event; just some blue jean shorts and a black tank top.

"I know, sweetie…" he told her, staring up at one of the paintings. "But for now, it can't be avoided. We have to bare with it until things are a bit more stabilized." He was dressed in much the same way – a black, sleeveless workout shirt and his favorite blue jeans.

"I know, but still…" she said, staring down at the papers. "It just seems so formal, is all. I wanna just go ahead and do the fun stuff again…"

"It's boring but it's important…" Z-No told her. "For both our sakes, we have to do all the boring no-fun stuff first."

"Doesn't make it any less tedious…" she grumbled, reaching into her purse for a pen. "So I sign this now, and we're good to go?"

"All that's left after that is the collaring ceremony," he replied. "You sign, and it's all official."

Kristina looked up from the paper, then smiled at him.

"So if I sign this…" she said in a hushed voice, "you're my Caretaker officially, right?"

"Yep."

"So I get to call you Daddy?"

"Of course."

"And you take care of me?"

"Yes…" he replied, looking away from the picture and over to her. "Why? What are you hinting at?"

"Well, I dunno…" Kristina asked, closing the folder for a second before getting on her tiptoes to whisper in his ear. "What if I need my Daddy to take care of me in the first quiet room we find? What if, like, hypothetically, I need Daddy to drag me somewhere private and use me like the filthy little fuckdoll I am?"

"Hypothetically?" Z-No replied, smirking. "Well, you've been on your best behavior here recently, and look amazing today… so I think your Daddy would be more than happy to acquiesce to such a request. Hypothetically speaking, of course."

"Good," said Kristina, opening up the folder again. "Cuz I'm not gonna lie… just the idea of putting this all down in writing has me excited."

Z-No smiled, looking away from the painting long enough to watch her sign the last page of their little agreement. As she handed the folder back to him, he made a show of shaking her hand, as if they were congratulating each other on a business deal well struck… then he leaned in and growled the next orders into her ear.

"Head towards the signs for the sculpture exhibit in exactly 15 minutes," he commanded. "Don't. Be late."

And with that, it was done. He was hers and she was his, officially and until they got sick of each other. Z-No made his way through the admittedly light Tuesday morning crowd of art enthusiasts and back to his car… but for a moment, he thought he could smell something.

Something familiar was in the air… and not in the good way either.

He spun around a bit, looking for the source of the scent… and he found nothing. But when he got out to his car, he found something; a small batch of orchids – both white and gold and white and purple – stashed under his drivers' side windshield wiper, along with a card signed 'For Kuro."

He bristled at the mere presence of them, picking the card and burning it at once. He decided, after looking up the symbolic meaning of the orchid, he would give the flowers to Kristina.

Fuck off, Carina… he thought angrily. *I'm a free man now. You do not control me.*

And with that, he headed inside to find his girl.

The collaring ceremony was that Friday, and it was a reminder for Z-No what happened when Tasha and Tati had something to celebrate. Those two women had a unique way of doing the absolute most when it came to a celebration. He hadn't been to the Dojo in nearly a year before the Anniversary party, so he had no idea how much they'd done to make the place look as nice as it did... but with his return and the increased involvement, he was indeed privy to how much things had changed.

The place was decked out in decorations, from table covers to streamers and balloons. Everything was bright, cheery, and colorful... there had even been frilly lace lain down upon the floor to make what was just bland grey concrete look ephemeral and glowing.

Z-No, who had essentially lived in the Dojo at one point during its construction, barely recognized the place.

"Holy shit..." he whispered aloud.

"Don't you love it!?" asked Vergil, setting down some decorations to sprint over and clap his hands excitedly. Dante, who was awkwardly trying to figure out center pieces, wandered over and gradually moved his beloved a few steps back from Z-No.

"We did manage to reign it in, believe or not," he said. "Tasha was able to get us a discount on materials through one of her party planner contacts… and dear Cortez here has been decorating his ass off ever since.

Z-No blinked a bit, startled.

"What?" asked Dante.

"It's just… it's weird as fuck to hear you guys address each other by your real names…" Z-No admitted, chuckling slightly. "Especially down here…"

"Dude… really?"

"What? I've never even heard you use my real name once!" Z-No countered.

"You use Morticia and Titania's real names," Dante shot back.

"I knew them before the Dojo," said Z-No. "You guys I met here."

"Still, I at least have an excuse;" Dante said. "Your name is long as shit."

"2 letters longer than your husband's," Z-No said with a smirk. "That aside, are you really saying you'd rather be called 'Maurice' than 'Dante'?"

Dante made a disturbing grunting noise, then sighed and held his hands up.

"Remind me why I don't kill you?" he asked.

"You'd be unimaginably bored without me," Z-No reminded him.

The two chuckled, then set about getting the last few things set up.

Z-No was hanging some more balloons when Tasha and Tati walked in.

"What's he doing working!?" screamed Tasha.

"H-he volunteered!" Vergil replied, stepping back reflexively.

"It's *his* big day!" Tasha yelled back. "Have you ever heard of a groom working on decorating the church the day of his own wedding!?"

"My uncle did," said Z-No. "He was in the basement fixing pipes until the bells chimed."

"I got us a discount on the chapel where me and Cortez by fixing the roof there," said Dante. "Got done 6 hours before the ceremony."

Tasha threw her hands up, growling in frustration. Tati giggled and put a hand on her sister's shoulder.

"Now, now…' she said, soothing the younger of the pair. "It's just fine, love… just fine. We'll have the whole thing ready and prettied up before the guest of honor makes it in."

Tasha mumbled something under her breath.

"Still, guys… we only have about 2 hours," said Tati. "Showers in 1, dressed in 30. We must look out best, all of us."

Dante, Vergil, and Z-No all saluted, then watched the pair leave with Tasha still grumbling.

"So, please go start getting ready?" said Dante. "Because as much as I hate when Tasha is right, it doesn't make sense for you to be sweaty on your special day."

"Not before the ceremony is over, at least!" countered Vergil with a chuckle.

"'Tez, I 'clair fo' *LAWD!*" shouted Dante, all the southern gent coming out of him.

Z-No, meanwhile, shook his head and took their cue. It was, indeed, time to start getting ready. Everyone needed to look sharp, and he had to be the sharpest of the bunch.

The other members of the Dojo – 10 pairs in total, with a few orbital members here and there – poured in about 10 minutes till time for the show to start. They'd been given a later time, Tati said, because Z-No was still a founding member and they wanted the décor to be a gift from the other founders to him. A gift, Tasha reminded him, he'd almost ruined by coming in early and working.

Z-No couldn't help but laugh thinking about it now. He was in his tux, sporting his mask, in the upstairs part of the Dojo with the others as they waited for Kristina to be led in. Soon enough, Gomez escorted her inside gingerly, telling her when and where there were steps since she was blindfolded for the sake of the 'ritual'.

It all seemed overblown to Z-No... but maybe that was because he was in a hurry.

Once Kristina was close enough, he took her off his arm and let her grab hold of his. After a few encouraging words to let her know it was, indeed, him, he escorted his new submissive down the stairs and into the main lobby of the Dungeon, where the lights were off and the noise was minimal.

"Darling..." he said, caressing her cheek softly as he undid her blindfold. "I've brought you here today, among our peers... to ask you to be my submissive and let me be your dominant. I've wanted this for longer than I can say… longer than even I've know, I think. And for the life of me, I can't figure out why I waited so long."

This drew a slight chuckle from the crowd, which was quelled shortly.

"So… my question now is…" he paused, holding up the play collar he'd picked out for her. It was purple (one of his favorite colors), and green (one of hers), with a golden d-ring in the middle. Hanging off of said ring was a matching name-tag, inscribed simply with the name he'd chosen for her: 'Babydoll', all one word.

He could hear a pin drop in the room as the assembled audience awaited an answer.

"That is… the dumbest question… anyone's ever asked me," said Kris, shaking her head before smiling boldly. "Of course I accept, you overly dramatic goof!"

She threw her arms around him, then, and kissed him, as the entire group erupted into cheers and yells and whistles.

Z-No managed to break the kiss long enough to turn her around and put the collar on her, which was met with more raucous cheering. Someone from somewhere had brought in a bottle of champagne, which popped and fizzed everywhere… and with that, Tasha and Gomez as the owners of the Dojo's physical property welcomed their new member Babydoll into the fold. The doors to the play room of the Dojo opened, ever so slowly… and amidst the throng of cheering people, Z-No scooped his precious princess up in his arms and carried her over the threshold and into their new life together.

Now it was official. And for the first time in what felt like a long time… with champagne suds in his rapidly growing hair, the sound of his cohorts cheering in his ears, and the warmth of his darling Kristina in his arms… Z-No

felt, for the first time in a long time like he was truly happy.

Epilogue

"So you're sure?" Tati asked as the party went on. She'd been pulled outside by Dante abruptly. At first she'd been reluctant to leave, but he said something... one thing that could make her drop almost anything

"Would I even bring it up if I wasn't?" Dante snapped at him. "You know I hate even the sound of her fucking name after what she did!"

"Alright, alright..." Tati replied with a sigh. She reached into his pocket, pulled out a pack of smokes, and lit one for herself before offering Dante one as well.

"Trying to quit," Dante reminded her. "Besides, I didn't even know health nuts like you could smoke.

"I save 'em for special occasions..." Tati replied, putting her smokes and lighter away. "So, what ya got?"

"Definite confirmation of a few choice property acquisitions," said Dante, handing over his phone. "Along with that, there's a bit of money changing hands, from some familiar sources. And it's all being done slightly in shadow, but there's not much effort to hide who's behind it."

"She get sloppy?" asked Tati.

"I doubt it," replied Dante. "She wasn't hiding the names from the banks or the brokers... just from us. And now that it's too late for us to stop her, she doesn't care if we know."

Tati stared at the phone for a while, then glanced over at the door they'd just left. Behind that thick metal door, down some stairs, and in a soundproof romper room... her friend Z-No was now having the time of his life with several others he loved and cherished.

Tati didn't have the heart to rain on his parade. She'd so rarely seen him smile these past few months. The thought alone of ruining his evening with this news soured in her stomach like milk.

"You're to tell no one about this," she said. "Not your husband, not *my* husband, and certainly not my sister."

"Yes'm," said Dante.

"I want every contact you can muster. Start pricing things out in the noise-maker department." She threw the cigarette down, stomping it out. "We can't stop the move, but we can make sure she doesn't enjoy her stay."

"Got it," said Dante.

"For now..." she sighed, rubbing her head. "Just go back into the party. I'll be in soon."

Dante did as he was told. Dante ALWAYS did as he was told. Such a good soldier, Dante... he'd forgotten he left his phone with Tati. She glanced down at the screen of it again, seeing the name in text as the search confirmed her deepest fears.

A new house had been purchased, not even 15 miles outside the city, by one Carina H. Bingham.

The cur was coming home.

Made in the USA
Middletown, DE
29 August 2021